CW01020579

Interior and Cover design by RJ Kinner

ISBN 979-8-9880683-0-3

THE OTHERWORLDS

Book One

RJ Kinner

For Grandma and Grandpa B.

"Jump, and you will find out how to unfold your wings as you fall."

Ray Bradbury

PROLOGUE

<u>Color Clouds</u>

The dark gash in the fabric of reality rippled.

As if torn from an invisible curtain, the space between spaces had been gnawed open, leaving a gaping tear flapping in the breeze. Beyond the tear, creatures moved. Dark things. Deeper than shadow, blacker than night.

The pitch-darkness stood in great contrast to the vibrant world around it. Innumerable clusters of clouds danced and swirled around each other, never seeming to touch. Weaving peaks of blue and gold gave way to shadowy canyons of pink and maroon. The sky was obscured by undulating psychedelic hues, dwarfed by the colossal cloud formations rocketing into the air. The punch of blackness was shocking in comparison. Invasive, somehow. Even the intense-colored clouds around it seemed to dim in proximity.

Scattered among the mists were floating islands of craggy rock. Some were mere boulders, others large flat surfaces with enough space to walk on. Two travel-worn figures stood at the edge of a large island near the black void, one man and one woman. They pulled their coats more securely around them and studied the rippling hole. An anxious silence leaked from it, as if at any moment something could claw its way through.

"Do you think it'll be safe here?" asked the man. "They're going to find out eventually. They always do. What then?"

The wind caught a nearby small island and sent it crashing into another. The boulder tipped, its fragile equilibrium disturbed. It plummeted out of sight, a harsh reminder that one false step could end in tragedy.

The woman paused, nudging a pebble wedged in the cracked surface with her foot. She tilted her head to the sky.

"It's funny, there's no sun in this world." She stretched her hand forward. "Look at those clouds. They're self-luminous. They make their own light. Does this system have a sun? A moon? I wonder if you could see a moon at night." She chuckled, a dreamy expression overtaking her. "I wonder if there *is* a night."

The man smiled, accustomed to receiving indirect answers like this. "Do you think it'll be safe here?" he repeated.

The ceaseless shift of the saturated nebula before them swirled. Colors without names danced and spun like some great atmospheric ballet, with only the wind as the choreographer.

The woman stared at the silent black void. Her eyes glazed over, marveling at something no one else could see in the darkness.

"I . . . I wonder if there is a night."

ONE

Commander and Sergeant

The speaker crackled through the heavy plastic earpiece. I yanked the banana-shaped phone away from my ear. It didn't help. My eardrum took the full force of the painful static.

"Can you hear me?" I yelled into the banana. "Alice?"

The static abated. Gradually, Alice's voice returned to full volume. ". . . good *God*, Lily. You don't have to scream! I can hear you fine."

I shifted the phone to my other ear and picked up another floppy cardboard box. "Sorry, sorry. It's this stupid landline. Something must be broken."

"You've been there three weeks. Why haven't you gotten that fixed yet?"

I cast a sidelong glance at the room littered with half-packed boxes. The usually empty dining room table was stacked to the ceiling with random objects: teacups, blankets, books, stained throw pillows, casserole dishes, chipped bone china, and a broken lamp. At the rate I was packing, I would be here for the rest of my life, trapped in a cluttered oblivion.

I narrowed my eyes at the phone. "Yeah . . . I'll add that to my list of things to do."

"What about your phone?"

"No joy."

"Still no signal?"

"It's as dead as my hope of ever seeing the light of day again."

A snort echoed across the line. "Oh, don't be such a drama queen. It's just packing. You're not building a rocket ship."

I shifted one of the boxes with my foot to avoid crushing a set of small ivory figures. My other foot was stuck between an old-fashioned butter churn and an empty propane tank. I tugged upward. It wouldn't give. It left me stranded in the vast sea of cardboard boxes. My only lifeline was the old corded banana phone I'd stretched from the kitchen to the dining room (not a small feat, by the way) to contact the outside world. Alice, my best friend since grade school, was currently bedbound due to a broken leg. This was her first day back from the hospital after a plethora of surgeries, and the first time we'd had a chance to really talk since I started my sojourn in the Oregon wilderness.

I jerked my foot from its confines and stumbled into the table. Objects wobbled. A tarnished silver candlestick tipped onto a pile of crumpled blankets and rolled off the table. I winced as a great shattering noise followed the fall. Ah, yes. The box of picture frames. I'd . . . deal with that later.

I cleared my throat. "Have you ever had to box up two people's entire life before, Alice dear?"

"Well, no, but—"

"In the middle of nowhere?"

"No—"

"By yourself?"

"*No*, but—"

I heaved another box onto the table. "Then shut it."

She giggled. "Wow. I've never heard you so determined before. Or touchy. You've been up there too long by yourself."

I flipped the phone to my other shoulder and picked up another box full of . . . corks? Who keeps a box of corks? "No kidding."

"Remind me why this job was delegated to you?"

"I was closest. My parents have work and couldn't take time off. They're still waiting to hear about schedules."

"What about your brother and his wife?"

"Oliver and Dolly just moved to Ohio for his new job."

"Okay, strike that, then. What about relatives? Did they have any besides you guys?"

"Who, my great-aunt and uncle?"

"Yeah."

"Nope. Just us. Everyone else on my dad's side of the family is dead. Great-Uncle Terry and Aunt Susan were siblings, and since neither of them had any kids—" I bent to toss a pack of embroidered handkerchiefs into another box. "Packing up their house is my job now."

"Wow. Bad luck for you. So . . . what about the library? Aren't you supposed to be starting work soon?"

My teeth ground together. "I *was*."

5

"They're going to give that admin position to someone else if you're not careful," Alice warned. "Like *Brenda*. You'll be sent back to shelving. Bye-bye steady job in between semesters. Bye-bye benefits."

"Don't remind me." I grabbed my roll of packing tape and sealed the box of corks. "I'm trying not to think about it."

"Well, since you haven't decided on a major—which I *still* can't believe, because you're a college junior, for God's sake—you could always get a job with a moving company."

I shuddered. "Who would willingly choose this as a profession?"

The phone crackled again. "I dunno, maybe people just like organizing stuff. Or maybe it's a front for the mob."

I laughed. It turned into a sigh as I considered how much of the house had yet to be packed. The kitchen, the study, two sheds, and the enormous barn outside. I dreaded the barn most of all.

"So . . . how're you doing?" Alice asked. "After the funeral. Well, *funerals*."

I paused from reaching for the next box and wiped some sweat from my forehead. "I'm all right, I guess. I can't believe they've been gone a month already. I keep expecting Uncle Terry to come bounding through the door, dragging in a cool stick, or rock, or some animal bone he found." I smiled. "Or Aunt Susan to walk in with a whole jar of mushrooms she picked herself. They were always outside doing stuff like that. It feels like they're going to come home from one of their outings any minute." My smile faded as a pang of loss settled in my stomach. "But . . . they don't."

"Any leads on what caused the accident?"

"No. But that doesn't mean much. Terry and Susan were well into their seventies. They probably just got distracted on the road, and . . ."

I trailed off. Talking about them hurt. Between packing up their belongings and cleaning, there hadn't been time for me to grieve. For now, it was something I needed to shelve. I had one job while stuck alone in the old family homestead: get everything ready to be trucked off to storage, where treasured heirlooms passed down through generations would rot in obscurity. The thought made my insides curl.

"It must be hard for you," Alice said. "To lose both of them at once."

I swallowed the lump in my throat and nudged an empty Tupperware tub from my path. "This may be an obvious sentiment, but I feel like we didn't have enough time together."

"You met them when you were, what, fifteen? That's over seven years, Lily. It's longer than I had with my grandparents. Let alone my grandparents' siblings."

"I know, but there's still so much I don't know about them."

"Like what?"

"I dunno, lots of things." I tucked a stack of books into yet another box and taped it shut. "What they did for work. The reasons for moving back to this house together. Why they never contacted us before Grandpa Masters died. Or—here's a great question—why did they leave the house and *everything* to my parents?"

"Well, like you said, you were the only ones left."

"I guess," I mumbled. "The lawyers said their will was complicated. They may have left us the house, but we can't sell it."

"Why not? You guys could definitely use the money. It's not like there's a huge work industry in— What's the town again? It had a weird name."

"Stars Crossing. Don't bother looking for it on any map. It's not there. Anyway, it's part of the conditions of the will. If my parents try to sell it, the property reverts back to some historic-preservation society." I shook my head. "But the attorneys said it had a lot of loopholes, so they're looking into it. I just hope they find an answer before my parents' life savings gets wiped out from lawyers' fees. What's left of their savings, anyway."

"Do you want to sell it?"

"*I* don't. I mean, this house—or farm, or whatever it is—has been in the Masters family since, like, the 1800s. You can't just sell something like that. But my parents can't handle the taxes on it either. It's a conundrum."

"Sounds like they've put you in golden handcuffs."

I laughed. "I know. I wish I could ask them why. Or ask them about *anything*. I swear, Alice, I've known them all this time, but I couldn't tell you the first thing about them. That's weird, right?"

"Hm." A shuffling against the receiver signaled Alice had repositioned in bed. "I don't think it's weird. Some people just don't talk about themselves much. Maybe they were retired CIA or something? Or maybe *they* were part of the mob!"

I huffed a breath through my nose. "That would make sense. I'll probably find spy equipment while I'm packing. Or a dead body. Whichever comes first."

The banana squealed with static again. I cringed until it subsided, turning to try to escape the noise. My foot caught on a pile of tablecloths I'd emptied earlier today from the pantry. I picked up the pile and tossed it onto the already overburdened table. An envelope fell out. Crouching to grab it, I pulled the flap open.

My stomach twisted. It was a hand-drawn Christmas card I had sent Terry and Susan the year we met. Had they kept it all this time? Judging by the hideous attempt at portraits on the inside, it was made during my "brooding teenage artist" phase. The words "Bestest Great-Aunt and Uncle Ever" were scrawled at the top. I folded it and shoved it in the back pocket of my jeans. This was one thing I could keep.

The static cleared. I started to ask another question, but Alice was talking to someone else on her end.

She sighed. ". . . Okay, thanks, Dad. I'll just be a minute. Hey, Lily, Nurse Dad has informed me that I need to take my meds. When are you coming back home?"

"No idea. Hopefully in the next couple of weeks, *something* will happen. Either someone will come out to help me, or I can go home. Do you have a date for the cast coming off?"

She exhaled an annoyed breath. "Not even sort of. The doctor said it's going to take a while for the bone to set. Two months, at least."

"Sorry for bringing it up."

She sighed. I could almost hear her eye-roll over the phone. "Stupid accident. That tree root was *clearly* not there before I tripped on it. Or that rock. Or hill."

I danced around the boxes at the edge of the cardboard ocean and finally stood on both feet.

"Well, thanks for chatting. Tomorrow I get to tackle the creepy barn. Pray for me."

"Glad to be of service. Please, call more! I'll just be . . . sitting here. Watching YouTube. Lamenting my lack of best friend to dote on my every whim."

I chuckled and glanced up at one of the five wall clocks in the room. It was evening already. I still had to close up the shed. "I should go. Got lots to do. For all eternity it seems."

"No problem, Commander. Be safe out there in the trenches. And the creepy barn. Sergeant Minnley, out!" she cried. "You, uh, can't see, but I'm saluting you."

I laughed again. "As you were, Sergeant." I put a flat palm to my forehead for a return salute. "Commander Masters signing off!"

We laughed at our inability to move on from the playground.

"G'bye, Alice."

"G'bye, Lily. Don't go insane!"

Click.

Two

A Mom Thing

After navigating my way back to the kitchen to hang up the phone, I glanced out the window.

It was a soggy day. The rain had let up in the last hour, and mists drifted between the towering pine trees. It was quiet, too. That didn't indicate much, because it was quiet every night. If there were neighbors nearby, I didn't know about them. Every few days, I'd hear the far-off noise of a barking dog, but for all I knew, I was the only person left on Earth.

I stretched over the sink to peek at the barn, and . . . yep. Still looked haunted. Out of the numerous creepy places on the expansive property, the barn was easily the most unsettling. Its simple structure and plain dark wood gave it a gray hue in the evening light, making it look staunch and cold, like it was cut from dark marble. The large windows in the hayloft could have been eyes. The wide door on the bottom level could be the mouth, agape in terror at the inky blackness inside.

I hadn't tackled *that* project yet. Even in broad daylight that place gave me the willies. Maybe if I had someone with me, it would be easier to swallow the fear, but I was well and truly alone. At least, I hoped I was well and truly alone. I didn't relish the thought of someone sneaking around the house, mirroring my footsteps so I couldn't hear them. Maybe I watched too many crime shows.

I sank back on my heels and retrieved my shoes from the hallway. The shed at the bottom of the small hill was still open from this morning's escapade to locate a hammer. The last thing I needed was some animal to find their way inside and make a nest. I unhooked the shed key from the peg on the wall and grabbed my jacket. The peeling wooden porch creaked as I descended the steps into the mist. The wind knocked around a small rusted tin sign nailed to the siding: "MASTERS: EST 1859."

Walking down the gentle slope to the lower property, I turned and looked up at the house, studying the clouded windows, the dark shingle siding, the peaked roof, and the general air of antiquity. Bits of moss and grass had sprung up from the old flagstone foundation, mostly covered by the splintering wraparound porch. The house and surrounding farmland had been in the family for years, passing from Masters to Masters with each new generation. At least, that was what I'd been told by the most recent caretakers: Great-Aunt Susan, and Great-Uncle Terry.

Grandpa Masters—unbeknownst to my family—had two younger siblings: Terry and Susan. When Grandpa Masters finally passed away six years ago after a long battle with Alzheimer's, not many people showed up for the service. Grandma Masters had died a few years before, and Grandpa had become a recluse. Growing up, I always knew him as a stoic, sour man who didn't seem to like me very much and smelled strongly of cough drops.

When Terry and Susan had approached us at his funeral, things changed. I felt like a connection that I was supposed to have had with my grandparents was filled. Terry and Susan were kind, eccentric people who had an air of worldly experience. We talked for hours, and they regaled us with stories about the family homestead back in Oregon, where they still lived. We'd heard Grandpa mention growing up there, but my parents had assumed it was sold off to some investor years ago.

A few weeks later, my mom, dad, older brother, Oliver, and I took a road trip to the Oregon wilderness to get to know them better. Over the years, it became a regular thing we did on holidays. I'd looked forward to those trips, but it always left me wondering about Terry and Susan. I'd read about con artists who made people believe they were long-lost relatives, eventually robbing the real family blind. Terry and Susan had made no attempt to steal my parents' meager savings, so I'd ruled out that theory long ago. But if they weren't con artists, then who were they?

They were an ongoing mystery to be solved, but their unknown past never bothered me. I'd figured one day they would trust me enough to cast off their secrets. It was only a matter of time.

As I came to find out, time had a way of being cut short.

Days after we'd gotten news of their fatal car accident, a formal letter printed on thick fancy stationery arrived at my parents' house, informing them of their newfound ownership of a home in Stars Crossing, Oregon. We soon came to find out that everything meant *everything*. All the property, all the buildings, and all the things therein.

Which also included the nightmare-inducing barn, which now I had to go through alone. Probably tomorrow. Alone. In the rain. Alone. With a dying flashlight. Did I mention alone?

I turned away from the house and continued down the slope to the shed, glancing up at the gray expanse of sky. It got dark so early here. Was that because of the rain? Or because of the lack of light pollution?

Peering inside the old metal shed, I grabbed the flashlight near the door and shook it until it stopped flickering. I shined it around the back of the structure, looking for any bats that may have nestled in for the night. The flashlight beam illuminated dusty boxes, plastic shelves, and covered pieces of furniture, but no bats. Satisfied, I switched off the flashlight and locked the door. On the way back to the house, I chanced a peek up the hill.

The barn stared back at me like it was issuing a challenge. Its gaping void of a door made the swirling mists look like ghosts out for an evening stroll. I didn't appreciate that.

After I got back into the house, I had just enough time to put the keys back on the peg when the phone rang.

I hopped over a few boxes and answered it.

"Hello?"

"Hey, sweetie, it's me."

"Hey, Mom."

"How is everything up there? Raining still?"

"Everything's fine." I shrugged off my jacket and tossed it in the general direction of the coatrack. "And it's Oregon. Of course it's still raining. How is everything at home?"

"Good, good. Your dad's got the late shift tonight at the factory, so I have the house to myself for a while."

"Are you going to do something fun? Get a pizza or something?"

"I may—in fact—go crazy and do *two* loads of laundry."

"Wow." I smiled. "A real wild child, aren't you?"

"You know it. So . . . how're you doing tonight? Gotten dinner yet?"

I chuckled. She was terrible at feigning casual interest. I knew she didn't like that I was up here alone. But that was reality, and we just had to roll with it.

"I'm fine, Mom. Any word on your work schedules?"

She inhaled. "As of right now? No. We still don't know about work yet."

"Okay, so another week?"

"More like another couple weeks. Maybe a month."

"Oh."

She sighed away from the receiver, but I still heard it. No matter the time or day of the week, she always sounded so tired. "I know it's lonely up there, and I know you're missing out on starting at the library, but until we know more about what we're doing with the house, the best thing for you to do is just to stay put."

"They're going to give my job away if I'm gone for much longer," I said. "Permanently."

"You can always find another job, honey."

"Like where?"

"Well . . . the hospital is always hiring, and—"

"Do you really want both of us dealing with them? It's bad enough that you have to cater to their bureaucracy."

"It's a job, Lily. It pays."

I chewed my cheek. She had moved from her usual "honey" to invoking my name. I knew better than to press the topic further.

"Have the lawyers gotten back to you yet?" I asked.

"Nothing we didn't already know."

I tightened my grip on the phone. "Have you had any more discussions on . . . you know . . ."

"We still don't know if we can keep the house yet, honey."

"I know."

"I just don't want you to get your hopes up and—"

"I know."

There was a stretch of awkward silence.

She cleared her throat. "Have you eaten tonight?"

"Mom, don't worry about me. I'm fine."

"I know, but I have to ask, have you eaten tonight?"

I rolled my eyes. "No, Mom, I haven't eaten yet. It's only like seven o'clock here. I'll grab something soon, I promise."

"Okay, are you getting regular meals? I mean . . . are you okay up there by yourself?"

I leaned against the counter. "Mom, I'm fine. You don't have to worry. I'm taking care of myself."

"Of course you are, honey. I just—"

"I know. You worry."

"It's a mom thing," she said.

"It's a mom thing," I agreed.

The static warbled.

"Well, I'll let you go," she said. "Sleep well tonight. We'll be in touch as soon as we know something."

"All right. Say goodnight to Dad for me. I'll be folding laundry with you in spirit."

"Will do. I love you. Goodnight!"

"Goodnight, Mom, I love you too."

Click.

THREE

Of Mice and Pens

I hung the banana phone back on the wall and turned to look out the window. The soft *tick-tick* on the bubbly glass panes signaled the rain had picked up, and the fog had rolled in. I couldn't see the barn anymore.

Turning my thoughts to food, I sighed. Mom was right. I did need to eat something. I hadn't since this morning. But I was exhausted. My arms and back ached from bending over boxes all day. Maybe food could wait until later . . .

No. No, I needed to make something now, not later. I'd promised.

I settled on making pasta. That required minimal effort. Grabbing a pot, I started boiling some water and leaned against the counter.

My eyes wandered around the kitchen. It was a cozy little place: a mixture of wood paneling and river-rock backsplash. The creaky wooden floor had become soft and smooth from decades of shuffling feet. An old-fashioned porcelain range stood watch from the corner, no longer in use but keeping guard just the same. Luckily, a much newer gas stove had replaced it years ago.

I closed my eyes. The bubbling water. The wind whistling through the trees outside. The rain soaking the already saturated ground. It was strange to hear these sounds. I wasn't used to it being quiet enough to hear the rain. Everywhere I'd lived, there was always some kind of background noise. People, cars, the hum of streetlights. Here, the noisiest thing was me. It made me strangely self-conscious of my actions. Like somehow, disturbing the silence was against the rules.

The water changed from a gentle trill to a rolling boil. After waiting for the noodles to cook, I set a heavy ceramic pasta bowl on the kitchen table with a *clunk*. I opened the fridge and grabbed a few leaves of spinach, twisting them into pieces and stirring them into the pasta. There. At least it kind of looked healthy. Maybe that would make me feel better.

I listened to the rain while I ate and stared at the table. A sudden stab of understanding shot through me as to why Terry and Susan had lived here together. It was lonely, to say the least. Maybe I could give Alice another call? No, she was passed out from her pain meds already. Oliver? He was probably busy.

My fork scraped loudly against the bottom of the bowl. Glancing around the kitchen, my eyes flicked to the numerous cabinets and drawers packed full of dishes, cups, and utensils. All things that I would have to pack eventually. I shook my head—one room at a time. The chair squeaked against the floor as I pushed back and set the bowl on the counter.

I flicked off the lights in the kitchen and headed for the stairs, starting the ascent to the only place devoid of boxes. I hadn't begun to tackle the upstairs yet, which included a bathroom, two bedrooms, and the loft. The loft was a converted attic space and also happened to be Terry, Susan, and Grandpa's childhood shared bedroom. It was where my brother, Oliver, and I had stayed whenever we visited. At least we did until he got married last year. Now a queen-sized bed had replaced the two twin frames that used to be there, one of which had been moved to a bedroom downstairs.

I turned left at the top of the staircase and tugged on the long cord hanging from a square-shaped door in the ceiling. With a great squeak, a collapsed ladder stretched downward and bumped gently against the floor. I climbed the wide wooden steps, greeted by the soft glow of Christmas lights wrapped around the exposed beams of the loft. It gave me enough light to see the fluffy bed underneath the yellow stained-glass window. The pattern of the stained glass looked like a snowflake and according to Susan was something called a Metatron's cube. I'd asked her years ago what it symbolized, and she shrugged, explaining it was a just symbol for good luck.

I sat on the edge of the bed to take my shoes off and was overcome with a wave of tiredness. Everything in my body ached in harmony. I sluggishly changed into pajamas and crawled underneath the white flower-patterned comforter. I blinked at the familiar sight of the Christmas lights and sighed.

Tomorrow, I'd tackle the barn. For sure this time. No backing out again.

I closed my eyes and listened to the steady drum of rain pounding on the roof. After some time, I noticed an electrical hum. Was that the Christmas lights? They couldn't be using that much power, could they? The hum grew in pitch until it dissipated.

I snuggled deeper into the comforter. I just wanted to sleep. I'd take care of that tomorrow. For now, I was warm and dry and—

I was stuck.

It was dark, stuffy, and disorienting. I put my hands out and felt around me, but I was pressed in on all sides by . . . something. The stringy texture reminded me of the innards of a pumpkin. A mass of spiderwebs. I pushed against the wall, and it snapped back. How did I get here? Where was I? Uncontrollable panic welled up inside me. Small gasps of fear were replaced by screams as I kicked and struggled against the darkness.

Eventually, I stopped screaming, my throat raw. All was silent until the growing noise from outside my prison grew louder. It was like a cluster of static was hurtling toward me at high speed. It was so loud, I clamped my hands over my ears. What could it be? People? Maybe there were people out there who could help me?

I needed to see what it was. I needed to know.

I pushed with all my strength against the mass. I breathed deeply and pushed even harder, willing it to break. Instead of breaking, something strange happened in the blackness. A stab of pain shot through my head, and my vision moved outward.

I saw where I was trapped. A large round sack suspended on all sides by thousands of tangled stringy threads. The harsh orange light was unwelcoming and eerie. I watched myself struggle to pull apart the sack from the inside. It was so strange. I could still control my body, but I watched from afar.

Turning my attention away from the sack, I tried to see what the static sound was. Giant masses of amber-colored clouds floated around me, the sky a muddy brown. It was too bright here but somehow too dark at the same time. My eyes strained against the contrast. It was painful. The static increased.

The more I listened, the more of the garble I understood.

They were voices. And songs. And instruments. And ideas. A billion streams of consciousness overlapping. There was no order, just an indistinguishable frenzy of vocalizations. My ears rang, and my head was invaded by a splitting pain.

What was going on?

A much nearer gushing noise turned my attention back to my pod. Black liquid seeped through the thousands of strands into the sack. I felt the cold sludge ooze onto my skin.

I panicked, and something slipped. It was dark again. I was back in my body, the rushing of black liquid cold and suffocating. I started screaming again. The black liquid filled the pod, passing my head in seconds.

I didn't scream for much longer after that. There wasn't anything after that.

Nothing.

Just darkness.

My eyes cracked open. Soft yellow light filtered in from the window above me, making an oval shape of color on the bed. I eased myself into a sitting position.

What a strange dream. Even stranger, I couldn't remember falling asleep before it started. I didn't usually dream, so to have one that felt so . . . real was odd for me. I stretched my arms in the air, alarmed at how sore they were. I sighed. I had overdone it while packing yesterday, and I was going to pay for it today.

"Oh my *God*!" I breathed, picking myself up from the floor. "Don't *do* that to me!"

"Grrmeow."

"You almost gave me a heart attack!" I said. "My heart actually exploded."

The cat licked its paw and preened, unconcerned.

"Where did you even come from?"

"Grmeow."

"Were you Terry and Susan's?"

"Grmeow."

I sighed. "I'm not going to get any information from you, am I?"

"Grmeow."

I knelt and held my hand out to him. He gave a tentative sniff and pushed his head into my fingers. I scratched behind his ears, which activated the purring mechanism. He started drooling.

I chuckled. I had forgotten how good it felt to have another living thing interact with me, even if it was just a cat. He flicked his tail in the air and sauntered in the general direction of the stairs. I followed, glancing at the large metal storage shelves next to the stairwell.

Now that I had my newfound friend, this place didn't seem half as scary. I didn't know why I thought it was so terrifying in the first place. It was just a barn, after all. Why was I getting worked up over nothing?

There was no railing for the old stairs, and the barn was tall enough that falling would end in probable death, so I took out the flashlight and picked my steps carefully. Reaching the top, I was greeted by my furry pal. He seemed to be waiting for me.

"Hi," I said. I shined my flashlight on the wall, hoping to find another light switch, which I did. I clicked it on, tearing free a mess of spiderwebs.

The more I listened, the more of the garble I understood.

They were voices. And songs. And instruments. And ideas. A billion streams of consciousness overlapping. There was no order, just an indistinguishable frenzy of vocalizations. My ears rang, and my head was invaded by a splitting pain.

What was going on?

A much nearer gushing noise turned my attention back to my pod. Black liquid seeped through the thousands of strands into the sack. I felt the cold sludge ooze onto my skin.

I panicked, and something slipped. It was dark again. I was back in my body, the rushing of black liquid cold and suffocating. I started screaming again. The black liquid filled the pod, passing my head in seconds.

I didn't scream for much longer after that. There wasn't anything after that.

Nothing.

Just darkness.

My eyes cracked open. Soft yellow light filtered in from the window above me, making an oval shape of color on the bed. I eased myself into a sitting position.

What a strange dream. Even stranger, I couldn't remember falling asleep before it started. I didn't usually dream, so to have one that felt so . . . real was odd for me. I stretched my arms in the air, alarmed at how sore they were. I sighed. I had overdone it while packing yesterday, and I was going to pay for it today.

I located my clothes, settling into the same dusty jeans as yesterday. I was going to be poking around a mucky old barn; no need to do more laundry than I had to. My eyes flicked to the clock on the nightstand. Was it really only six thirty in the morning? A quick look out the window revealed today's weather would be very much like yesterday. I groaned. On my way to the ladder, I felt the bulbs of the Christmas lights. They were warm but not overly hot. I unplugged them just in case the humming from last night meant they were going to explode or something.

In the kitchen, I poured a bowl of cereal. The carton of milk escaped my grasp and sloshed a healthy amount onto the counter. Blotting the mess with some paper towels, I sat on the hard kitchen chair and stuck a spoonful in my mouth. Each bite tasted bland and unappetizing, but I kept eating anyway. I stared at the back of the box, and my thoughts wandered to the dream. Most bits were hazy, but I remembered the pod and the darkness inside. In fact, I didn't think I'd ever be able to forget the penetrating darkness. The suffocating blackness. Drowning.

My chewing slowed to a stop as my appetite evaporated. I pushed the bowl away from myself and stood to gather my jacket, shoes, phone, and a small flashlight. Shrugging on my jacket and taking a much-needed deep breath, I walked out the front door.

There were a total of four buildings on Terry and Susan's property: the house, the two metal storage sheds, and the barn, all of which were situated at the bottom of a valley surrounded by soaring pines, evergreens, and oak trees. A clearing around the house and barn let in a small circle of light. Everything else was shaded by the imposing expanse of the forest.

I made my way toward the barn, ignoring all thoughts of axe murderers waiting for me around the corner. I stopped short of breaching the threshold. It was an odd place to put a barn. The entire foundation had been sunk into the remains of a large granite deposit. I could still see the chisel marks and chipped pieces that had been patiently stripped away. Why build this massive barn here, when there was a perfectly good flat area where the sheds now stood? Why bother to blast away huge chunks of rock?

I peeked my head into the opening and shuffled inside. There were stalls on the lower level that probably used to house livestock at one point. Old tack, ropes, farming equipment, and tools hung from large square nails driven into the walls. Everywhere I looked was roughly the same color of grayish wood, spiderwebs, and dust.

It was quiet. The light drizzle behind me dissipated as I walked further inside, like walking into a vacuum. A chill in the air made me step back. There was an uneasy feeling here, one that was hard to ignore. My stomach churned. My hands became clammy.

The diluted light from the clouds could not penetrate the threshold, so I hunted for a light switch. Did they even have electricity in here? Eventually, I located a pair of switches behind some wooden planks.

"Aha," I mumbled. "Found you."

I leaned sideways and clicked on the pair of old switches with a *cur-chunk*. The hum of electricity buzzed above me as two old metal lamps came to life, casting a soft orange glow onto the colorless scene. There, that was a little better.

A small thumping noise preceded a loud rasp directly behind me.

"*Grrrmmmeooow.*"

I whirled around. My feet tangled in each other, and I fell backward with an undignified squeal. I looked around frantically for the noise, but nothing was there.

"Grr-meow."

I looked down. Sitting in front of me was a very dirty black cat. His tail twitched as his bright yellow eyes surveyed me. He meowed again, which was less of a meow and more of a feline gurgle.

"Oh my *God*!" I breathed, picking myself up from the floor. "Don't *do* that to me!"

"Grrmeow."

"You almost gave me a heart attack!" I said. "My heart actually exploded."

The cat licked its paw and preened, unconcerned.

"Where did you even come from?"

"Grmeow."

"Were you Terry and Susan's?"

"Grmeow."

I sighed. "I'm not going to get any information from you, am I?"

"Grmeow."

I knelt and held my hand out to him. He gave a tentative sniff and pushed his head into my fingers. I scratched behind his ears, which activated the purring mechanism. He started drooling.

I chuckled. I had forgotten how good it felt to have another living thing interact with me, even if it was just a cat. He flicked his tail in the air and sauntered in the general direction of the stairs. I followed, glancing at the large metal storage shelves next to the stairwell.

Now that I had my newfound friend, this place didn't seem half as scary. I didn't know why I thought it was so terrifying in the first place. It was just a barn, after all. Why was I getting worked up over nothing?

There was no railing for the old stairs, and the barn was tall enough that falling would end in probable death, so I took out the flashlight and picked my steps carefully. Reaching the top, I was greeted by my furry pal. He seemed to be waiting for me.

"Hi," I said. I shined my flashlight on the wall, hoping to find another light switch, which I did. I clicked it on, tearing free a mess of spiderwebs.

The weak light flickered, revealing the outline of boxes stacked in the center of the room. Lots of boxes. Some were cardboard, some were wood, but all were stacked in a perfect pyramidal shape.

I walked around the pyramid. It was a little taller than me and twice as wide at the base. Mouse droppings covered the floor—apparently, my little friend was a vegetarian—joined by a thick layer of grainy dust.

Curious, I picked one of the top boxes and pried open the flaps. Holding the flashlight in one hand, I shined it into the box and saw—

Pens. It was filled to the brim with . . . pens.

Inside the plain cardboard box were several hundred pens of various sizes and styles. Many of the pens seemed old, others like they were bought yesterday. All stacked neatly. All placed with care. A few were broken in pieces, some were cracked, and some were covered with a dry dark substance. Probably ink.

Okay, maybe this was the only crate like this? I opened a few more from the base. They were all the same, simply filled with pens. A gurgle-meow resonated below me. I looked down to see a pair of bright yellow eyes peering up at me.

"Pens, huh?" I asked. "You know anything about this?"

The cat cocked his head. His stare was . . . unsettling. It seemed a little too intelligent. Too knowing. Were all cats like that?

I skirted past the boxes to the windows on the far side of the room and peered down at the distant muddy ground below. Through the dirty glass panes, I had a vantage point of the house and the two sheds. I undid the corroded latch on the bottom and heaved upward. It stuck at first, but after a good tug, the window came open. I leaned outside and looked up at the roof of the barn. Despite it being so old, the siding and shingles were well maintained. Upon further inspection, the timbers above were new and had been stained brown to look old from a distance. Odd. Why hide the fact that you have a new roof?

I withdrew from the window and closed it. Considering the room, something occurred to me.

The ridge beam was off-center.

The rafters were exposed, so I could see where the ridge beam lined up with the wall, and the two windows on the opposite side were off-center by quite a bit. How had I not noticed that when I walked in? I went back to the windows and walked heel to toe from sidewall to sidewall, taking a measurement. Going back downstairs—carefully—I walked the same spot underneath the windows from one side to the other.

It was off by almost ten feet.

Heading back upstairs, I ran a hand over the boards. There were gaps between them, I could probably get them off if I had something to wedge between them. I traversed back downstairs and hunted for a tool closet until I found a rusty crowbar. Excitedly I hurried back up the stairs, where I found my little friend waiting patiently next to the open boxes of pens.

"Well, well, well," I said, crouching. "I wonder what architect in their right mind put the roof ten feet off-center."

I stroked his head. He nudged my palm with his nose. "Grmeow."

"You're right, they wouldn't."

"Grmeow."

Hefting the crowbar in my hands, I scrutinized the wall. I had heard older properties like this contained secret passages or rooms, mostly used for smuggling during prohibition or as a hideaway. But what was it doing in the barn? Weren't things like that usually hidden in the main house? I ran my hand along the boards, starting from left to right. As I got closer to the windows, I felt a slight draft.

Four

<u>Tetherball</u>

It . . . wouldn't open.

"Oh, come on," I mumbled.

The handle turned, but no matter how hard I pulled, the door wouldn't budge. After yanking for an embarrassing amount of time, I sat on one of the crates full of pens and huffed. I could try to crowbar my way in, but the door was metal and looked too sturdy for me to handle alone.

My little friend meowed.

I sighed and scratched behind his ears. "Well, looks like we won't get in there after all. Not until I can find a key or something." I brushed off dirt from my hands. "How about we give you a name, huh?"

He looked indifferent.

"Okay . . ." I cleared my throat. "I suppose I could just call you Cat, but that seems a little on the nose, right?"

His yellow eyes bored into me.

"Well, it is," I murmured. "Don't look at me like that."

He hopped off my lap. A *poof* of dust rose from his fur. He certainly was dirty, like he had just crawled out of a cave. Or a tomb.

"How about . . . Catacombs?" I tried.

He cocked his head and sat. "Grmeow."

"Do you like that?"

He flicked his tail and meowed again at me.

I laughed. "Okay, Catacombs it is."

After a moment of purring, Catacombs stretched and sat facing the strange metal door. He turned to look at me.

"What?" I asked. "I tried to get it open, but it won't give."

Catacombs rotated in place and sat against the door. It budged. He lay down, and it budged some more with a small *squeak*.

Rising, I tried the knob again and nudged it forward. It opened a crack. I closed my eyes against my own stupidity and put my head in my hands. It was a *push*, not a pull.

Catacombs stretched again and flicked his tail.

"I am so glad you were the only witness to that," I said.

I grabbed the knob again and pushed. The door swung open.

A small white room filled with cobwebs lay beyond the door. A poorly boarded-up broken window on the back wall was the source of the draft. The acidic odor of paint wafted from a nearby cluster of empty tin cans. A few brushes lay near them, bristles full of dried paint and black grit. The floor felt almost spongy from the many uneven layers of white paint slopped into now-dry puddles.

In the center of the room was . . . a tetherball pole.

It was the only description that came to mind. A tall copper-colored pole jutted up from a large wide-brimmed metal bucket. There was no ball or rope, just . . . a pole in a bucket. A large amount of dirt filled the metal bucket, obscuring the bottom.

I stood in shocked silence. Out of everything I had expected to see, this was not even on my radar. Catacombs sat beside me and meowed.

I walked around the room, circling the tetherball pole as if it were some strange animal. What was it? Some childhood relic that someone felt was too precious and hid behind a false wall? Maybe it was too heavy to move?

I stepped forward to grab the pole but was jerked to a stop by an overwhelming sense of danger. Horrible nausea rose in my throat, and I wasn't sure if I was about to throw up or scream. My heart pounded. My vision darkened. I drew my hands back and turned to run out of the room, but Catacombs rubbed against my leg. The crushing fear disappeared. I was fine.

What was going on?

This was not normal. Nothing about this room was normal. I needed to leave. Right now.

Nudge.

And I was fine.

Catacombs slunk to the corner of the room and crouched low to the ground. His tail swished as he readied to pounce on something behind the paint cans. In one swift motion, he leapt and swatted at a small spider that had made a home there. He munched on it and licked his paw while he waited for me to do something.

I turned my attention to the base of the pole. The metal bucket was wide at the mouth but not half as deep. I shook the pole, freezing cold to the touch, but it didn't wobble. In fact, I couldn't budge it. It was probably welded to the base of the bucket.

The "dirt," upon closer inspection, wasn't really dirt but large oily brown beads that moved like sand. I reached in and attempted to grab some, but the pebbles were slick. I tried to get to the bottom of the bucket by scooping them to one side, but the nature of their slipperiness made them always stay level.

I moved to stick my hand in and touch the bottom, but my common sense kicked in. Who knows how long this thing has been here? There could have been broken glass or rusted nails in there for all I knew. I carefully reached into it, using the pole to find where it connected to the bottom. It was a weird feeling, all of those pebbles sliding past my arm. They didn't give any resistance against me. Like they weren't even there.

The bucket was much deeper than I thought. And cold. I was almost up to my elbows. Now past my elbows. Any second now, I would hit bottom.

Any—any second now.

I was now up to my shoulder.

I wiggled my arm. Was this a false-bottom floor? Did I just put my hand straight through a hole in the wood? That must have been it.

I rose and backed away from the bucket.

A hole in the floor. That had to be it. What else could it be?

Slightly disturbed, I backed out of the room, ran past the stack of boxes, and trotted down the stairs. Striding over to where I imagined the room would be above, I scanned the ceiling.

Nothing. Not even a crack.

I frowned. Maybe there was another hidden room or a space between the two levels? I needed to see what was at the bottom, then I could find out where the other room was. Taking out my phone, I again ascended the stairs. Kneeling next to the bucket, I clicked on the camera app and waited for it to load.

It occurred to me how silly I must have looked, waiting on the floor clutching my phone, staring skeptically at a bucket with a pole in it.

Keeping a very tight grip on my phone, I lowered my arm back into the bucket, soon up to my shoulder in the strange slippery beads again. I clicked the side button a few times to get some pictures, twisting my wrist to capture several angles. I pulled my arm out and sat back on my heels.

Flicking through the numerous photos, I was confused. All of the pictures were black, except one at the end.

Instead of darkness, there was light.

There were no distinct objects or any identifying features, only fuzzy vibrant pinks and oranges. Sweeping swaths of saturated colors blurred together into a confusing array of curiosity.

I sat back on the floor and put a hand to my head. Was I dreaming? Was this one of those dreams where you think you're awake, but you're still asleep? I flexed my fingers and felt the pain of the splinters I'd acquired pulling the wood off the wall. That felt real.

Catacombs emerged from the other room and sat beside me. I gave him a pat.

"Grmeow."

"No, I don't think I'm going insane."

"Grmeow."

"Yes, I know I'm talking to a cat."

"Grmeow."

"No, that does not make me crazy by default."

He stretched his back into an arch and spent a few minutes cleaning his paw. He glanced at me before sauntering over to the bucket and hopping onto the rim.

"Hey, what're you—"

With a casual lean, Catacombs fell sideways into the bucket. The brown beads sloshed in a single wave before becoming still.

I stared open-mouthed. After a moment of stunned silence, I came to my senses.

"Catacombs?" I called, getting to my feet. I rushed over to the bucket and tried to push away some of the beads, to no avail. I didn't hear anything below. Nor did he reappear.

Okay, well *now* I had to do something.

How far down was that drop? Cats were agile, but what if he had been hurt, still stuck in the barn somewhere? I couldn't just let him die. In the last hour, I had gotten attached to the little guy. At least I could take a peek and make sure he was okay. But how far down was that room? I couldn't just poke my head in to see, but the pole looked sturdy enough. Maybe I could slide down into what was evidently another secret room?

I rushed back downstairs to the tool closet where I had found the crowbar earlier. Hanging above the shelves were a few coils of thick rope. I grabbed one.

I ran back up the stairs. The exposed beams on the sidewall opposite the white room looked sturdy enough, so I tied one end of the rope to it. Rolling it out, I fastened the other end around my waist and pulled it tight. I didn't trust my arms not to give out halfway down the pole. I wasn't sure how long the drop was from the bucket, but it couldn't be more than a few feet. Using the rope was probably being overly cautious, but the last thing *I* needed was a broken leg.

Mounting the pole fireman style, I slid past the strange beads and watched the ceiling disappear. A thought occurred to me:

Maybe this was a bad idea.

Five

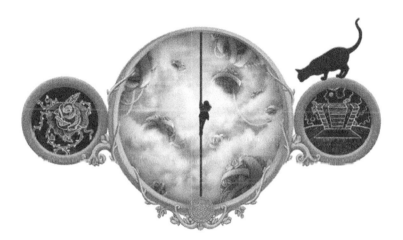

<u>Roseland</u>

The slippery brown beads pressed against my face.

I slid at a snail's pace down the pole. A bead came dangerously close to getting in my mouth, revealing the horribly bitter taste coating them. I clamped my teeth together. Another one stuck to my eyelashes. My eyes scrunched shut instinctively.

This room below was much farther down than I'd figured; I was still sliding after a minute's time. The pole never buckled or swayed throughout the descent. My clammy hands stuck and squeaked on the freezing-cold metal.

My eyes were still shut tight when I gradually slid to a stop.

A cool breeze rustled my hair. The swirling wind had a fruity smell to it, almost floral. I inhaled. Lavender, lilac, oranges, and something else. Roses. The air smelled strongly of roses.

I cracked open my eyes. The bright warm-toned light obscured my first glances with overwhelming color. The saturated oranges and pinks seemed blended into the very fabric of the air.

My eyes adjusted and widened. Gargantuan sphere-shaped islands floated in place in the distance, and wispy clouds drifted lazily between them. Like small moons in stasis among the pink-and-orange clouds, they sat suspended by nothing. Strange white vines and pink vegetation embedded themselves in overlapping layers, resembling bizarre enormous rubber band balls.

I craned my neck to see some of the nearest orbs. Others in the distance were so large they obscured the horizon. Twisting together, white vines and vegetation made up bridges connecting the small planets, hanging from them like swirling ribbons.

For an uncountable passage of time, my hands were clamped to the pole. It was the only thing I was fairly certain was real, so I clung to it for dear life. My panting breath caused no echo, getting more ragged with each passing moment. Faint music floated past my ears. Not a melody but a tinkling collection of notes. It seemed to be part of the atmosphere. As natural as the air I was breathing. It belonged here more than I did.

Evidently, this was not the secret room I thought it was.

Time passed. I realized my arms ached. I took my eyes off the immense scene and looked down. Below me was a large orb, big enough to appear almost flat from my vantage point. The pole went all the way to the sphere.

I slid down the remaining feet but was stopped by a tug around my waist. The rope from the barn. Fumbling with the knot, I untied it with a few tugs. My shaky arms held out long enough for my sneakers to touch the ground. I unclenched my hands and stumbled back from the pole.

A gust of floral-tasting wind swept by, and my eyes watered. I blinked away the tears and rubbed my eyes. I rubbed them again, but it didn't erase what I was seeing. I tried again. Everything was still there. The sweeping clouds, the floating islands, the strange color-tinted air. I swallowed but couldn't eliminate the taste of the impossible world.

That left me with only one conclusion: it was real.

"*Grrrrmeow!*"

A gurgling meow snapped me out of my stunned silence. The unpopped bubble of shock and disbelief erupted in a shrill, unbecoming scream.

"*Gaaah!*"

I whipped around to see Catacombs staring up at me from atop a cluster of thick spongy vines, eyes twinkling.

"Stop doing that!" I yelled.

He flicked his tail. Did he look smug?

I glanced at the pole and remembered his lack of opposable thumbs. I heaved a few hyperventilating breaths. "How did you even get down here? And a better question: Where is here? Where am I? What is *this*"—I gestured wildly at my surroundings—"doing in a barn in a backwater town in the middle of nowhere? In *Oregon* of all places!"

Catacombs patiently waited for me to finish. He licked his paw. To my amazement, I found myself waiting for a reply. From a cat.

"Great." I sat next to him on the cluster of vines and put my head in my hands. "I'm now arguing with a cat."

"Grmeow."

"No, I don't feel any better. Sorry for yelling at you."

"Grmeow." He pressed his head to my leg. I gave him a pat.

Sighing, I peeked up. Everything was still there. Nothing had disappeared yet or shifted into anything else. Was that a good thing? Did that mean I wasn't dreaming? Maybe I had fallen and hit my head, and that meant this all *was* a dream. That possibility made me feel a tiny bit better. A very tiny bit.

Looking back the way I had come from, my gaze followed the long copper pole until it disappeared into a perfectly round hole in the sky, made visible by the large brown beads. Staring at it made my brain hurt. It was just so . . . *there*. A hole in the sky. The rope from the barn swayed in the wind.

I blinked and stood, shuffling a few steps forward on the sphere. Some of the vines encasing the strange ball sprouted outward and twisted together. These pockets made flower shapes, like some crazy pink-and-maroon roses on steroids. The roses were everywhere, with clusters of smaller ones the size of a breadbox and huge ones the size of castles.

This sphere was large, connecting to another nearby smaller sphere via vines. I tiptoed over the spongy ground until I became used to the way my steps sank into it. Like walking on wet sand.

Catacombs trotted ahead of me and headed for the vine bridge. Not knowing where else to go, I followed. I had the impression that Catacombs had been here before, which made him more qualified to lead than I was. He leapt onto the sloping cluster of vegetation that twisted into the next enormous orb island. It was wide and seemed sturdy. I tested a step onto one of the vines and put my weight on it. Nothing strained; it felt solid. I crept forward just in case.

Halfway across, I made the mistake of looking over the side. A tsunami of vertigo plowed into me as the reality of just how high I was settled in. Thousands of feet dropped into the clouds below, probably more. The fluffy pink-and-orange clouds looked deceptively solid, but it made me dizzy to think there was a bigger drop beneath the cloud layer.

My legs wobbled. I backed away from the edge and shuffled up the remaining bridge, breathing a sigh of relief when I stumbled onto the sphere. This one was bigger than the last, with an almost flat top. The smaller vegetation had been cleared away from the center, and in the middle was a cluster of trapdoors.

They were all different shapes and sizes. Square, round, hexagonal, octagonal, and even a triangular-shaped hatch. I counted seven in total, all of them inscribed with a variety of symbols. I recognized a few of them: an infinity sign in a circle, a pentagram, Celtic knots, Mandarin characters, and in the center, the symbol from the loft. That same strange snowflake-looking sign. What was it doing here? Where did these hatches come from? Who put them here?

And the most important question of all: Where was I?

"Grmeow," came a gurgle behind me.

I turned to see Catacombs peering up at me with a tilted head. He sat near a large iron-banded trapdoor.

"Grmeow."

"What?"

"*Grmeow.*"

I paused and turned. "Do you . . . want me to open that for you?"

"Grmeow."

"It must be rough not having hands, huh?"

"Grmeow."

The hatch was a simple square door made of wood and held together by rusty iron bands. Crouching, I grabbed hold of the cold handle. It was easier to move than it looked, but the door was heavy. I tugged upward, and it creaked open.

The hole beyond it was dark. Not true blackness but a deep echoing well of deep greens and purples. Faint, pulsating glows of light moved within. A musty, damp smell wafted from the hatch, permeated by the pungent odors of cinnamon and sage. Something rumbled.

The strange light moved again. I leaned closer and squinted. What was that?

Two hands pressed on my back and shoved me from behind. I reached for the edge of the trapdoor but missed. My stomach dropped as I fell forward, tumbling headlong into the darkness with a startled yell.

Six

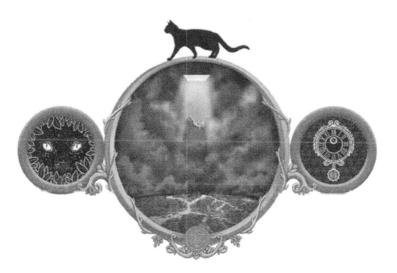

Roger That

I had no sense of direction as the wind rushed past me.

My arms flailed to grab something, *anything*, to stop my fall. My hands clawed at empty space. I twisted, flipping onto my back, the square of pink light from the trapdoor in the sky rapidly growing smaller. It was my only point of reference as I tumbled into oblivion.

I was probably screaming, but the howling of the wind drowned it out. A sudden *whoosh* preceded a deluge of water soaking me in cold droplets. I sputtered against the spray, turning in uncontrolled circles. A blur of light flashed past my vision in rapid bursts, followed by patchy darkness.

Something springy hit my side and flipped me over. Dark slender silhouettes of branches reached upward, backlit by an ethereal glow from beneath. I put my arms over my face. The branches ripped past me, breaking and bending as my weight slammed into them. One caught the sleeve of my jacket, violently jerking my right shoulder. I screamed as it popped into a position it shouldn't have. The branch snapped, and I was falling again.

Before I could continue screaming, I hit and slid off of a leafy patch of brambles and slammed into the ground. Everything went gray.

Disjointed thoughts returned at a sluggish pace. Was I still falling? I didn't feel like I was falling anymore. My body was pressed into something soft and spongy. The sharp odor of wet dirt and strange spices assaulted my nose. I cracked open my eyes.

Tiny squiggles of bright glowing blue blurred into focus. Curling strands of moss twitched and swayed. Small insects piddled between the strands, upset at having their path blocked by something as large as me.

I blinked, coughed, and rolled onto my back. Horrible pain shot through my right shoulder. My arm flopped against the ground, but it didn't hang right from my shoulder. It was out of place. Limp. I blinked again and sucked in a delayed shuddering breath.

Towering purple trees looked down at me, taller than any skyscrapers I'd seen. Their bark was a dark plum color, and their branches stretched out at sweeping angles. A vast canopy of plump foliage blocked out most of the deep-green sky. The light was strange. Backward. Instead of being lit by the sun, everything was underlit by patches of glowing blue moss. I raised my left hand in front of my face. Angry cuts and scratches crisscrossed my palm, lit blue from the patch of moss beneath me. Unfamiliar birds cawed in the distance.

After my breathing returned to normal, I sat up. Nothing seemed to be broken, but my shoulder was definitely dislocated. The pain had dulled to numbness, but it flopped disturbingly. I swallowed nausea away and cradled my right arm, rising on shaky legs. The small clearing was ringed by dense rainforest-like vegetation. Blue patches lit up the surrounding shadowed forest, stretching in all directions.

I looked up from where I fell. I couldn't see the trapdoor anymore, only a rolling expanse of dark clouds far above the trees. Flashes of electricity popped behind the clouds, which seemed too thick for even lightning to penetrate.

As I turned in a circle, a low growl stopped me in my tracks. No, it was a hissing noise like a snake. The chilling hiss echoed from everywhere, it seemed, increasing in volume. The hair on the back of my neck prickled. I looked behind me.

A strange creature, head low, entered the clearing. Its spiny, fur-like scales were patterned with swirls that gleamed fluorescent green. Its large head was shaped like a cat. Steely wide-set reptilian eyes stared me down, lean coiled muscles twitching under the folded, scaly skin.

I stumbled back. The creature followed, silently moving through the brush. My sneakers hit something hard, and before I had time to move my foot—

Snap!

The stick broke in half, echoing through the clearing. I cringed. The creature showed no indication of having heard the stick snap, continuing to advance with tight, calculated strides. Its tail flicked, the smooth curve interrupted by acid-green-tipped spikes. They flexed at vicious angles.

My back bumped against one of the colossal trees, rough bark crinkling against my jacket. The creature stalked forward with a low hiss. I pressed my left hand behind me and felt the end of a broken branch. I grasped it, heart pounding. It wasn't big enough to defend myself with, but maybe it could make a good distraction. Did I dare try to run? How far would I be able to go before it caught up with me?

What other options did I have? Be mauled here or get mauled a few yards from here. Maybe if I ran, I would at least have a chance.

The tiger-lizard stopped advancing, muscles on its hind legs twitching in anticipation. I'd seen cat fights before, enough to know it was about to strike. I didn't have much time left to make a decision. My thoughts turned to how painful it would be to get eaten alive. I tried to swallow, but my throat was too dry to manage it. The edges of my vision darkened.

The creature's eyes widened, and I flung the stick from behind my back. The unanticipated movement startled it, buying me a split second to dash for the nearest opening in the trees. It leapt behind me, missing my head by inches as its large muscular frame got stuck between two narrow trunks. I tripped over roots and bushes, pumping my shaky legs as fast as they would go. My shoulder bounced horribly and popped again. The muscles in my arm spasmed. I gasped, sucking in a whimper as I sprinted forward.

A raspy hiss of a roar bellowed behind me. I didn't look, weaving between the trees and following the patches of blue moss. They were my only light source. I had no choice but to follow them.

Something whizzed past my ear and thudded into a nearby tree. More thuds. Something flew past my ear. I chanced a look. Stuck into the nearest trunk was a spike from the tail of the creature. It was longer than my forearm, buried deep into the purple wood. Green acid from the tip ate away the bark from the inside out.

The hissing growl followed close behind me. I realized something: this thing was playing with me. Playing with its food. It could catch me at any time. This chase was on *its* terms. My labored breath came in gasps. The ground became increasingly uneven, great deposits of shale hidden beneath the dense vegetation, shifting every few steps.

A sharp sting pierced my right leg. I lost my balance and tumbled into a nearby shallow ravine. Rolling over stones and twisting roots should have been painful, but all that mattered was the excruciating pain in my leg. Someone had injected liquid metal into my bones; I was sure of it. Someone had set fire to my veins. The flames now devoured them.

Rolling to a stop, I clutched my leg and screamed. I looked for the flames but saw nothing. A gash on the side of my knee leaked through my torn jeans, a fizzing green slime coating the wound. The pain increased. My vision darkened. I tasted blood.

I tried to push myself against the ravine wall, but the dirt crumbled. The creature stalked toward me, but it was so hard to see. My ears rang. Everything went black, white, and yellow all at the same time.

The dark outline of the creature moved, its long slender tail poised in the air.

My eyes were still open. Everything had been reduced to shapes.

Another shape appeared in front of me. A flash of pink light, and then—

Nothing.

Just darkness.

The world had been erased. Only obscurity and fuzzy thoughts remained.

I didn't remember anything before the darkness and couldn't see anything beyond it. Warbling noises echoed through my head, but I couldn't understand them. Voices, maybe? I floated on the edge of . . . something. What was that word again?

The voices grew loud. Demanding. Pulsing static consumed me like a radio struggling to find a station. My head hurt. So did other things. In fact, the other pains sharpened as I focused on them.

I floated. But in what? What was that word?

I was bobbing. Bobbing on the surface of—

Consciousness.

My fingers twitched, and my eyes snapped open.

Everything was blurry. And bright. I lay on my back, staring at an old-fashioned globe lamp suspended above my head. The soft yellow light of the humming bulb was comforting, contrasting against the dark wooden ceiling. I blinked, and the details on the lamp sharpened. Little pink painted flowers adorned the frosted glass. The paneled dark ceiling above was carved with extravagant Victorian-style vines.

I swallowed, throat raw and sore. My head spun from the effort of focusing on so much detail. Gathering my strength, I scrunched into a sitting position. A blanket fell to my lap, a dark film passing over my eyes as the pain in my head worsened. My jacket was nowhere to be found, but my skin was damp like I'd just recovered from a fever. A hesitant move of my shoulder confirmed it was back in place. I rolled my arm, alarmed by the sudden movement as it almost popped out of socket again. I cradled it to my chest and shuddered.

A dull ache flared in my leg. Pulling back the blanket, I frowned. My jeans had a hole cut in them, just below my right knee. A large gash ran from the back of my leg to the front, but it had been sewn up. Yellow thread crisscrossed the cut, the brown alcohol stains still visible.

I blinked and looked around the room. I was in somebody's study or a small library or something. Bookshelves stood proudly against the walls, an abundance of chairs and tables clustered together in pockets. Dark oak and cherrywood paneling covered the ceiling and floor. Exotic artifacts dotted the space: tribal masks, framed bits of parchment, and expensive-looking paintings of various styles. A large ornate rug dominated the center of the room.

I sat on an opulent antique chaise longue in the corner. Swinging my legs off the side, I prepared to stand. A table and chair sat near me, so I used it to hoist myself up. Putting some weight on my bad leg, I tested if I could walk. It was painful, but nothing compared to the pain earlier. I limped around the room. All was quiet except for a ticking clock on a nearby shelf. It had no hands.

There were three doors in this room: one on either side of me and one straight ahead. Heading for the closest of the three, I staggered to the handle. It swung open with a light push.

The door led to a long hallway dimly lit by wall sconces. Another door stood on the other side. A thin strip of light gleamed from the crack beneath. Halfway down the hallway, my leg stiffened, my vision blurred, and my ears rang. Falling to my knees with a loud *clunk*, I held my spinning head in my hands.

The door at the end of the hallway opened. A muffled cry of surprise echoed down the hall as I passed out again.

"Well, I didn't think you'd try to get up so fast."

I was aware of being propped against a wall. The voice seemed miles away from me, pinpointed only by the occasional sound of tearing paper and the corresponding pain in my leg.

The voice heaved an exasperated sigh. "Ugh. These were some of my neatest stitches too."

I opened my eyes. My leg came into view first, the gash covered by a red-stained gauze pad. A blurry shape knelt in front of me.

"Ow," I groaned.

I attempted to sit up but was pushed back.

"Easy. You need to sit tight for a second."

I blinked. The blurry shape focused into a guy. He looked to be in his midtwenties, maybe older. The dark circles under his eyes and rough complexion made it hard to tell. He wore a gray long-sleeved shirt, stained jeans, and hiking boots. Rummaging around a nearby duffel bag, he pulled out a fresh pack of gauze, folding it into a thick square. He grabbed some scissors and held out the gauze.

"Can you hold this for me?" he asked.

I took the gauze and held it taut for him to cut, which he did. He ripped off a piece of medical tape, swapped out the bloody gauze for the new square, and taped it to my bleeding leg.

He zipped the duffel bag closed. "Is that too tight?"

"Uh." My throat was raspy, so I cleared it. "No. Where—"

"Hang on, let's get back to the other room so we're not on the ground."

I nodded. What was I going to do, argue?

He grabbed under my arm and lifted me into a standing position with ease. We stumbled back to the room I woke up in, and he steered me back to the chaise lounge. I sat down, panting.

"Okay." I huffed. "I'm off the floor. Can you tell me what's going on—I'm sorry, what's your name?"

"Roger," he said. "And you are?"

"Lily."

"Nice to meet you, Lily."

I fumbled for words. His response was so . . . ordinary and polite.

"It's . . . nice to meet you too, Roger."

He slid the nearby chair next to the chaise and sat. "First things first, does your mouth taste like you just downed an entire tube of toothpaste?"

I stared at him, waiting for the punchline.

His expression was even. He was completely serious.

"Um, n-no?" I said.

"Well, then you won't be dead within the next hour, so that's progress." He rose and grabbed a silver pitcher from a tray on a serving buffet across the room. Looking inside, he nodded and reached for a cup. "You want some grape juice?"

Again, I was too stunned to speak. The ordinary nature of the question floored me. My mouth floundered for a moment before I stuttered, "S-sure."

He grabbed two crystal cups and poured a deep-purple liquid into each glass. Walking back to his seat, he handed me one and took a drink from his.

"Thank . . . thank you." I took a sip. It was indeed grape juice. The fruity flavor coated my raspy throat. The familiarity of it calmed me. It seemed to make breathing a little easier. My leg hurt less, too. Even though the juice was ice cold, warmth flooded through my extremities like I had just sunk into a hot bath.

He cleared his throat and leaned back in the chair. He seemed bored. "Okay, you probably have some questions."

I stared at him. "You're damn right I have some questions."

SEVEN

Sandwich Apocalypse

Roger drained the remaining grape juice in his glass and raised an eyebrow. "Shoot," he prompted.

"Okay, for starters, who are you?"

He gave a wry smile. "That's an easy one. My name's Roger Owens. I was in charge of surveillance today for The Forest, Sector 14."

"Sector 14?"

"Yeah, you know, the one between 13 and 15?" He shook his head and set his empty cup on the table. His eyes, a deep brown color, looked at me with a measure of disdain. "I swear, do people even bother to *read* the cartography manual before they go on duty anymore?"

My head spun. "Manual?"

He frowned. "Which Gate did you even come from? Nearest one is a three-day hike. I didn't see you until the Tigris had already tripped two of the sensors." He narrowed his eyes. "Which was *also* weird, because no one's passed through that sector in almost a month, and . . . and . . ."

Roger trailed off as he read the confusion on my face. An understanding blossomed behind his eyes, and he paled. He leaned forward. "How much do you know about . . . any of this?"

"Um."

Judging by the sudden change in his demeanor, I was not who he thought I was. I had stumbled into somewhere I wasn't supposed to be. Before I could weave together a modicum of an intelligent answer, the string of events from the last few hours tumbled from my mouth at an uncontrollable speed.

"So I was worried about this cat who jumped down into what I thought was another secret room in the barn, so I went down what I thought was, like, one of those portable tetherball poles? And I ended up in this place that's . . . somehow another world? Like some real-life Narnia stuff. But it had all of these trapdoors, and the cat, he kept appearing in front of me for some reason. And then I opened a trapdoor and got pushed inside by . . . I don't even know what. Someone? But I fell a long way and ended up in this forest, and then I got chased by that tiger thing. Sorry." I sucked in another breath and wondered why I was lightheaded. "Tigris? And then I woke up here, and I was alone, but now you're here. And I don't know how I got here, but that's all I know up to this point."

Roger stared at me, mouth open. His attentive expression had progressively degraded to one of disbelief as my tirade of nonsense continued.

He pinched the bridge of his nose. "You . . . fell through a trapdoor and ended up in the sky. You don't know where you are, and you landed in the *only* place in the *entire* Forest of Luminescence where the Tigris has its *only* den?" He threw back his head and laughed. "Wow. You have even worse luck than I do."

I looked down. The way he put it made it sound as if I had done everything on purpose.

He stood. "So you aren't a Jumper, I take it?"

"A Jumper?"

"You've never heard the term before?"

I shrugged. "I've heard the word, but probably not in the context that you're talking about."

"Well . . . shit," he said matter-of-factly. "This is not how I thought this day would go."

"That makes two of us."

He laughed, seemed to come to the realization that this predicament wasn't funny, and coughed. "Well, at least you're safe now. You've been out for a long time. I was getting worried you wouldn't wake up. Right now, the best thing you can do is sleep. Tigris venom is no joke. The longer you give it to leave your system, the better." He turned to the door. "I'm going to make some . . . inquiries."

"What? You're not just going to *leave* me here, are you?" I looked around the room. "Where even is here? Where am I? What happened after I passed out? What's going on?"

Roger sighed. "It's . . . Look, I can explain things later. As for what happened after you passed out, there's not much to tell. I brought you back here after dealing with the Tigris, patched up your leg, popped your shoulder back in, made sure you weren't dying, etcetera, etcetera. But you're safe now. There's no safer place than Gifts—" He bit his lip. "I'll . . . explain that later, too. Also, did you mention something about a cat?"

I blinked in surprise. Out of every topic in my psychotic rant, *that* was the detail he remembered?

I nodded, stopping when dizziness overtook me. "Yeah, Catacombs. Well, that's what I named him anyway. I think he was my aunt and uncle's. He's probably still back at the floating rubber band ball place."

"Floating rubber band balls?"

"The, um, other place I mentioned. That other . . . world." I leaned against my knees as spots obscured my vision. Sitting up was becoming a battle. I swallowed. "I don't know what else to call them."

Roger surveyed me. "All right. You're lucky that quill just grazed you. If it had entered your bloodstream directly . . ." He blew a breath through his teeth. "Well, complete nervous system failure usually occurs in sixty seconds or less. I'm amazed you're even conscious right now." He turned to leave again. "What did you say your name was again?"

"Lily. Lily Masters."

Recognition lit his eyes, his expression shifting from casual interest to understanding. "Masters?"

I blinked. "Is something wrong?"

He shrugged, pushing open the door. "No, nothing. It's nothing."

"Roger?" I called.

He turned.

"Um, thank you. For saving my life, I mean. It wasn't your job to help me, but I'm glad you did."

He flashed a small smile. "Actually, it is my job. Get some rest. You're safe here."

Roger pulled the door shut with a *click*, and I was left alone.

The small ticking of the handless clock staved off the deafening silence. I stared at the cup of grape juice in my hands, willing my numb brain to form coherent thoughts.

Did everything in the last few hours really happen? Was I almost eaten alive? I'd ruled out the possibility I was dreaming because I was in too much pain to be asleep. My leg throbbed, the cuts on my hands stung with every movement, and my shoulder felt like it would pop out of socket at any time. My stomach growled. I tried to ignore it. How long had I been unconscious?

Experimentally, I tried standing. It was painful but not impossible. I hobbled to the buffet counter to pour myself another glass of juice. My stomach grumbled again.

"Quiet," I muttered.

Turning to stumble back to the lounge, I stopped. There was something on the couch that hadn't been before.

A sandwich.

A diagonally cut peanut butter and jelly sandwich sat on a plain ceramic plate. I glanced around the room. Had someone walked through when I wasn't looking? No, I would've heard the door open. I would've heard footsteps. The plate had just . . . appeared.

I crept toward it, prodding the sandwich before picking it up. It seemed normal. Just a PB and J, nothing spectacular. I put it down and moved it to the table. Lowering myself onto the lounge, I sipped my juice until the glass was almost empty and swished around the remaining contents. The diluted color of purple distorted the cut crystal into elongated shapes. I turned to set the glass on the table and stopped.

There were now two sandwiches.

I rubbed my eyes, glancing around the room to see if anyone had come through. I looked at the plate again. There were now three sandwiches. I blinked. Four sandwiches. Blink. Five.

"Um, Roger?" I called. "There's a plate of replicating sandwiches here. Is this normal?"

Silence. In the time I had looked at the door, three more sandwiches appeared.

Before any more could materialize, I grabbed half a sandwich and stuffed a large portion in my mouth. Chewing rapidly, I swallowed and cast a hesitant glance at the plate. The pile had stopped growing.

I had ended the sandwich loop and saved the world.

Hooray.

I finished the sandwich and slumped sideways. Every inch of my body ached and throbbed in varying degrees of misery. Maybe I should try to get some sleep. I had endless questions, but sleeping sounded better than trying to figure them all out on my own. I didn't feel in any danger here. Maybe it was all right to rest.

The room seemed to be getting warmer, like an electric blanket being pulled over me. A low hum in the air reverberated through my body. It soothed my many aches. There was something else. A presence in the room with me. Inexplicably, the knowledge that I was being watched over by some unseen force washed over me, calming my questions and fears.

I lay against the lounge and watched the globe lamp above me dim. A weight on my eyelids pulled them closed and eased me into unconsciousness.

It was dark. Again.

My hands pressed against the slimy, pumpkin-like walls of my confines. As before, panic welled up inside me. I wanted to scream until my vocal cords wore out. I wanted to thrash and fight against the pod until there was nothing left of me.

But I had learned from last time. I inhaled the stagnant air and forced myself to calm down. I knew where I was trapped. At least, I knew what it was. The strange sack suspended by thousands of strands. I'd been able to see outside before, but how? How did I do it last time?

I felt around the pod. They were unbearably stringy, and too stretchy to move. No matter how hard I pushed, the walls didn't break.

I remembered this. The pushing, willing myself to see outside. And then—

I pushed at the wall until I couldn't push anymore, and suddenly I could see. I was outside the sack again; at least my vision was. I could see thousands of threads suspending the pod, connecting to the clouds. I remembered the threads doing . . . something last time. The memory was so fuzzy. What was it?

A loud noise approached, enveloping me from all sides. The crackle and whistling of the great wall of static surrounded the pod, so loud my eardrums bled.

But this time I didn't cover my ears. This time I listened.

And this time I heard.

The jumble of voices untangled themselves. Songs, poems, books, instruments, incoherent thoughts, hopes, dreams, unfulfilled wishes, angry promises, and a million other things echoed through the clouds. It was too much. I couldn't pick one voice to follow out of the throng.

"Hello?" I called.

Immediate silence.

"H-hello?" I stammered. "Where am I?"

The silence held. And then—

"They are coming"

Every voice spoke at once, magnifying the words to an impossible volume.

"W-what?"

"THEY ARE COMING," the voices screamed.

The din was too much to bear. The voices staggered into their own separate voices and rhythms but all shouting the same thing.

I whirled around to look back at the pod. Black liquid seeped through the threads. I tried to keep calm and stay outside of the pod, but the panic dragged me back inside. I screamed. The black sludge filled the pod. Everything went black. Nothing could escape the black. There was nothing.

Nothing.

Just darkness.

EIGHT

Reunion

Something swatted my face.

I tried batting it away but couldn't find the offending swatter. A weight on my chest shifted. The smell of peppermint and old tobacco permeated the air. I opened my eyes to see what the commotion was.

Intense yellow irises stared at me, inches from my face. The dirty black fur surrounding them twitched as a wet nose sniffed, whiskers tickling my cheek.

My head, in the middle of rising, smacked back onto the wooden curl of the chaise lounge.

"*Ow!*" I yelped.

Catacombs leapt gracefully off my chest and perched next to the plate of remaining sandwiches. The dimmed lamps brightened to full illumination as I swung my legs off the couch. A flash of dull pain reminded me of my limitations, so I stayed seated.

I rubbed the back of my head. "Why do you keep *doing* that?"

A chuckle echoed from somewhere. I looked around the room to see who had entered. No one was there.

I stretched my neck, groaning at the headache already spreading behind my skull. Judging by the pounding pain, I'd been asleep for a few hours at least. My body ached less than it did when I had fallen asleep, but my mouth felt like it had been scrubbed with hay. I smacked my lips.

Peeling back the bandage on my leg, I prepared for a messy sight. I frowned at the bloodstained gauze. The gash, when last Roger taped it, had been bleeding, crisscrossed with stitches that had torn in some spots. Now, a thick white line replaced it. The stitches had completely dissolved.

How was that even possible? This wound looked days if not weeks old. I wasn't asleep for *that* long, was I?

Catacombs hopped to the floor. He sniffed at the gauze in my hand and the scar on my leg. His whiskers twitched as he peered up at me with a tilted head.

I reached to pet him. "Where'd you run off to?"

He sat.

"Where d'you think I ran off to? I was trying to find out whether you were dead or not! Jeez, lady. I was only trying to show you the Gate, not giving you an invitation to hurl yourself in."

I froze.

Someone was talking. Their voice didn't come from one direction but from between my ears or from a pair of headphones. Except I wasn't wearing headphones.

I glanced around, searching for a person or a speaker mounted on the wall or *something*. Catacombs rubbed up against my still-outstretched hand. I jumped.

He blinked. *"Hey, don't be scared. Sorry, I didn't think you'd freak out so much."*

I stared.

"To be honest, I thought you'd be used to the weird stuff by now."

I continued to stare.

"I mean, it's been, what, almost two days registered in your body clock? Three days? Earth time is funky."

My mouth dropped open.

Catacombs's ear twitched in the direction of the door leading to the hallway. He stretched. *"Looks like you're about to get the lowdown. I'll come back when you've . . . adjusted. Later."*

Sauntering to one of the tables, he walked behind a wooden leg and vanished.

I sat on the lounge. Did that just—

Voices approached from the hallway. The mumble subsided as the door creaked open. Roger poked his head around the frame. He spotted me and advanced.

"Hey," he said. "You're awake. Good. I, uh, brought some people to . . . talk to you."

He pushed open the door all the way and strode inside, four people trailing him. Two men and two women.

They all looked as though they had returned from a long trek in the mountains. Dressed in hiking shoes and varying degrees of coats and protective clothing, they were worn down and dusty. The man on the far right was in his sixties, bundled in an old leather jacket. He had a wrinkled face and an air of someone who had seen too many hard years go by. The other man was in his late twenties with kind eyes and a jovial smile. He looked familiar.

The two women standing next to Roger were roughly the same build, shorter and athletic. One of them was African American, with coffee-colored skin and long intricately braided hair streaked with the occasional patch of gray. The other woman looked younger, maybe my age. Her light auburn ponytail was tucked into a thick beanie that framed her pale freckle-covered face. She also looked familiar, but I couldn't place her, or the younger man. They had similar features. Siblings maybe?

The group stared me down. Roger hung back in the open doorway, arms crossed.

The older man in the leather jacket stepped forward. I stood, surprised to find my leg didn't hurt at all. He nodded politely and stuck out his hand.

"Hello, miss," he said. His voice was gruff. "My name's Edgar Vasquez. You mind telling us yours?"

I glanced at Roger. No readable expression showed on his face. I warily grabbed Edgar's hand and shook. It was rough and calloused.

"Uh, Lily. Lily Masters. I'm—"

Edgar gripped my hand and leaned in to scrutinize my face. He stared into my eyes. I looked back. His irises were a cold glacier blue. A broken blood vessel in his left eye created a dark blotch. His pupils swept back and forth rapidly, as if searching for something. After a tense moment, he let go of my hand and stepped back.

"Well"—he turned to the group behind him—"she is who she says she is. As far as I can tell."

Everyone seemed to relax.

"That's a relief at least." Replied the African American woman. She had a rich voice that carried an accent of another country. "She's just another Wander. I don't see why we're making such a fuss. Let's process her and get back to work." She glanced sideways at the others. "Let's not forget, we have more pressing matters to attend to."

"Bea," the other woman muttered, "we couldn't forget if we tried."

The woman, Bea, looked down.

"I don't think she's another Wander, considering the Gate she came through," said the younger man. He approached me, a curious expression upon his features. He smiled. "Well, I never thought I'd see the day—Hey, Ed, maybe it wasn't so bad that John retired early after all, eh?" He chuckled and extended his hand. "Terry Masters. I believe we're related somehow."

My stomach dropped. That was how I recognized him.

It was . . . Uncle Terry.

I put a hand to my mouth. My eyes filled with tears.

His smile faded. "Uh-oh. What did I do?"

I stared at his face. He looked so young! But his eyes were as they had always been, the same faded hazel as mine. I'd thought I'd never get to see them light up again when he laughed. But here he was in front of me. Tears of shock from the sudden rush of emotion fell down my face.

Terry looked concerned. The younger girl from the back came and stood next to him.

"Susie," he whispered. "Do you want to locate some tissues?"

Susie?

The woman was Aunt Susan. Her familiar gray hair was now a light auburn, and the wrinkles creasing her features were gone. She nodded to Terry and rummaged through one of the bookcases, returning a moment later with a handful of tissues.

Handing the bundle to me, she looked at my face and realization dawned.

"You know us, don't you?" she asked.

I stared at her. What was I supposed to say? That I'd buried them in a cemetery a few weeks ago? I wiped my face with the tissues and nodded.

"Can—" My voice broke. "Can you . . . tell me what's going on? Where am I? Why is there a plate of replicating sandwiches?"

Terry's eyebrows furrowed. "Replicating sandwiches?"

Edgar's gaze flicked to the plate on the table. He turned to Roger. "You haven't introduced her to Giftshop yet? She might take offense to that."

Roger shrugged. "I thought it might be too much at once. Apparently, Giftshop likes her anyway. Look at her leg. It was an open wound only a few hours ago."

Edgar bobbed his head. "Right. All right. Okay." He turned to me. "First off, do you mind telling us how you're related to Terry and Susan? That might give us a starting point."

I sniffed and tried to compose myself. "They're my aunt and uncle."

Susan's eyes widened, and Terry smiled.

"No kidding? You're John's daughter? I can't believe it!" He shook his sister's shoulder with vigor. "Susie, we have a niece!"

"John?" I asked. "Oh, wait a minute. You mean John Masters? That's my grandpa, not my dad. My dad is his son, William." I shook my head. "Sorry, I guess that makes you my great-aunt and uncle. Actually, when we first met, we called you 'great-aunt' and 'great-uncle,' but you said to shorten it to 'aunt' and 'uncle' because you said it, um . . . wasted time . . ." I trailed off. They were staring at me.

Terry and Susan looked at each other sideways.

"So you're . . . our great-niece?" Susan clarified.

I nodded.

"Well, it's good to know we are still alive to meet our grand-niece!" Terry said. "How about that?"

I looked down.

"Uh-oh," Susan said. "Bad news?"

I glanced up. How had I just attended a funeral for these people? They were barely older than I was!

"You, um, both passed away a couple of weeks ago. Car accident," I said. "I'm sorry."

Their faces paled. Susan let out a rushed breath and lowered her head.

Terry, as usual, was first to regain his happy demeanor. "Hey, that's all right. It had to happen eventually. It's not like it was your fault. Well, actually." He narrowed his eyes in mock suspicion. "I don't know . . . was it your fault?"

I laughed. "No, it wasn't. But thanks for the vote of confidence in your future descendants, Uncle Terry."

The group chuckled. Some of the tension in the room eased.

Edgar stepped forward. "I think that gives us a good starting point. Can you walk?"

"I think so."

"Good." He opened the door to the hallway. "Follow me."

He led the group to the door at the far end, intricately carved with many types of flowers and other flora. It was a beautiful piece. I couldn't begin to guess how much effort went into carving it. Everything in this building had the same level of craftsmanship, right down to the baseboards. Who took the time to make it all?

Edgar pushed the door open with a *squeak*. The cozy room was covered wall to wall in paper. Newspaper clippings, old black-and-white photographs, sheets of paper, and maps obscured a large portion of the walls. An enormous wooden desk sat in the center, topped in various books and interesting knickknacks. A fire snapped and whistled in a black marble fireplace.

Edgar strode into the middle of the room and inhaled slowly. "Right. I haven't done this in a *very* long time, so Bea, Terry, Susan, would you mind lending a few words here and there?"

Bea, Terry, and Susan nodded.

Terry leaned against the wall. Bea and Susan sat on a nearby couch, Roger remaining in the doorway. Taking the hint, I found a seat on a neighboring wooden chair.

Edgar leaned on the desk, palms flat against the cluttered surface. "All right, miss. What I am about to tell you in the next few minutes will most likely drive you insane. Older and much wiser people have gained this knowledge and subsequently lost their minds. I've seen it happen before, and I'll probably see it happen again. At this moment, it is my obligation to give you an out."

He glanced at the others, eyes shifting to each one individually before settling on me. "You have a choice: You can learn who we are, what we do, and why we do it. You can discover wonders of the universe, the likes of which even the greatest minds on Earth could never dream of. You can unlock a new world. A new reality. If you want to."

Edgar folded his arms. "Or you can leave. You can walk away right now and save yourself a whole mess of pain and suffering. We can make you forget all you have seen, heard, and felt in your time here. You can walk out of here like nothing ever happened. If you choose to continue, there will be a price for this knowledge. It may not come tomorrow or the next day or in the next hundred years, but someday the bill comes due. It may cost your life, or the lives of those you love. You must be prepared to pay that price."

His chilly blue eyes bored into mine. "But the choice is yours. Are you in, or are you out?"

Silence.

I looked down at my palms. The angry welts and lacerations had been inexplicably healed in the last few hours. Between the cuts, I spied the splinters I had acquired when pulling down the false wall in the barn. He was right; whatever I stumbled into had led me to danger. I had almost been killed already because of it.

But the wonders of what I had seen baffled me. The rose-colored world, the strange glowing forest, this house that was more than it seemed . . . Were there more places like it? The possibility sparked something in me that I'd never felt before. A curiosity. A thirst for answers. Exploration. It pushed me forward when I could have stopped prying. Back in the barn, I could have left it alone. It would have been easier to leave it alone.

But this secret, whatever it was, left me digging for answers. I wanted to find them.

I looked up. "I'm in."

Edgar's mouth twitched. "Then let's begin."

NINE

Jumpers

Edgar rose from leaning on the desk and paced.

"Many centuries ago, people around the world began noticing . . . anomalies in their everyday lives. They were subtle things. Visual distortions, strange animal behavior, unexplained mechanical failures. Things that didn't look quite right but had no explanations as to *why* they didn't look quite right. Ripples, if you will. Ripples in the fabric of reality. One day, people saw movement in them."

"Movement?" I asked.

"Shapes. Animals. Noises. Other life than what existed on Earth," he said. "Back then, many assumed that they were gateways to Hell, or Purgatory. But some . . . some believed otherwise. It was as if certain spots on the fabric of reality had been rubbed bare—by time or some other force—and we could glimpse something on the other side."

Edgar paused and looked at the others for help.

Susan cleared her throat and took the reins. "One day, in 1859, things sort of . . . snapped. Like an elastic band that couldn't take any more stretching. Throughout history, the ripples—or shifts, as they came to be known—were observed, but nothing ever came of them. They were just sort of *there*. But in September of 1859, things changed. The shifts split open into what we now call Gateways."

"Gateways?" I asked.

Susan glanced at Terry. He nodded, turning to face me. "Have you ever seen a crocheted blanket?" he asked.

Susan rolled her eyes. "You and your stupid blanket analogy."

He ignored her. "When you stretch the blanket, some of the stitches get wider and expand, while others stretch so much the holes look closed. But no matter how you stretch the blanket, as long as you keep tension in one place, there is slack in others. Get it?"

I blinked. "You lost me."

Terry held his hands out as if playing cat's cradle. "Imagine the blanket represents this universe, give or take a few octillion light-years in scale. As far as we can figure, during the Shift in 1859, the tension in the universe shifted. Doors that were previously closed were left wide open, and no one knew what to do about it." He looked to Bea, who nodded.

"A call went throughout the world, to launch expeditions and locate the newly opened Gateways," Bea said. "I doubt any of those expeditions knew what they were getting themselves into. Over time, the accessible Gates were found, documented, and cataloged. Unfortunately, not before many souls wandered into them and were lost."

"What do you mean wandered into them?"

Bea shifted in her seat, an annoyed expression flashing across her face. "Ordinary people—not unlike yourself—stumbled through the Gates out of curiosity, or in a search for riches, or what have you, and got themselves killed in the process. After witnessing the staggering loss of life, people began to understand. The Gateways were more than a safari trip. They were not some cute parlor trick they could view from the sidelines. The horrors and the beauty that lived inside were real. And they were dangerous."

Edgar cleared his throat, shooting Bea a sideways glance. "Over the next few years, the more . . . let's just say *adventurous* people volunteered to venture inside and explore. This was controversial, particularly in religious circles. After much debate, one team of highly trained and experienced explorers were chosen to enter a single Gate. They were given the most advanced technology they could find, equipped with the most information possible. Seven people entered the Gate. Only five returned."

He looked to Bea again.

"When they returned, none of them could make sense of what they'd seen," she said. "They babbled of places that were neither Hell nor Earth. They spoke of plants and creatures far beyond reckoning. They told of the Otherworlds."

There was a short tense pause.

Susan turned to me. "The remaining five who had returned from the Otherworlds dedicated their lives to guarding the Gates. They understood the dangers of what would happen if . . . things started getting through to Earth. Take the Tigris, for example; by far not the most dangerous thing connected to our world, but can you imagine what would happen if it got out in a crowded city street? The carnage of just that one mistake would be . . . horrific."

Terry shuddered. "Fortunately, most of the Gates don't open straight into Earth; most of them are linked by what we call Connector worlds. Think of small fringe bubbles connected to bigger bubbles. They link Earth to the Otherworlds by filling the gap." He nodded to me. "You came through one on your way here, by the sound of it. They're not usually very big. Pockets of space between larger spaces."

"Despite Connector worlds," Edgar said, "it fast became apparent that the original five wouldn't be enough to protect all the Gates. Over the years, people joined the fight. Officially, their only job was to keep people from wandering in.But . . . well, the kind of people crazy enough to join up weren't exactly the type to follow the rules. They explored, mapped, researched, and cataloged all they could find beyond the Gateways. Some explored too far and were never seen again."

I sat sideways against the chair and propped my head on my elbow. "Just how many Gates are there?"

"There are thirteen known Gateways on Earth," Susan said. "Seven are only ever open at one time. On the same day every year, they switch. The seven Gates that were previously closed are opened, and vice versa."

"Why?"

She shrugged. "We have no idea. But for the last two hundred years or so, they've switched on October 31, regular as clockwork."

"Are you serious?" I looked around the room. "It switches on Halloween?"

Susan smiled. "Haven't you ever wondered why that day in particular feels different from any other day? The strange foreboding feeling as night approaches? That odd . . . energy in the air?"

"I always thought it was from eating too much candy," I mumbled.

The group chuckled.

"Anyhow," Terry said. "As people started mapping, they discovered Gates *within* the Gates. Even though there are only thirteen Gates connecting Earth, there are more Gates connecting to those Gates, and so on. It seems when the blanket shifted, it caused a ripple effect, opening Gates across this universe. I can only imagine the chaos in the worlds that link straight to each other without the benefit of Connectors."

Everyone but me shuddered.

Terry cleared his throat. "But that's where we come in. To this day, we guard the Gates around the world."

"We make sure that if anyone wanders into the Gates, we get there first and get them out," Susan explained. "No matter how stupid they were to end up there in the first place."

"We are guardians," said Bea.

"We're explorers," said Terry.

"We're conservationists," said Susan.

Edgar looked at them all.

"We're Jumpers."

It was quiet. The sudden dam in the river of information made my head spin. I looked at the ground, feeling many pairs of eyes scrutinizing my every expression.

After some time of silence, Susan leaned forward. "Um, how— Are you all right, Lily?"

I looked up, intending to say something, but no words escaped. Closing my mouth, I stared at the floor.

"Give her a minute," Bea whispered. "That was a lot to take in. Though we might have broken her. You know some people can't handle it."

I blinked at their varying degrees of concern. "No. I'm fine. I'm fine. Definitely . . . fine."

The cat was right. I should be used to crazy stuff now, right? An uncomfortable pang of realization shot through my stomach; I just referenced a cat as a credible source of advice.

"Do you . . . need a drink?" asked Terry. The others shot him a look.

"No, no, I'm fine. I just . . ." I put my head in my hands. "My brain hurts."

Edgar nodded. "Yep, that'll happen."

"Okay." I shook my head. "So you guard and protect these portals to other worlds. Right. That's normal. Okay. What do you do for jobs? How do you make money to live if you're doing this all the time?"

They chuckled.

"Out of all the things to worry about doing this job, money is at the bottom of the list," Bea said. "We get compensation."

"Compensation?" I asked. "So someone pays you?"

"Yes and no," Terry said. "It's not exactly a nine-to-five job. More of a . . . choice of lifestyle. Let's just say our needs are taken care of."

"What if you get tired of it? What if you want to do something else?"

"Those who discover the Otherworlds tend to have issues leaving it behind," Susan explained. "The knowledge that we, as human beings, make up such a minuscule percentage of the known universe causes a lot of people to withdraw from the rest of the world. As time goes by, it becomes difficult to relate with anyone outside of the Jumper community. The only person I've personally known to completely withdraw from this life was John—er, your grandfather."

My stomach gave a funny jolt. "Wait, Grandpa was a part of this too? But he was, I don't know, so . . . *Grandpa*."

Terry snorted. "He always was a little . . . reserved, even when he was part of the community. Never one to be part of anything, liked to keep to himself. Mom and Dad always thought he had a screw loose. But he

74

was as involved in this as we are, mapped and explored just like the rest of us. Then he met Lorraine, who I assume became your grandmother?" He asked. I nodded. "A nice girl from Idaho. She's sweet and quiet; they really are perfect for each other. Back in our time, they'd just gotten married, and John . . . left."

Terry shook his head. "He dropped everything and ran. No explanation, no note, nothing. I know it was his decision, he needs to live his life as he sees fit, but after everything we'd been through together. Our family. Our friends. He left them all."

I looked around the room. Everyone was shaking their heads.

"I don't understand," I said. "Why was it such a big deal that he got married and left? Can't he just come back?"

"Of course he can. Nobody disowned him," Terry said. "But it . . . our relationship will never be the same. The level of trust is broken. For him and for us. Jumpers don't usually settle until they retire for good because, well—" He glanced at Bea and Edgar. "We may call it a job, but it's a duty. We take an oath when we're sworn in to willfully give our lives for each other and the people of the Earth. And . . . it happens. People die all the time. You can be as prepared as you want, take every precaution, check every box, but it's never enough. You try your best to keep each other alive, but—"

Terry looked hard at the floor. Susan put a hand on his shoulder and squeezed. "Sometimes, things just happen. So, to abandon those who count on you to do your job . . . it causes a lot of hurt. Especially if they don't give a reason for leaving."

It was quiet. Everyone but me looked at the floor, countenances dark.

"So how are you two here?" I asked. "In this time, I mean."

The group shared a look.

"Er," Edgar said. "We . . . don't really know."

"What?"

"We used a Teleporter to get back here, in our time," Susan explained. "And we found ourselves fifty years in the future. No idea how or why we got here. Nearly gave poor Ed a heart attack when we waltzed through the door. Us too. The dorky twenty-year-old Ed became a grouchy old man in an instant."

"Hey," Edgar called. "This grouchy old man can still kick your collective asses. Watch it."

Terry and Susan chuckled, backing away with their hands raised.

"Teleporter?" I asked.

"Oh." Bea realized. "She hasn't been introduced to Giftshop yet."

"Right," Edgar said. "Maybe we should—"

A frantic beeping sound came from his coat. He reached into an inside pocket and pulled out a large round compact. It was bronze in color, metal wires sticking out the top in a zigzag array. He flipped it open, looked at the contents, and groaned.

"Son of a bitch," he muttered. He flipped the compact closed and shoved it back in his pocket. "We gotta move."

"Which Gate?" asked Terry.

"Not a Gate. Locals are causing trouble again." Edgar huffed an annoyed sigh. "I'm getting real tired of wasting resources on these idiots."

"Do you need us?" asked Susan.

"'Fraid so. Sorry to cut this reunion short. Roger," he called to the doorway. I'd completely forgotten he was back there. He hadn't said a word during the whole exchange. "You all right to introduce her and take her home?"

Roger shot Edgar a look and chewed on the inside of his cheek. "Sure."

Edgar rubbed the bridge of his nose. "All right. Don't bother processing her for now. Keep to the paths, no detours. Take her through Sal's. That might be safer. And for the love of God, *do not forget to sign her out.*"

"I know the rules, Ed."

Edgar gave him a long meaningful stare. "I should hope so." He turned to me. "We'll be in touch. Roger will explain further and get you back to Stars Crossing. Good luck, and we'll see you later. Till again." He waved to the others. "Come on, time to gear up."

Bea followed right after. Terry and Susan flashed bracing smiles in my direction.

"We'll talk more, we promise," Susan said. "Try not to let this drive you down the rabbit hole, okay? Everyone adjusts eventually, so give it time. Till again."

Saluting with two fingers, she followed Bea and Edgar through the door.

Terry waved. "See you later, beloved grand-niece." He threw his head back and pointed with a dramatic flourish. "To the rioting locals, and wherever else fate takes us!"

He ran after the others, leaving me, Roger, and a million questions in his wake.

Ten

Giftshop

The room was quiet after they'd left. The soft crackling of the fire marked the only sound outside my head.

Inside my head, however, squealed a muted flatline noise reverberating in the useless pile of mush between my ears. I could feel synapses in my brain firing, trying—and failing miserably—to make logical sense of the last few hours.

Eventually, Roger cleared his throat. I looked up.

He watched me from a safe distance, head inclined. "So . . . you good?"

"I'm okay," I said. "Trying to wrap my head around the whole infinite worlds thing."

"It gets easier after a while. Kind of. Most Wanders—"

"Wanders?"

"People like you who find Gates by accident. Most Wanders stumble into a Gate, scramble back the way they came, and make a beeline for the nearest bar. I can't say I blame them, either. Oh, I almost forgot—" He rummaged through his pockets and pulled out a small dart-shaped container filled with clear liquid. "The second part of your antidote."

"Antidote?"

"For the Tigris poison. You got part one when you arrived. This is just to neutralize any remaining toxins."

"Do I need to sit?"

He shook his head, rolling up his sleeves. "Just tilt your head back."

I pulled my hair away from my neck and did as he asked. Roger popped the dart-shaped container into a funny-looking syringe he pulled from his pocket. Unwrapping a new sterilized needle from a vacuum-sealed packet, he attached it to the syringe and ripped open an alcohol swab. The sharp smell of antiseptic assaulted my nose as he probed the side of my neck with his calloused fingers.

He swabbed the area. "This might pinch."

I braced myself, but it was unnecessary. The most painful sensation was a slight tug as warmth spread through my neck. My mouth tasted funny, like oranges. It passed. He held a cotton ball firmly in place and prepared a bandage.

I laughed. "Wow, you're really good with needles. That didn't hurt at all."

Roger's eyes flicked to mine. A dark expression flashed across his features. He pressed the Band-Aid to my neck and stooped to clean up the wrappers. It was only then that I noticed the long-healed needle marks on his arms. Track marks. They had faded over time, but the purple puckered dots shone clear.

I looked down. "Sorry. I didn't mean—"

"It's fine." He pushed down his sleeves. "What does your mouth taste like now?"

I swallowed. "Um, kind of fruity?"

"Not minty? Not like toothpaste?"

"No."

"Then congratulations, you are officially clear of Tigris venom." He tossed the wrappers in a nearby trashcan, disposing of the needle in a lidded red container marked with the biohazard symbol. "Gold star for you."

"Why is no toothpaste a good thing?"

"Tigris venom, for some reason, leaves a minty taste in your mouth. Like you've just eaten an entire tube of toothpaste." He shuddered. "It's gross. Once that's gone, you're clear."

"Well, that's . . . good to know. Any of this information would have been good to know." I shook my head. "I wish Catacombs would've mentioned any of this before I got pushed through that trapdoor. Would've saved me a lot of trouble."

"You got pushed? Pushed by who?"

"I—" I stopped. "I actually have no idea. There wasn't anyone else around. Not that I could see, anyway. I mean, there was Catacombs, but he's pretty small."

Roger folded his arms and sat on the couch. "Oh, I wouldn't rule him out yet."

"You know he's a . . . cat."

"Yes."

"He doesn't have, like, hands to push with."

"Yes."

I was going to say something but shelved it for later. I had other questions pertaining to now.

"So, what is Giftshop?" I asked. "It sounded like you guys were talking about a person. Is it a code word for something?"

"Oh." He put a hand to his head. "Sorry, I keep forgetting you haven't been introduced yet. That's usually the first thing we do."

"You, uh, do this kind of thing often?"

"Well, not like *this*," he said. "You're the first Wander in a long time to get the full story."

I raised an eyebrow. "You know, between Jumpers and Wanders, you guys aren't very creative in the name department."

He smirked. "Names are funny. They aren't official, it's just what happened to stick over time."

"So what do you do with them? Wanders, I mean."

"Same thing I did with you. If they're hurt, we take them back here and patch them up. If not, we just wipe their memory and send them on their way. They don't remember a thing."

"Wipe their memory? What happens if you accidentally wipe *all* of their memories? Do they just become a shell of a person?"

Roger shook his head. "That's not how it works. The term *wiping memories* is a misnomer. You can't actually erase memories, no matter how hard you try. They always find a way back somehow. What we do is more like . . . rewiring." He stood. "But to answer your question about Giftshop, it'll be easier to explain in another room."

I pushed myself up from the chair. "Also, how is my leg—"

"I'm coming to that. Follow me?"

"Sure."

He led me through the room I'd woken up in, tugging open the only door that no one had come through yet. It led into another long hallway lined with picture frames and photographs. Several yellow hanging lamps lit the way. Roger stopped at a cluster of framed black-and-white photographs.

"We start," he said, "at the beginning: the early 1860s. After the Shift, the first Jumpers organized themselves into regional groupings, failing spectacularly at the whole 'protecting the world' thing. Because of technological limitations, communication and leadership were . . . well, to coin a phrase, complete shit. In an emergency, few people would be able to respond, let alone do anything about the problem. There was a lack of unity, infighting. The whole organization was one big mess, ready to explode."

He tapped his finger against an old photograph of a group of men, singling out two of them with scraggly mustaches and mischievous eyes.

"These two, Thomas Everbell and Samuel McNee, were out mapping a Gate one day. They came across a pair of 'peculiar round disks' wedged in the ground of a Connector world, as Samuel described in his journal." He reached into his pocket and pulled out a metal disc about the size of his palm. Its slightly arched top resembled an immobile silver button. The same snowflake design from the loft window had been embossed into the top.

"They picked them up, examined the pair, and moved on. Nothing out of the ordinary happened for about an hour. They started to make camp, talking about the day's progress and so on. Midway into the conversation, Thomas stops talking. Samuel turns around and discovers that Thomas is no longer at the campsite."

"That's not good."

"People disappearing during a mission isn't exactly unheard of," he said. "One of the *many* reasons we don't camp in an Otherworld anymore. A moment later, the metal disk in Samuel's pocket started buzzing, and he was transported here, with Thomas dazed and waiting."

Roger moved to the end of the hallway, stopping short of the door. "Needless to say, they were confused. They were suddenly in a house with fine furniture and lights that ran on something other than kerosene. And when they looked out the window— Well, you can see for yourself."

He pushed open the door, waving me forward.

A heavy purple velvet curtain blocked the doorway. I pulled it aside and staggered through the threshold.

It was an enormous room. The ceiling was so tall I could barely see the top. The walls were covered by bookshelves stretching almost as high, filled to the brim with books, strange artifacts, and ancient tomes. Many squashy red sofas and armchairs were arranged in clusters throughout the room. A large flagstone fireplace remained unlit. Unlike the other rooms, this one had windows. Huge, graceful, arching bay windows that extended all the way to the ceiling.

Through them, I saw the cosmos.

Billions of stars stared back at me. They glittered and gleamed like millions of diamonds in the darkness, splashing the expanse with a tidal wave of stars. The occasional slanted blob of faraway galaxies dotted the endless shimmering field. A silence echoed from the vast macrocosm. The totality of deep space seeped through the windows, bringing a sobering reverence with it. My eyes burned. Tears leaked from them as I sucked in a breath. I never knew a single snapshot of the universe could be filled with so much darkness yet so much light.

I wanted to say something. I wanted to describe the torrent of emotion inside me, but my mind was blank. A purple comet flashed by, leaving a trail of tiny diamonds fluttering behind it.

Eventually my floundering brain connected with my mouth. "It's so—" I broke off. The word *beautiful* was an insult to the scene.

"I know," Roger said. "I can't think of any words either. And believe me, I've tried."

We viewed it in silence. Our faint reflections in the blackness of the glass brought to mind how insignificant we were next to this . . . *infinity*. How could our minuscule actions matter in the slightest compared with such overwhelming grandeur?

Eventually Roger cleared his throat. "When Thomas and Samuel picked their mouths up off the floor, they found a table filled with the little peculiar devices, which we now know as Teleporters. Over time, others from around the world arrived. That was the day Jumpers found Giftshop."

"So what is Giftshop?"

He gestured to the whole room. "*This* is Giftshop. No one knows why she transported Samuel and Thomas here, and no one knows why she exists. But she gave us an edge in a fight we had been slowly losing. Supplies, technology, medical help, a singular gathering place. If the need was dire enough, she would provide it. She gave us . . . well, a way to continue protecting the Earth."

"So Giftshop is . . . this house?" I clarified.

He chuckled. "I wouldn't call her a *house* exactly. Unless your definition of a house is an omnipotent Winchester-like mansion that can manipulate matter and space and sometimes time and— Well, you get the point."

"So she's what we're standing in? Is it like a smart house or something?"

"That's one way to look at it. Although she far surpasses any technology that you or I will see in our lifetimes. Or the next millennia." He nudged me with his elbow. "Go ahead and say hi."

"Will she talk back?"

"In a way. Go on."

"Um." I looked around the room, feeling strange talking to empty space. Roger watched me expectantly.

"Hello?" I called.

Something in the room shifted. A breeze that came from nowhere bustled past me. I caught a whiff of pine, cinnamon, dust, and ginger. It was the exact smell that wafted from the box of Christmas decorations back home. The smell elicited an immediate feeling of nostalgia. Suddenly the room didn't feel so empty.

"Hello," I called again. "My name's Lily. It's nice to meet you. Formally at least. You, uh, make good PB and Js. At least I'm assuming that was you."

I spotted a nearby plate on a table with another sandwich on it, confirming my suspicion. The smell of peppermint floated by. The many lamps dotting the room brightened to a warm glow.

"Is that . . . how she communicates?" I asked.

Roger nodded, a faint smile spreading across his face. "Human olfactory senses aren't as advanced as some other animals, but they still tie to our emotions in a powerful way. What's special about cinnamon, and . . . trees? I didn't catch the last one."

I nodded. "Pine, yeah. They remind me of Christmas with my family. We used to go every year and cut down a tree up in the mountains, which my dad *always* insisted he could do by himself. When we got home, we'd pull out the decorations from this really ratty cardboard box my parents have had forever, and we'd spend the whole day decorating. My mom would make cookies. My brother would find something to break eventually. It was fun. It was the one time of year that everyone seemed truly happy. When things really felt like home." I sniffed the air again, but only peppermint remained. "So Giftshop ties different smells to memories that capture what emotion she's trying to convey?"

He nodded again.

"What did you smell when you first came here?"

He furrowed his brow. "Oof, that was a long time ago. I think it was campfire smoke and . . . I don't know what to call it, but that rain tarp smell? Those blue ones? Something like that."

"Did you go camping a lot as a kid?"

He blew a laugh through his nose. "You could say that. Anyway, besides Wanders, anyone who stays here for more than a few minutes should be introduced to her; otherwise, it causes . . . problems."

"What kind of problems?"

He rubbed the back of his neck. "Um, she tends to be a little . . . temperamental toward newcomers."

"Temperamental?"

"Well   normally, she won't let anyone in who she doesn't trust. But people are tricky. They're good at hiding things. A few years ago, a shape-shifter from an offshoot Gate near New York tagged along with a team until they got back to Giftshop. She trapped it in an infinite loop of hallways in the East Coast communities wing." He scratched his nose. "He was never seen again."

I swallowed. "So why wasn't I sucked into an infinite loop? I wasn't introduced until right now."

Roger shrugged. "Who knows? Maybe she just likes you. Sometimes it's as simple as that. I don't think you would've survived without her intervention. Your leg was so infected with poison by the time I got you here, I didn't think you'd make it."

"Wait, my leg— That was her? How is that even—"

"We don't know how she does it, but she just . . . speeds up the healing process. A lot. She also makes sure that any unwanted bacteria or organism gets scrubbed before we leave. Think of her as a kind of medical computer program. If she sees something in your system that shouldn't be, or some injury, she usually takes care of it."

"Why?"

"My guess? So we can keep doing our jobs and the world doesn't fall into utter chaos."

"Then why is she called Giftshop? And, for that matter, how do you know it's female?"

He shrugged. "It's just what stuck over time. And I don't really know, it *feels* like a female presence. Do you feel differently?"

I shook my head. He had a point. I couldn't pinpoint the reasons, but the strange presence did feel feminine. Like a bear guarding her cubs.

We watched out the window, lapsing into silence. I tried to find some cluster of stars that looked familiar, some recognizable constellation to make it feel less alien. The great expanse was so full, I could barely separate one star from the next.

I felt Roger's eyes on the side of my face, so I turned my head.

He looked away. "I, um—I have to take you back home now."

I swallowed. "Are you . . . going to wipe my memory of all of this?"

The smell of something harsh and acidic swept through the room. Sulfur.

He folded his arms. "No. Not now, anyway. Because you're related to Terry and Susan, they're going to want to ask you some questions. You've discovered us at a complicated time. There's been some . . . issues around here that have had us on edge. So until we can sort things out and process you, try not to wander into any more Gates. Please."

"What do you mean issues?"

He chewed his lip and rocked back on his heels. "There's been a breach in security. Things are going wrong that shouldn't be. Routine missions end in disaster. Entire teams go missing. But that's not your problem to worry about, so forget it."

I frowned. Out of all the things to worry about, security breaches around ever-changing holes in the fabric of reality seemed like a good one.

He waved me toward the door. "Come on. Time to go."

I nodded and turned. A subtle waft of green grass and creek water ruffled past me. At the end of every school year, we would pack up the car and camp in the mountains for a few days by a secluded lake. Oliver and I would swim, pretend to be pirates, make stick forts, and just . . . be kids. At the end of the trip, I never wanted to leave.

Roger leaned over to me. "I don't know what you did," he whispered, "but I think you have a multidimensional being that's going to miss you."

"Great," I whispered back. "I'll add that to my list of achievements for the day. Right next to almost getting eaten alive."

He laughed. "All right, you ready?"

"I just need to grab my jacket in the other room."

Tearing my eyes away from the windows, I went back through the hallway and entered the study. There were so many pictures I had skipped over. Most of them were photographs of people in groups of seven or more. A few of them were charcoal sketches of unfamiliar landscapes and other botanical diagrams.

My eyes swept around the room, settling on a coatrack that hadn't been there before. My jacket hung from it. Putting it on, I headed back down the hallway to where Roger was waiting, still looking out the window.

"You good to go?" he asked.

"Yep."

He looked at my left shoulder and smiled. "Looks like you have a souvenir."

Glancing down, I spotted a round embroidered patch with thin black threads forming the same snowflake design that seemed to be following me. It had been seamlessly attached to my jacket.

"Giftshop?" I guessed.

"Giftshop," he agreed.

Well, it looked like I made a new friend today. Maybe that made almost being eaten alive worth it.

"All right," he said. "Let's get you signed out."

ELEVEN

<u>Tally Marks</u>

"So what does *signing out* mean? Do I have to draw some weird mystical symbols to leave or something?"

"Nope. Just sign your name."

"Oh."

We walked—or rather, I followed—single file down another long narrow hallway that branched off of the room with the view of the universe. Small alcoves lined this corridor, filled with marble statues. Engraved bronze plaques wrapped around their pedestals.

"How big is Giftshop?"

"No one knows for sure," said Roger. "When Thomas and Samuel first came here, it was scarcely more than a closet. As more people joined up, Giftshop expanded to compensate. Now we find new rooms once in a while."

"Hm. Okay then. That's probably normal," I mumbled. "Sorry for all the questions."

"No worries, it's my job. Part Jumper, part medic, part Giftshop history docent. Fire away. Ask as many questions as you want."

"I'll hold you to that."

"I have no doubt."

I smiled. "Are we really floating in space?"

"Looks to be. At least the illusion of floating in space."

"What happens if you open a window? Or if one gets broken?"

"Giftshop doesn't have any windows that open. Most of them are big viewing bays, like the one we just came from. I don't think she'd allow anything, or anyone, to break her windows without there being some serious Hell to pay."

We arrived at the door. The long line of statues stretched from one end of the hall to the other, situated in little alcoves sized perfectly for each marble likeness. Each statue was unique. The different ages, sizes, and clothing were astounding.

"Who are all of the statues of?" I asked.

Roger stopped short of opening the door. "Those . . . are the people who didn't make it back."

I looked back at all the faces. The intricately carved features looked so alive. At any moment they could walk right off their pedestals, it seemed.

"Oh."

He studied his feet. "It happens more often than it should. If you're here long enough, you know most of them by name. At least in this hallway. There are others specific to each community."

"Who makes them?"

"Giftshop, probably. Most of the time, if you die, only a picture shows up. Sometimes, a statue shows up for one person but not for another. No one really knows why. In some cases, you can guess. Like him."

Roger pointed at a statue a few paces away wearing a puffy coat with a bundle of rope slung over his shoulder. He looked my age, maybe younger, eyes alert and bright.

"His name was Miguel. We grew up in the same outpost. On his first mission, he got separated from his team, who got trapped in a cave on an ice-covered Connector. An avalanche started not long after. Miguel set off a charge to divert it, killing himself in the process. He was eighteen."

"I'm sorry."

Roger's eyes swept over the statue. "Like I said, it happens all the time."

He pushed open the door, and I followed. The hallway let out into a room halfway down. It was a large space, with a few tables and bookcases. The dominant feature was a looming crystal chandelier, sparkling with white bulbs. Adjacent from the hallway, a large book rested on a wooden pedestal. The pages were yellow and stained, crossed with neat black lines in even rows to form a ledger. Scribbles and blotches of ink had taken up half the page already.

We approached it. Roger rummaged through his pockets and took out a pen. His mouth curled into a grimace. "Um, you wouldn't happen to be carrying a pen, would you?"

"No."

He sighed. "Great. All right, so Giftshop has certain rules that must be followed. One of those rules is signing out on the Guest Book whenever you leave."

I pointed at the ancient yellowed ledger. "Is that the Guest Book?"

"Yes. Whenever we leave Giftshop, we sign out on the Guest Book. So wherever you go, make sure you have a pen with you at all times."

"Why do you have to sign out?"

"No idea. It's just how things have always been."

"What happens if you don't?"

He chewed the side of his lip. "Not good things."

"What not good things?"

He pulled the collar of his shirt down to his right shoulder. On his back, raised white scars looked as if they had been burned in by a hot poker in a tally mark formation. I counted five scars: four straight and one going diagonal across all the others.

I winced. "Who did that to you?"

"Giftshop."

"Seriously?"

He shrugged to fix his shirt. "I always forgot to sign out when I was a kid. After a few times, I got the message."

"So, what, if you don't sign your name before you leave *every* time, you get scarred for life? What happens if you forget a pen? Or if it's an emergency?"

"You get burned. Which brings us back to the issue at hand. We don't have two pens."

"Why can't we just share?"

"You can't use the same pen for multiple people or else it doesn't work. Otherwise, we'd all bring pens collectively and just leave them here." He shook his head. "It took a long time for people to figure out all you had to do was sign your name. Before that, people just came here as seldom as possible."

"How'd they find out?"

"Honestly? I think Giftshop got tired of the constant complaining. She put the Guest Book in the middle of dark hallways so people would trip over it. Eventually they caught on."

I snickered. "Why don't you leave pens here for people to use?"

"They disappear. Always. Once, um—somebody—brought a bucket of pens to leave here. The next time they looked out the window, the bucket was floating past it."

I narrowed my eyes. "Was that person you?"

". . . maybe."

"You brought a *bucket* of pens?"

"What? I thought it was a good idea!"

"Why does it have to be pens? Why not pencils?"

"I think it has something to do with the ink, or at least the permanence of it. Plus, you can't erase yourself from the Guest Book if you use a pen."

"What about erasable pens?"

"I—" He paused, a surprised expression on his face. "I actually don't know."

The air crackled. A voltaic shudder rippled through the room. An almost imperceptible flash of light made me blink before an oval-shaped hole appeared out of thin air. For a moment, the stuttering caws and squeals of alien creatures were audible. A dark, person-shaped figure flew out of the hole, sliding on the polished wood floor until it came to a stop. The portal closed.

"Hello, Leo," said Roger, unfazed.

The figure swiveled on his back. He looked to be in his midthirties dressed in strange mismatched clothes covered by a light brown duster. Most of his face was obscured by large rusty amber-colored goggles.

"Hullo, Roger," he said. "Long time no see. How've you been? Still stuck on surveillance?"

Roger folded his arms. "Yeah."

"Aw, that's a shame." Leo got to his feet. "You should be back out in the field. Nothing ever happens in that sector anyway."

"It's all right. I don't mind."

Leo's gaze shifted to me. He pushed the goggles up to his forehead, revealing bloodshot pale green eyes. "Who's this?"

Roger glanced at me. "Just another Wander. I'm taking her back home now."

"What, from the Forest?" He eyed me with interest. "That's odd . . . not really a hub of activity. Where'd you come from?"

Roger shook his head. "Nah, from the Edge. Ed found her. I'm just taking her home. He and some others are dealing with the locals at the moment."

"Paris?"

"Yeah."

"Ah, I see. Idiots. We have to put up more Errands around that Gate; they're just getting too rowdy. Maybe when the so-called 'crisis' has passed, eh?"

"Yeah, maybe. Hey, you got an extra pen?"

Leo shook his head, producing a single pen and signing on the bottom line in the Guest Book. "Sorry. Fresh out. What happened to that big bucket you brought?"

Roger's cheeks tinged pink. "It . . . doesn't matter. Anyway, Leo, this is Lily. Lily, Leo."

Leo held out his hand. "Nice to meet you, Lily."

I returned a polite smile and grabbed his hand. My palm stung. Probably from the splinters. "Nice to meet you, Leo."

He let go, stuffing the pen back in his pocket. "Sorry to run off, but I gotta get going. I'll see you later. Rog, get yourself out of that surveillance station, even if you have to stir up trouble yourself."

With a cheerful wave, he crossed into the hallway and disappeared through the door with a *squeak*.

Roger shook his head. "Poor guy."

"What do you mean? He seemed so happy."

"Don't be fooled. He just lost his sister a few months ago. He hasn't been the same since. I think he's in the denial stage right now."

"What happened?"

"No one knows. He was the only one there. Things went . . . bad. Anna was just in the wrong place at the *really* wrong time. She was always a bit on the odd side, but sweet. We all miss her."

"Do siblings usually work together in teams?"

He nodded, walking up to the Guest Book. "Yeah, but not always. They just work together better than most. Anna and Leo worked together especially well; I think they've mapped more Otherworlds by themselves than a full team combined. They've been out as far as you can go and still come back."

He rummaged through his pockets, pulled out a pocketknife, and snapped it open.

"What are you doing?" I asked.

"We don't have two pens."

"So what, you're going to sign out in blood?"

"Yeah. Hurts less than if you don't sign out at all."

"Wait, you don't have to—"

Before I could stop him, Roger tugged the pocketknife, making a cut on the back of his thumb. Dabbing a finger on the small cut, he drew the initials RAO onto the old paper.

"What does the *A* stand for?" I asked.

He went through his pockets again and pulled out a pen, accompanied by a Band-Aid. Uncapping the pen, he handed it to me. "Here, sign out below mine."

"You didn't answer my question."

"No offense, but you're over your question limit."

"I believe your exact words were 'fire away.' Is it something embarrassing? Like a really girly name? Come on, I won't laugh."

He raised an eyebrow, waiting for me to take the pen.

"Fine," I mumbled. Grabbing the pen, I signed my name below his, noticing Edgar's name a few lines above ours. Roger applied the bandage and shoved the wrappers in his pocket.

"So . . . are we going to use those Teleporter thingies to get home?"

Roger shook his head. "Teleporters only link to Giftshop, and the last place you established a connection. My last connection happens to be where the Tigris was about to eat you, so that one's out. Do you remember what Terry said about Connector worlds?"

I nodded.

"Well, the seven Gates open right now on Earth all have them, and they all have a connection here. I think Giftshop rigged it."

"You said there's thirteen Gates altogether, right?"

"On Earth, yes. Only thirteen."

"And seven Gates are open, but they switch every year?"

"On October 31, yeah."

"Doesn't that mean one Gate is always left open?"

"Correct," he said. "There is always one Gate that stays open. It's located in the United States."

"Really? Where? Is it on top of the Empire State Building or something?"

"Nope. It's in a small town in Oregon that almost no one has heard of, in the hayloft of an old barn."

"You're kidding."

"Nope."

"The barn at Susan and Terry's house?"

He nodded. "The same. The Earth side was boarded up before my time, so I've never been through that way. But I've heard Ed talk about when it was in use."

"Why did it get blocked off with the false wall?"

Roger shrugged. "Some sort of . . . organic substance started growing, blocking off the connection to Giftshop. and every other Gate inside it. Terry and Susan put up a false wall from the Earth side."

"Why?"

"Because there's no point in keeping it fully guarded since the Connector was completely blocked off. Waste of manpower."

"So how are we getting back?" I asked.

He turned away from the Guest Book and headed for an arch-shaped door in the corner. "To borrow from Terry's blanket analogy: when a crocheted blanket stretches, the stitches that open tend to be clustered together."

"Okay . . ."

"So, it's common for multiple Gates to open in the same general area. Usually it's in twos, but occasionally they open in threes. Stars Crossing is home to two Gates. You found one."

"Where's the other?"

"In the basement of an old diner called Sal's. That's where we're headed."

Twelve

Sal's

The heavy wooden door creaked as Roger pushed it open.

We stepped into a large circular room. A total of thirteen doors lined the walls, all different sizes and styles. Some were carved with outlines of various landscapes, others with geometric shapes and divots. Some were riveted together with bits of mismatched steel. They reminded me of the conglomeration of trapdoor styles in the rose world. Looking down at the marble floor, I groaned in exasperation at the snowflake design inlaid in brass among the stone.

"Okay, what is the deal with this pattern? I keep seeing it everywhere I go."

"The Metatron's Cube?" Roger said.

"I think that's what Susan called it. I couldn't remember the name."

"It's a symbol for the Jumper community," he explained. "It was the first symbol associated with Giftshop, since it's what was on the Teleporters when Thomas and Samuel found them."

"What does it mean?"

"In short terms? It represents the known universe. The big things, the little things, and everything in between. I think it's supposed to remind us of the interconnected nature of life or energy or something like that. The name comes from the Bible, the archangel Metatron who guarded the tree of life."

"Does that represent you guys?"

He cocked his head. "How do you mean?"

"Well." I gestured around the room. "You guys are protectors of the Otherworlds, right? All these worlds filled with such strange and wonderful creatures. Seems akin to the tree of life. Kind of."

Roger chuckled, his eyes crinkling as he considered the Cube. "I've never thought of it like that. I suppose it's flattering to be compared to an archangel."

I turned in a circle to see all the doors. Which one had we just come through? With all of them closed, I had no reference point anymore.

"So this is where the Gates connect to Giftshop?" I asked.

"Yep. Almost all the Gates that are open right now connect to here. One way or another. Except for the one you came through. What did you say it had? Floating rubber band balls? That Gate has been blocked for a long time. Before I was born, actually."

"You said it was blocked by some organic substance. What is it?"

"See for yourself. It's that one."

He pointed to a plain door made from a dark grainy wood. I grasped the cold handle and pulled. A tangled, stringy mass obscured the doorway. The strange vegetative vines curled and twisted in tight conglomerations, thorns sticking out between the fine pale strings. A rotting stench emanated from it. My hand reflexively covered my mouth.

"What *is* it?" I asked through my fingers.

He pushed the door closed and waved his hand in front of his face. "No one knows. One day, it started growing from the Connector side of this Gate. It's been this way ever since."

"Have you tried cutting through it?"

"Only a couple hundred times. It grows back too fast."

I considered the door for a moment, frowning. "Do you think Giftshop did it?"

"I don't think so. It was probably some natural phenomenon. Sometimes, plant life acts strange next to Gates. Something to do with the electromagnetic properties, I think. It grew on every Gateway in that Connector, so that's the most logical answer. But it doesn't matter, since we won't be going through this Gate."

Roger strode to the opposite side of the room. He grabbed the peeling painted handle of a blue door decorated with orange flowers. Glancing at me sideways, he cleared his throat. "Just, uh, try not to fall off, okay?"

"Off of what?"

Roger opened the door. The flood of bright light assaulted my eyes. Squinting, I stumbled through the threshold and craned my neck.

Twisting spires of white bone-looking rocks soared into the sky. They tangled and braided together, connecting in sweeping DNA-shaped arches. Wispy blue clouds drifted between the peaks. The sky was a deep shade of lavender. A flock of silver birds shimmered on the summit of one of the spires, squawking loudly while drifting in a V-formation. The air smelled of rain and something else I didn't recognize. Something tangy and sharp. Distantly, craggy rings of rock orbited the outer atmosphere.

Roger waited until I was done gawking at the world.

"Do you ever get used to this?" I asked, neck still craned.

He looked around. "Not fully. But it loses its kick after the first hundred times."

He walked forward. I followed until I made the mistake of looking down. We stood on a twisting white arch barely wider than a car. Like the rose world Connector, nothing stood between me and the clouds below. *Instant death* were the words that came to mind.

"Hey, you coming?"

I looked up. Roger was waiting for me. He didn't look scared, so why should I be?

Keeping my eyes fixed ahead, I started walking. Roger strode forward without hesitation. I tried my best to imitate his confidence. Eventually, a large blotch of white came into view attached to the other end of the bridge. It looked like an overturned bowl, holes littering the surface in a spongelike manner. Several similar formations of them were scattered in the distance.

We stepped onto the island. Roger climbed to one of the holes toward the middle, about as wide as the bucket from the tetherball pole.

"This is our stop," he said.

I clambered after him, losing my footing a number of times. Staring into the darkness of the hole, I swallowed. "Here? How can you be sure? They all look identical."

"Trust me, I've been through here more times than I can count. This Gate leads to Sal's, and nowhere else."

"You technically *are* the expert here," I mumbled. "So do I just . . . jump into it?"

"Sure. You'll end up in the basement of the diner. It might be a little disorienting at first. Not all Gates connect right-side up, if you catch my meaning."

I swallowed again, my throat becoming increasingly dry. "Am I going first?"

"If you want to."

"What if I don't want to?"

"Then I'll go and leave you stranded here by yourself."

I thought.

"Okay, I'll go first."

"Right."

I approached the hole. It dropped straight down into darkness. The hairs on my neck stood up at the thought of falling into the unknown.

"You can slide in, if you want," he suggested.

I nodded and sat on the edge. A few deep breaths later, I inched forward and closed my eyes. The drop wasn't as far as it looked from the top. I slid at an angle until my feet hit something hard. Squatting, I felt around. My hand bumped into a round handle, the metal cold and smooth.

I twisted the knob. The door opened beneath me, and I fell into the ceiling.

It was a bizarre sensation, like getting turned around underwater. All sense of direction was forfeit. I lost momentum halfway through and fell onto the hard floor with an "*Oof!*" The hatch sprung closed, a click following soon after.

Sitting up, I rubbed my sore tailbone and waved some dust from my face. The room I had fallen into was small. Crates and cardboard boxes were stacked against the stone walls. A single bare light bulb flickered above me, lighting the dust particles aglow.

I eased to my feet and stretched. A loud thump rattled the trapdoor. It opened, and Roger emerged, grasping onto the edge of the hatch to keep from falling out. Righting himself, he closed the door and brushed himself off.

"There," he said. "That wasn't so bad, was it?"

"No, but you were right, definitely disorienting." I cracked my neck. "I have a question."

"Surprises never cease."

I narrowed my eyes.

He glanced at my expression and smirked. "I'm kidding. Go ahead."

"Why did you tell Leo that Edgar found me instead of you?"

He looked down and folded his arms. "Remember how I said we were having security problems?"

"Yeah."

"Right now things have gotten tense. People don't know who to trust. Some even think we have a mole."

"You think it's Leo?"

"Of course not. I've known Leo for years. I'm just trying to be careful."

"What's the Edge?"

"Just another Gate. It links through a series of Connectors to the catacombs below Paris. People stumble into that one all the time, so it was pretty believable."

"Why does it need to be believable? Why not just tell the truth?"

Roger chewed the side of his cheek. "As of right now, no one in the Pacific Northwest community knows the second Gate in Stars Crossing is open. Everyone—including me—thought the Connector was blocked on all sides. But now, we know at least one way is open. It might explain the security breach. Or it might be a coincidence."

"So what do we do now?"

"We take you home and pray nobody upstairs is feeling chatty today. If anyone talks to you, act like you just got your memory wiped."

"So just act oblivious to everything?"

"You got it."

"Cool. I can do that."

Roger crossed the room to an old wooden staircase and started up. I followed. It was dimly lit, and the sagging steps bent and creaked under our weight. Loud voices accompanied by the clattering of dishes and silverware drifted from beyond the door at the top. Roger pushed open the squeaky door, flooding the stairwell with light.

It looked like a cross between a mom-and-pop cafe and a fifties diner. The vinyl on the plentiful squishy booth seats had been rubbed bare from repeated use. Fire-engine-red barstools sat at a long Formica counter, little lamps lighting the bar. Most of the booths and the counter seats were full. Everyone chatted and clattered their utensils against their plates, fully engaged in their separate conversations. Roger leaned on the end of the counter, waving at a middle-aged waitress wearing a short apron and a loose-fitting dress. Her hair was pulled back in a messy red bun.

"Hey, Rhonda," he called.

She glanced up and smiled, peering over her glasses. "Howdy, stranger. Haven't seen you here in a while. You still grounded?"

He rolled his eyes, head flopping downward. "Good Lord, it's just *surveillance*. I'm not under house arrest! Why does everyone keep assuming it's a punishment when I get assigned surveillance?"

"Oh, gee, I don't know." Rhonda leaned her head back and counted on her fingers. "Might it be because last year you got assigned surveillance after you let dozens of flying snakes into the diner? Or maybe it was because of the time you tried to raise a lion cub in Giftshop? Or the tuxedo incident? Or that time when—"

"All right, all right. I get it," he grumbled. "Does Sal have any cars available?"

She shook her head. "Sorry, Gurdall just took the last one. He should be back in about half an hour, though. Do you want a booth?"

Roger thought for a moment and then sighed a little. "Sure. Can we get one in the back?"

Her eyes flicked to me. "Everything all right?"

"Everything's fine. Just had a rough day. Not up for a lot of conversation."

Rhonda stood on her tiptoes to see across the diner. "You can take the corner booth. Do you two want something to eat?"

Roger brightened. "Do you have any cinnamon rolls left?"

She smiled and turned toward the swinging door behind her. "I'll bring you some. Seat yourselves."

Roger gestured for me to follow him. We passed an assortment of people on our way to the booth, none of whom looked up from their discussions. Many of them had maps and papers strewn about the table, talking low and fast. The booth Roger headed for was next to a window, showing that the diner was situated in a large clearing in the middle of a forest. The ambient green glow from outside turned the white curtains a pastel shade of emerald.

Sitting down across from each other, we waited.

"So . . ." I cleared my throat. "Flying snakes, huh?"

He glared across the table. "Shut up."

I snickered.

Rhonda approached with two plates of delicious-looking cinnamon buns and set them on the table. "That all for you today?"

Roger slid his plate to him and grabbed a fork. "Thanks, Rhonda. As always, your generosity knows no bounds."

She bent a dramatic bow and returned to the counter, smiling.

Roger dug into his cinnamon roll with a contented sigh. I used a fork to strip a piece off the top of mine and tried a bite. It was delicious, though an unfamiliar spice left me puzzled as to what was in it.

The minutes that passed in silence weren't uncomfortable, just quiet. Roger leaned on his elbows and watched out the window, eyes flicking to every movement of birds or rustle of wind.

"Why is being put on surveillance such a bad thing?" I asked.

He turned his head from his window watch. "It's not, really. I think people in this job usually crave excitement and adventure. Being still in one place makes them restless."

"Not you, though?"

He shrugged "I don't mind the quiet. Sure, surveillance gets kind of boring, but sometimes boring is good. Y'know?"

I nodded.

He looked around the diner. "My dad used to say this job was for the adrenaline junkies of this world. The kind of people who were insane enough to throw themselves headlong into any situation and keep doing it day after day. Even if it means sacrificing their lives."

"Do you think that?"

"A little. I've seen some people do some crazy things. But also, I think most Jumpers have a good heart. They know what's at stake, and they do something about it. It's not like any of us are perfect, not by any stretch of the imagination, but we try our best to help people. At any cost."

The door on the far side of the diner opened with a squeak. A short man dressed in a fluffy winter coat walked in and handed Rhonda some keys.

Roger swung his legs from under the table and stood. "And there's our ride."

I stood as well.

Urgent beeping noises swept across the room. People at every table rummaged around their pockets and pulled out the same compact-like devices that Ed had used. Short, tense looks were exchanged, and everyone gathered their belongings in an organized frenzy. Those seated at the bar jumped down and ran to the back door leading to the Gate.

Roger's face drained of color. He stopped an older man running past wearing a cowboy hat. "Jonesy, what's going on?"

Jonesy turned, his round face flushed red. "Not sure yet. Just got a message from Ed to meet back up. Finish what you need to do and get back to Giftshop."

Roger's eyes dimmed. "Not another one."

Jonesy shrugged. "Hey, it could just be a meeting. But you know how things are right now. I'll see you there. Till again."

"Till again," Roger mumbled.

Roger watched Jonesy join the others before he waved me forward. Rhonda tossed a pair of keys to him as we passed the counter. She gave him a weak smile as we shuffled out the door.

We were greeted by a chilly gust of wind. The darkened gray sky hid any indication of the current time of day. I pulled my jacket tighter around me and glanced around the small parking area. The number of cars outside the diner seemed disproportionately small compared to the number of people inside.

Roger hefted the keys in his hand and beelined for an old red farm truck that looked like one good pothole would finish it off. He tugged open the door and entered the driver's seat while I rounded the truck to the passenger side. It took both hands to pry the door open. The smell of oil and musty fabric seats permeated the air. He turned the keys in the ignition. The engine started unwillingly. Warm air flowed weakly from the vents, adding a new smell of gasoline to the truck.

Roger tapped his thumbs against the steering wheel and stared at the diner. He let out a—probably unconscious—elongated sigh.

"Listen," I said, "I can just drive myself home and then bring the car back later. It sounds like you need to go."

He shook his head. "I have to make sure you get back. It's protocol."

"What exactly went on back there?"

He tugged the gearshift into reverse, twisting to look out the clouded back window. "Team leaders have these communicators called Chatterboxes—the little round things—which relay messages from other leaders. They work almost wherever you are, even across multiple Gates. The last time they called a group meeting was about a month ago. Ed received a message from a team requesting backup. Urgently."

"What happened to them?"

He pushed the gear shift into drive and pressed on the gas pedal. The engine sputtered forward down the muddy lane.

"They died."

Thirteen

Car Talk

The car ride continued in strained silence as swaying pine boughs flew past the window. The roads Roger took didn't look familiar to me. This didn't indicate much, as I'd seen so little of Stars Crossing in the last month. We turned from one back road and onto another, eventually coming to a paved stretch of highway. We hadn't seen a single car since leaving Sal's.

The quiet cab held tension. Roger's posture and face had set into rigid tautness, the stress clearly visible from his white-knuckled grip on the steering wheel.

"What did you do before you were a Jumper?" I asked.

"In a word? Nothing," he said. "I was raised in the community; grew up on a Jumper outpost a little ways northwest of here."

"Outpost?"

"Kind of like a camp but more permanent. There are pockets of them all over the world. I called the one I grew up in Tree Town, but it doesn't have an official name."

"Why Tree Town?"

"Because it's basically a village of tree houses." He chuckled. "Most kids want a tree house in their backyard. My entire childhood *was* a tree house."

"Is there a Gate out that way?"

"No. Jumper outposts serve a lot of functions. Supplies, medical help, housing, that sort of thing. They're usually situated on large swaths of land away from cities. A good place to raise kids if you have them."

"I thought Jumpers don't have families until they retire."

"Sometimes it just . . . happens. If they want to settle, they retire early or stick around in the community to do low-risk odd jobs. Usually."

"Usually?"

"Some people keep exploring full-time and have a family." He shook his head. "It always ends in disaster."

We lapsed into silence again. The hum of the engine revved as Roger turned onto another curvy highway. The truck hit a bump, and the entire cab shuddered.

"You mentioned your dad earlier," I remarked.

He shot me a sideways glance. "Yeah."

"How does he fit into all of this? Is he a Jumper too?"

"Not anymore."

"Oh. How does he feel about you being one?"

"Well, I'd imagine he'd be happy that I kept the tradition going after I said I'd quit."

"You'd imagine? Do you guys not speak?"

He gripped the steering wheel. "No."

There was an awkward stretch of silence.

"My dad," he said, "died when I was sixteen."

"Roger, I—"

"It's fine."

I looked down at my hands. "What happened?"

"Don't really know. One day he just . . . didn't come home. No one was with him. He always mapped solo, the idiot. My guess is he ran into trouble and didn't make it out."

"How do you know he didn't just get lost? Didn't you guys send out a search party?"

"No one knew which Gate he was in. They sent a search party, but there was no need."

"Why?"

"Pictures showed up in Giftshop about a day later."

I looked out the window. A deep pit of sadness sank into my stomach. My never-ending string of questions had, until now, felt like I was uncovering some great mystery. Now I realized what seemed novel and new to me was the reality of what people lived every day. The pained fatigue in Roger's eyes was real. The statues in Giftshop were real people. Bea was right. This strange and wondrous world I'd walked into was real. And it was dangerous.

"I'm so sorry," I mumbled. "I didn't mean to bring it up."

"Forget it."

The truck rumbled as we rolled up to a stop sign. I recognized this intersection. A few more turns and we'd enter the main road through Stars Crossing.

"Um." I cleared my throat. "What do you do if someone comes into Sal's? Not a Jumper, I mean."

He pulled onto the much smoother road, and we passed our first car. "Not many people wander that far into the wilderness. On the off chance that people do get lost, we have deterrents."

"Deterrents?"

"Roadblocks, I guess you'd call them. Devices that . . . encourage people to go a different direction. The most common one is called a Fool's Errand."

"What does it do?"

"You know that feeling when you get close to a cliff? Or an open flame?"

"Yeah."

"A Fool's Errand messes with those internal instincts. If you get too close to one, you feel uneasy, like when you're getting close to danger. Every animal that feels fear can be affected by it. It's an inborn survival trait."

"That would explain the fear I felt at the barn. Even from far away, I felt unnerved just by *looking* at it. I just thought the place was haunted."

"That's usually what people think."

"What do they look like?"

"They can be a lot of things—insects, rocks, junk. It depends on what blends into the area so people don't mess with them."

The endless expanse of trees parted. Shabby buildings peeked from between them, the largest of them an old stone courthouse in the center of town. Tattered awnings and splintery wood telephone poles leaned haphazardly over the roadway. People were out, despite the rain, strolling on the cracked sidewalks. We turned onto a side street at the very end. A figure on the corner waved at the truck. Roger waved back.

"Do the locals here cause trouble? Being close to the two Gates, I mean."

He snorted, slowing to let an elderly couple cross the street. "No, definitely not. They're Jumpers."

"Really? How many?"

"The whole town."

"*What?*"

"Mm-hmm."

"You're kidding."

"Nope. Jumpers founded this town after the Shift. Why else do you think it would have such a dramatic name like Stars Crossing?"

I watched the couple as they crossed to the sidewalk. There was nothing out of the ordinary about them. I thought of all the times I had passed people on the street, in the grocery store, at the post office, and never thought twice. They hadn't *seemed* like Otherworldly explorers. Even the town itself screamed "nothing to see here, folks," which I realized was probably intentional.

"Are they all still active?" I asked.

"Oh, no. No, most people who live here are retired, your aunt and uncle included. You won't see it in any public town history, but the Masters family name is significant here. They helped settle the valley."

"Huh."

"That's why I recognized it when you told me." Roger turned onto another winding road. "Well, that and the fact that Terry and Susan just showed up in Giftshop fifty years younger."

I sighed. My brain was so occupied by other information, I hadn't thought about them since we left Giftshop. I leaned my head against the window. "I still can't believe that. I mean—" I paused. "They're . . . dead, aren't they?"

"I expect so. In this time."

"Then how are they here?"

"No clue. But it's happened before."

"It has?"

"It's rare, but yes."

"Why? What causes it?"

"No one knows for sure. Sometimes it happens right before a widespread event. Sometimes they're only there for a few minutes, then they disappear. Personally, I think we get a little extra help."

"Help from who?"

"I don't know. Maybe the same force that led us to Giftshop? There's someone—or something—that keeps an eye out for this little planet. Could never explain that, either."

Roger turned onto the long winding driveway that led to Terry and Susan's. I looked up at the clouds and watched the rain splatter against the road.

"Has anyone ever found . . . um, you know, other beings in an Other-world?"

"How do you mean?"

"Aliens."

Roger cracked a smile. "Besides the thousands of different animal and plant species, you mean?"

"No, people like us. Humanoid. People who can talk and build things."

He frowned. "You mean intelligent life-forms? To my knowledge, no. It doesn't mean they're not out there. It just means that we haven't found them yet."

"Don't you find that odd? With all the Otherworlds you've been to, you haven't found any evidence of intelligent alien life?"

"Not really. It's a big universe. We've barely scratched the surface."

An inharmonious vibration against my leg made me jump. My head smacked into the window with a *thump*. Pulling my phone out of my pocket, I blinked at the date and time. According to the screen, only four hours had passed since entering the Gateway in the barn. That couldn't be right. I probably just needed to reset it.

"Does technology work in the Otherworlds? Or Giftshop?" I asked.

"Not usually. In Giftshop they shut off completely. Every once in a while, you get a Connector where your phone will work. You even get service in some of them."

"How—"

"Don't ask me how. I have no idea."

The outline of the house was visible through the trees now. Its many chimneys and pipes sticking from the roof were absent of smoke, the bubbly windows devoid of light or color. A pang of loneliness shot through me at the sight of it. I'd forgotten how nice it was to be around other people. Returning to an empty house seemed even more depressing than before. Roger pulled the truck a few yards behind my car. We stepped into the rain.

Roger blew a low whistle through his teeth as he surveyed my car. "Wow. That looks like you took it through a brick factory."

I frowned. It was the epitome of a poor college student's ride: small, dirty, and held together by duct tape. I'd bought it a few years ago from a friend who was kind enough to sell me a car that actually ran. The windows didn't roll up or down, the mirrors were held on by electrical tape and fishing wire, the front and back windshields were severely cracked, and it had four different brands of tires, all supposedly refurbished. But it worked. Kind of.

"It has . . . character," I allowed.

"Hm."

I mounted the steps, the scar on my leg twinging. "How did you know how to get here? I was going to give directions, but you never asked."

"My dad used to come here. He'd take me along."

"Really? Why?"

"He would visit with Terry and Susan, I think. I'm not sure about what. I was never allowed to listen."

He climbed the stairs to the front door and checked his watch. "Sorry, I have to make sure you're in your house before I can leave."

I swung open the door and stepped over the threshold. "Okay, I'm in. Sorry for being deadweight."

"You're not. Just bad timing is all."

"Are you going to drive back?"

"I think so. It's slower, but we might need the truck."

He turned to leave but paused. He seemed to debate something in his head before turning back to me. "Hey, um, now that you know about all of this, don't—don't go looking for trouble."

"Don't try to go back through the Gate and die, you mean?"

"Something like that."

"Don't worry. My plan is to stay as far away from *all* of this as possible."

He looked down. "Good. That's . . . good."

There was an awkward silence. Roger's face tinged pink.

"Thanks for putting up with all my questions," I said. "And taking me home, and saving my life, and— Well, you get the point. Are you going to miss the meeting now?"

"Nah, they still have to recall everyone from out in the field. I'll be fine." He tugged open the cab. "I'll . . . I mean, we'll be in contact. Please . . . just be careful."

Roger slammed the door and started the shaky engine. He reversed and waved as he drove out of sight.

I watched the truck disappear around the corner, feeling as if it had taken the last of my strength with it. I was alone now. The realization of it overwhelmed me. The only person I could talk to, who could confirm my sanity, was gone. The companionship of another person not only distracted me from the mind-breaking reality I had discovered, but it distracted me from my exhaustion. My entire body felt shaky, worn out. I sat on the floor, my legs outside of the open door, and put my head in my hands. I closed my eyes.

Reality sank in. The knowledge of the Otherworlds, Jumpers, Giftshop, the strange things I'd seen, was any of that real? *Really* real? Was it all—somehow—just a dream? A hallucination? What could I possibly trust if everything before now was just an illusion? I couldn't think straight. My entire view of the world, of the universe, had been shattered in a matter of hours. For some reason, I wanted to scream. I wanted to redirect the flow of hysteria outside my body. Outside my head.

I needed to focus on something.

I needed to ground myself.

The cold floor seeped through my jeans, so I focused on that. I inhaled the warm aroma of the kitchen. The smell of cold rain wafted through the open door. Little droplets splashed against my fingers. Birds chirped. Swaying pine trees creaked in the breeze.

It wasn't enough.

Breathing deeply through my mouth, I blew out an unsteady breath through my nose. My lungs filled with air. They emptied. The steady pump of my heart continued on despite everything. It was strong, unwavering. There. That was something to hang on to.

Just breath in.

And out.

My frantic mind calmed, and I untangled myself from the threshold and shut the door. The cold wind dwindled, blowing between the thin cracks in the uneven doorframe. Looking down, I cringed. I needed a shower.

My clothes were splattered with dirt and blood from my tumble down the ravine. On my way to the stairs, I pulled out my phone and restarted it, hoping to reset the clock.

I glanced back at the kitchen. Before anything else, I should call my parents. I'd been gone for at least two days, maybe more. I hoped my mom hadn't tried to call in the time I was gone. Knowing her, she'd enlist the FBI because I didn't answer back within an hour.

I dialed the number and listened to it ring. The speaker crackled. A man's gruff voice answered.

"Hello?"

"Hey, Dad, it's me."

"Hey, Lil, how you been? Haven't talked to you in a while. Your mom always hogs the phone when you call."

I smiled. It was good to hear his voice. "Sorry about that. And tell Mom I'm sorry I didn't pick up her calls the last few days. I was . . . busy doing things in the barn."

Some static rattled the phone. "Oh, really? She mentioned she talked to you last night."

I paused.

"Really? She said last night?"

"Around seven, she said, while I was at work. Why?"

I scratched my forehead. "No reason. The—the days blend together here." I leaned against the wall. "S-sorry for the short phone call, but I have to go."

"Why?"

"I just remembered I left something in the barn," I lied.

"Are you all right? You sound funny."

I didn't like lying, but what was I supposed to tell him? That I'd just wandered into a multidimensional hole and discovered a band of people who secretly kept the Earth safe from boundless otherworldly dangers?

"Everything's fine. I guess I'm just getting loopy from packing. I'll try to call you later this week, okay?"

"All right, not a problem. I'll be home the regular times, if you want to chat."

"Will do, Dad. Love you."

"Love you too, Lil."

Click.

A deep silence lingered in the kitchen. I leaned on the counter and looked up to the barn. It seemed so unassuming. You would never guess what was inside if you didn't go looking. But I didn't want to look anymore. My curiosity meter had drained to nonexistent levels, and I had a feeling it wouldn't recover anytime soon.

For now, it was nice to just stand here. Nice and quiet. Nothing trying to eat me, nothing supernatural was happening, everything was normal. In fact, just standing here, I could believe that everything in the last few days had been one big confusing dream. That was it. Just a dream.

"So, have you adjusted yet?"

I jerked back from the window, searching for the voice.

"Down here."

I looked down.

Catacombs sat on the floor, tail twitching. *"Hi there."*

"Why do you keep doing that?"

"Because it's entertaining."

I blinked at the dirty black cat. His eyes surveyed me with an amused smirk. "Okay, are you actually real, or did I just completely crack?"

"*No, I'm real. Then again, that's exactly what someone who wasn't real would say.*"

I sighed. "How did you even get in here?"

He hopped onto the counter, trailing dusty pawprints behind him. "*I have my ways. But this time I walked in when you were having your little freak-out moment. Hilarious.*"

"Thanks. I'm glad my shattered perception of the world amuses you."

"*Don't mention it. So are you adjusted yet?*"

"No."

He sat.

"*Well, you better start fast, because we got problems.*"

Fourteen

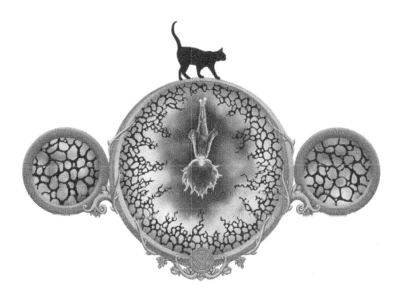

Problems

"What do you mean problems?"

"I mean big problems. Gargantuan ones. Big humdinger type of problems."

"Are you talking about what happened at Sal's? Because Roger—"

He paced (can cats pace?) on the counter. *"No, no, no. Well, yes, that's an extension of the problem, but no."*

"Then what's the problem?"

He rolled his eyes. *"What isn't the problem?"*

"Good God, between you and everyone else I've met in the last two days, I am *sick* of the cryptic answers!" I said. "What's happening?"

"You sure you can handle it?"

"Yes!"

He peered at me with luminous yellow eyes. *"Fine. It's your funeral. I was just sent to get you."* He stretched, tilting his head back in a haughty roll. *"You might want to grab a pen."*

Jumping down from the counter, he pranced behind the leg of the kitchen table and disappeared.

I glanced at a mug filled with pens on the counter. Grabbing one, I shoved it into my pocket and waited. For what, I didn't know.

I jumped as a vibrating sound came from my jacket. I thought it was my phone until I remembered my phone was in my pants pocket. Reaching into my jacket, my hand closed around a small metal disc the size of my palm, buzzing ferociously. I pulled it out. A Metatron's Cube had been engraved on the front, the surrounding metal scuffed with divots and scratches. It was a Teleporter that Roger showed me earlier. How did it get in my pocket?

A crackling sensation snapped in the air like a dozen sparklers popping in unison. The hair on the back of my neck stood on end. I felt dizzy. A static noise consumed my hearing, my vision vibrating to gray spots and blotches. The world pressurized into the small shaking disc in my hand.

The bubble of pressure around my body popped. I could breathe again. My ears rang from the static popping noise, and a sudden wave of nausea overtook me. I doubled over, blinking until my vision returned to normal. An ornate rug was below me. Many pairs of feet were pointed in my direction.

The nausea subsided. I looked up.

I was back in Giftshop, in the room covered with maps and photographs, staring at a large group of people lit by glowing patches of rainbow. Strange lights moved about them. I blinked. The strange lights were weapons—weapons made of color. Swords, spears, maces, blunt objects, and sharp implements. I blinked again. Were they made of glass? No, they looked more solid and were all different colors. They glowed from the inside out.

My gaze, distracted by the odd sight, turned to the faces of those holding the weapons. A large group of maybe thirty people. Their alert expressions told me that I'd just crashed their party in the worst way possible.

"Um." I gulped. "Hi."

"Stand down, everyone," called a familiar voice. Edgar stepped through the crowd of tense faces. He shoved his hands into the pockets of his worn leather jacket and stared me down. "Hello again, miss."

"Hello."

"I'm guessing you didn't do that on purpose?"

"No."

He tilted his head back to the ceiling and narrowed his eyes. "You just have to be theatrical, don't you?" he grumbled. The statement wasn't directed at me.

A few people behind him lowered their weapons. Most didn't.

"Ed, no offense, but we have no idea who this is," said a woman in the crowd. Her white-blonde hair was tucked into a braid, the glowing orange mace she carried casting harsh light against her already sharp jawline. "She could be anybody. Any*thing*. Giftshop has been wrong before."

Most of the group murmured in agreement. Distrustful glances were exchanged.

Edgar shot a look at the group, and they quieted. "I don't expect you to take anything at face value, Irene. But she's been here before; actually, she just left. It seems Giftshop knows something we don't."

"But we don't know anything about her," called a man from the crowd. I couldn't see his face. "She could be the one who cut off communications with Laura's team. I say we put her in the Quiet Room until we get some answers."

The room mumbled in agreement.

"We can vouch for her," interjected another familiar voice.

Terry and Susan pushed their way to the front, putting themselves between me and the group.

"She was with us earlier today," said Susan. "She left here with Roger."

"It's true," came Roger's voice. He stepped forward and addressed the crowd of paranoid Jumpers. "We were at Sal's when we got the call. She wouldn't have had time to cut off communications, because she was with me the whole time, and I just barely got back."

"I can second Roger," called a man from the right, who I recognized as Jonesy. "She was with him at Sal's."

The room was quiet. An unbearable tension gripped the silence. Every muscle in my body tightened. The group began to murmur, quietly at first, then working up to a low rumble.

"That's enough," Edgar barked. The rumble ceased. "Paranoia will get us nowhere. For all we know, Laura's team came to a new Gate and simply lost contact. You all know it happens."

"Then *why* the hullabaloo?" someone called.

"Out of an abundance of caution, I'm enacting a search chain."

The room groaned.

"We know for sure that they went through a Connector outside of Twisting Caverns a few hours ago, so we start there and see where that gets us. Gurdall," Edgar addressed a short man in a fluffy winter coat, arms folded. "Your team will set up surveillance in the Caverns in case they circle back. Alert us as soon as you get a visual."

Gurdall nodded and waved a handful of people to follow him. They disappeared through the side door, shooting dubious glances in my direction.

Edgar turned to the woman with the orange mace. "Irene, you and your team stand by here for backup. We'll call you if we need you. For now, pick up any new situation that comes through. You're on a skeleton crew until we get back. Got it?"

Irene nodded once, lips tight and thin.

Edgar pulled open his Chatterbox and grimaced at the contents. "Everyone else, gear up and sign out. We meet in the entry hall in fifteen minutes."

The remainder of the group headed for the door. Many gave suspicious looks my way as they passed but made no move toward me. In the shuffle, I recognized Bea. I waved, but she looked away, holding her head high.

Only Edgar, Terry, Susan, Roger, and I remained. The once crackling fire in the black marble fireplace had dulled to spitting embers.

"It seems," said Edgar, "that we are in a mess of problems."

Terry rocked on his heels. "Amen to that."

Edgar put a hand to his forehead. "All right, let's start with the basics. I'm guessing that you found a Teleporter in your pocket?"

"Yes."

"And you pulled it out."

"Yes."

"And it started buzzing."

"Yes."

"And now you're here."

"Yes."

"And she didn't even scream this time when I came to get her. I'd consider that progress."

I looked around, spotting Catacombs perched on a stack of books, nonchalantly licking a paw.

Edgar narrowed his eyes at the dusty black cat. "So it was you that led her into the barn, I take it?"

Catacombs lifted his tiny shoulders into what I assumed was a shrug. *"Hey what can I say, she followed. Well, except when she fell into the Forest. That wasn't part of the plan."*

"Hey," I interjected. "In my defense, I didn't fall. I was pushed."

"Pushed?" asked Susan. "Pushed by what?"

I shook my head. "I dunno, but I didn't fall in on purpose."

Catacombs hopped off the fireplace and onto the floor. *"Hate to break it to you, but there was no one else around; you just kind of tipped over."* He swung his head to Roger, eyes half-closed. *"And before you ask; no, I didn't push her. Despite popular opinion, I don't want to see all humans destroyed."*

"That's up for debate," Roger mumbled.

Catacombs hopped onto the paper-covered desk. *"By the way, tree-boy, you catch all those snakes in the diner yet?"*

Roger chewed the side of his cheek. "How's your flea problem?"

Catacombs's hackles stood on alert. He hissed.

Edgar sighed. "We don't have time for this. Listen, miss, I don't know why you're back here any more than you do, and there's not much I can do about it right now. We lost contact with a team over an hour ago, and our window is closing to find them."

"Window?" I asked.

His fists clenched. "It's almost time for the Gate switch. In a few weeks, the Gates that connect to Earth will swap, and getting to the team will be almost impossible."

"Why almost impossible? Won't they still be connected to Giftshop?"

"In a way," Susan said, "but when the Gates close on Earth, we can't access them through Giftshop. The Teleporters' connections to Giftshop are severed until they reopen next year. They'll likely be dead by then."

"Can't they just wait it out?"

Everyone exchanged glances.

"Time works differently in the Otherworlds," Terry said. "It's always in flux. The farther you go out, the worse it gets. Depending on what Gate they're in, hundreds of years could pass for them in one year on Earth, or it could just be a few minutes. Without Giftshop to regulate their position in time—which she does through the Teleporter system—there's no way to tell."

Edgar glanced at his Chatterbox again. "All right, let's gear up. Lily, you can follow for now until I figure out what to do with you."

I nodded sheepishly and followed the others as they shuffled out of the room. Why was I always the problem child?

We detoured to the Guest Book room and took turns signing out before continuing down an unfamiliar corridor and descending a steep flight of stairs. At the bottom was a large metal door lined with iron and bolt nails. Edgar gave it a hard shove. It swung open and let the low murmur of conversation into the stairwell. We entered.

Unlike the other rooms I'd seen in Giftshop, this one was carved entirely from stone. People milled about, busy sifting through backpacks and cases of supplies. Racks and stands held shafts and empty handles, similar to the weapons I'd seen earlier but without the blades of light. Cubbies carved from stone took up most of the space. Individuals crowded around them, extracting various clothing, survival gear, and medical supplies.

Edgar, Roger, Terry, and Susan followed suit, splitting up to access separate cubbyholes. I followed, feeling out of place. Roger dug around a cubicle marked OWENS with a brass plate while Terry and Susan rifled through ones stamped MASTERS. Edgar's plaque read VASQUEZ—PA-CIFIC NORTHWEST REGION LEADER.

Roger pulled out a pair of arm guards. They were made of leather, straps running from one side to the other. One long curved piece of leather covered the back of his forearm, imprinted with an array of vine scroll work. A thin piece of metal was visible on the sides.

"What's with the glowing things?" I asked. "How do they work?"

He tugged on a bracer and glanced back at me. "Living things, specifically the human body, give off energy. These help us concentrate it in one place and use it to our advantage. Weapons, tools, whatever you want to call them."

"So . . . you power them? Like a battery?"

"More like a beacon. It gives a place for the energy around us to gather. There are stories of people, a long time ago, who didn't need tools like these to use the energy around them. I think it's a myth."

He held out his arm, and a curved oval of light appeared. It was a rosy-pink color, extending almost all the way to the floor. He let out a breath, and the oval disappeared.

"How do you turn it on and off?" I asked.

"Concentration. It takes time and practice to get a consistent flow, but it's easy to maintain once you get the hang of it."

I looked around. The others were doing the same quick check. Colors popped in and out of view around the room.

"Why are they all different colors?"

Roger shrugged. "It's different for everyone."

"All right," Edgar called. "Let's move out."

There was an immediate shuffling toward the door. I followed behind Terry and Susan, with Roger in tow. We ascended a long flight of stone stairs that ended in a small wooden door at the top, barely big enough to walk through. To my surprise, we were back in the circular room with thirteen doors. The group shuffled to the center, ready and attentive.

"Right." Edgar cleared his throat. "This is not classified as a recovery at this time. Our only consideration is to reestablish communications with

Laura's team. The search radius will be three Gate jumps, but we will expand as needed. Any questions?"

"What are you doing with *her*?" someone asked. "She's not coming with us, is she?"

"As I'm sure you're aware, it's against protocol to bring civilians on assignments," Edgar said in a somewhat harsh tone. "Lily will wait here in Giftshop. Anything else?"

The gathering was silent. A low hum hung over the room. You could have heard a pin drop.

It was shattered by the shrill chorus of Rick Astley's "Never Gonna Give You Up."

Everyone, including me, jumped. A burly man frantically searched through his pockets.

"Sorry, sorry, everyone," the man apologized. "Max changed my ringtone before he left, and I don't know how to change it back."

He yanked his Chatterbox free from his pockets and flipped it open, squinting at the contents. His face paled.

The hum hanging above our heads grew louder. The pitch shifted. It was faint, just on the edge of hearing. An electrical, static hum. The same as in the loft. What was that?

"Payton?" Edgar prompted. "What is it? Does Irene need something upstairs?"

Payton stared at the bronze-colored compact. "It's— It says it's from Laura."

The electrical hum increased. My ears began to ring.

Edgar stepped forward. "What? What does it say?"

"I—" Payton adjusted one of the wires. "It's just letters and numbers, Ed. Pages of it."

"Coordinates?"

"No. Random letters and numbers. I can't pick out any patterns. It maxed out the message limit." He swiped a finger on the bottom of the Chatterbox. "It has a subject, oddly enough."

"That can't be from Laura," called a woman's voice from the back. "She never uses the subject line."

The hum grew. I rubbed the side of my aching jaw. No one else seemed to be bothered by it.

"Does that say anything?" asked Edgar.

"It just repeats the same words over and over."

My teeth seemed to vibrate from the inside out. The back of my throat tasted bitter. The hum tripled in volume.

"What does it say?"

Louder.

"It just says . . . They are coming."

The world went black.

Something snapped behind my eyes. A painful rip inside my head sent me spinning into the deep. I fell backward, waiting to hit something. Nothing caught me. I kept falling.

Down, down, down.

The blackness parted. Unnatural amber clouds swirled past me. Dark sweeping shadows. Great swaths of blinding light. It stirred something in my memory. I remembered the dreams I had all but forgotten. I remembered the pod, the strange heightened vision, the voices, the darkness.

I remembered the darkness.

T h e y a r e c o m i n g.

For a brief moment, I caught the message again, but the wind ripped it away. My plunge into the colossal cloud banks slowed. I drifted instead of hurtled. The muddy red sky shone through for a fraction of a moment before it was again obscured.

My erratic breathing grew louder. Distantly, I heard the now-familiar sound of a billion voices. This time I sat on the sidelines, the echoes drifting from afar. A well of silence emanated below me. I looked down.

Waves of blackness consumed my view, continually tossing and turning in an endless expanse. But this sea was nothing natural. It moved like metal blocks shifting, ripping, tearing at each other in hungry ferocity. As I neared, it shifted. It reached for me in spiny twisting masses. An eerie silence covered the mass. There was no light, no sound.

Nothing.

Just darkness.

A light pressure against my arm. Fingers wrapped around my hand. My head was cradled by something. A pressure on my wrist indicated someone checked my pulse. I felt them. These sensations were as real as the black creeping mass, somehow. I knew they were. If I just focused on them hard enough, maybe I could—

I drifted too close. The black abyss brushed against my face.

The crushing pressure around my body only increased within the next passage of time. How long? I didn't know. Time meant nothing. Nothing meant anything. There was only pain, and the crushing hollowness of the shifting black sea.

And then all at once it was gone. Like a vacuum seal breaking loose, I was released. Gasping for air, I bolted upright. The circle of concerned-looking people jumped back. They stared at me in bewilderment.

"Well, guys," said a man's voice from the other side of the circle. "Apparently she's not dead."

My vision wobbled. I couldn't seem to get enough oxygen into my lungs. Something dripped from my nose. I swiped a hand across my nose. It came away red.

Right by my side sat Terry, Susan, Edgar, and Roger. All of their faces were white.

I rubbed the base of my throat. It was sore. "What just happened?" I asked. My voice was raspy.

Everyone looked around at each other and then back at me.

"Um, we thought you could tell us that," said Susan. "You collapsed and started screaming. A minute later you— Well . . ."

Terry gulped. "You . . . you died. You stopped breathing, and your heart just . . . quit. We thought you had a heart attack or something."

"Do you remember anything?" Edgar asked.

I thought back to the crushing hollowness and shuddered. "I-I remember everything."

"What did you see?"

"I was . . . somewhere I've dreamed about. This time it was like I was dreaming wide awake. But things were different."

"Different how?"

"It's—it's hard to explain. This time I felt like I was watching from the side, and there was . . . something else. Something new. Something dark."

Edgar's eyes flashed. "What did this place look like?"

"There were . . . clouds. Clouds and voices. It was like . . . a billion thoughts at once. I know that sounds insane, but it's the best way I can describe it."

"Oh my God," Bea whispered. "She saw the Collective."

A heavy silence washed over the room. The group looked at me as if I were some dangerous creature. Some even stepped away from me.

"What does that mean?" I asked.

"It means"—Edgar stood—"we're running out of time."

Fifteen

Traps

Edgar's words echoed in the small space. Though I didn't know what he meant, it was clear that whatever had just happened wasn't good.

The room spun. My head throbbed like someone was trying to escape my skull with a jackhammer, the metallic tang of blood coating my mouth. I stood on shaky legs, almost tipping over. Roger grabbed my arm to steady me, his face white.

Edgar looked hard at the floor. After mentally debating something, he exhaled a tight breath. "We have to move," he mumbled. "Lily, can you walk?"

I swallowed. "I dunno. What—what just happened?"

"We can talk on the way, but we need to move. Roger, keep an eye on her."

Roger shot him a look. "You can't be serious, Ed. You're not thinking of taking her *with* us?"

"I am."

A mumble of dissension swept through the room.

"Look at her," Roger said. "She's in no condition to—"

"Under normal circumstances, I would agree with you," Edgar cut in. "But these aren't normal circumstances. If she can access the Collective, then it gives us an advantage that we haven't had before. You want Laura's team to end up like Steven's? Marguerite's? We didn't even have a chance to recover *bodies* last time."

Roger looked down.

"Ed," an older woman said from the circle, "she doesn't even know what she can do yet. These things take time. Ed, she's not—"

"I know, I know." Edgar rubbed his eyes. "But if there's even a chance, I say we take it. Bea, what do you think? Can we make a go of it?"

All eyes turned to Bea.

Bea's gaze shifted to me, her face wearing an expression I couldn't place. Apprehension, certainly, but there was something else. A deep sadness. "It's . . . possible. She should be able to tune in to some extent now. I still don't understand how this is possible." She looked to Terry and Susan. "She hasn't had any relatives that exhibited signs, has she?"

"No," Terry said. "No, I can't think of anyone, unless they're way back in the family tree, but—" He stopped short and put a hand to his head. "Oh no."

"What?" Susan asked.

"John."

Realization dawned on her face, and she put a hand to her mouth. "How did we miss that?"

"You know him. Always keeps to himself. We thought that was because he was shy, but now . . ." Terry sighed. "That would explain this, though."

"Oh my God." Susan shook her head. "Poor John. All these years . . ."

I raised my hand.

The group's heads swiveled to me with bemused expressions.

"Hi, I'm still here," I said. "Can someone please explain what the hell is going on? Where are we going?"

"You don't have to go anywhere," Roger said, casting another look in Edgar's direction. "Not when we can't guarantee your safety."

"Safety?"

Edgar's eyes flashed. "Stop scaring her, Roger."

"Ed, you *know* that things don't always go as planned. Can you guarantee her protection? Can you guarantee *anyone's* safety?"

"Roger—"

"She's a civilian, Ed," the older woman from the circle interjected. "I'm with Roger. We took an oath to protect her. We can't put her in danger like this, even if it is just a rescue mission."

"She's right," said a man with shaved head. "You know how fast things can go sour. Remember those swarm of nocturiki last year? No warning. And that was at a surveillance station."

The group murmured in agreement.

"And what about our oaths to each other?" Bea asked. She clenched her fists. "Do we matter any less than they do? I say if there's a chance that Lily can access the Collective and help us find Laura and her team, then we take it."

The room was quiet. Most people looked at the floor, avoiding eye contact with me.

"Listen," I said. "I don't know what's going on, or the first thing about what you people do, but if there's any way I can help, I will."

Edgar's eyes brightened. "We'll do our best to protect you, but as Roger pointed out, there's no guarantee. But this is your choice. Will you try to help us get our team home safe?"

I looked around the room, then to Roger. His eyes swept over my face, and he slowly shook his head.

"I'll try," I said.

Edgar smiled. Roger looked hard at the floor and ground his teeth together.

"All right," Edgar said. "I'm upgrading this to a rescue mission. Lily, we can explain things on the way."

"Okay."

Edgar turned and strode to a door covered in overlapping silver scales. They gleamed against the lamplight as the door swung open, revealing a dark, damp corridor within. The group strode forward into the doorway, pulling out their weapons to illuminate the gloom.

Terry, Susan, Bea, Roger, and I followed them into the dimly lit hallway. It smelled of wet stone, dirt, and mold.

We walked in silence. It was a fairly narrow hall, just big enough to fit two people walking side by side. Terry and Susan walked together, Edgar walked with Bea, and I walked with Roger.

I cleared my throat and addressed the people marching in front of me. "So, uh, do you want to tell me what I just saw back there?"

Bea inclined her head toward me but kept walking. "It seems that you can observe the Collective, which is something we haven't seen for . . . a long time."

"What's the Collective?"

"A place where all of the memories of humanity are gathered. Every thought, every feeling, every emotion of all human existence is stored there. It is the lake that every stream of consciousness feeds into, if that makes sense."

"Huh. Yeah, okay." I nodded, then shook my head. "Not really. That doesn't make any sense."

Bea cracked a smile.

"So . . . the Collective is a place?" I asked. "Does a Gate connect to it?"

"No, it's not a physical place exactly," Edgar said. "It is a hub, a point in the universe that we all connect to, even if we don't realize it. It's not physical, I mean. It exists on another plane of being."

"Why can I see it?"

"For some unknown reason, there's a certain characteristic in your brain—some kind of abnormality—that gives you two-way access to it. Most commonly it's a genetic trait passed down by a relative. In your case, I believe it was your grandfather. Right, Terry?"

Terry nodded and sighed. "The idiot. I wish he would have told me. That must have been horrible, keeping that secret for all those years."

Susan put a hand on his shoulder. "You know he never lets us help him with anything. It's the wagon project in school all over again."

"Why did he have to keep it secret?" I asked. "Is being able to hear the Collective . . . a bad thing?"

Edgar glanced back at me. "Not inherently. But it makes people nervous. Think about it: you have unimpeachable access to anyone's entire life at will. Every memory, every embarrassing moment, personal information, deepest thoughts, *everything*. You could know every dark secret about a person, and they'd never know. It's a powerful gift, once you get the hang of it."

"But I have no idea how to use it. I barely even know what it does!"

"For now, yes," Edgar said. "But you'll learn."

I looked down at the smooth dirt floor as we walked. The pain in my head jostled with every footstep. For some reason, my brain seemed more squished into my skull than it had before. Was that because of what had just happened? Did I somehow have less space in my head because I could hear the Collective now? Maybe I was overthinking things.

"Anyway," Bea said, "you don't *have* to have the genetic trait to be aware of it, but it takes the choice out of the matter. It takes decades of meditation and study to achieve what you get naturally. How old are you?"

"Almost twenty-two."

She nodded. "That's about right. And you just started having those dreams?"

"A couple nights ago, yeah."

"Interesting. I wonder what sparked them."

"How do you know so much about this? Are you— Can you hear it too?" I asked.

Bea squared her shoulders. "No. But I knew someone who could."

The group slowed their pace as the hallway sloped downward. The smooth dirt floor became slick as it transitioned into stone.

"So what happens now?" I asked. "What am I supposed to do?"

"Just keep your eyes and ears open, miss," Edgar said. "That's it. Any information or impressions you feel, just shout it out."

"What do you mean information? If the Collective is just thoughts and emotions, how does that help us find Laura?"

"Think of it like this," he said. "Say you walk by a person on the street who's about to rob a bank. Before they do anything to physically rob the bank, their emotions, specific thoughts, and so on are connected and channeled into the Collective. Which is in turn connected to you."

I nodded. "So . . . even though they haven't robbed the bank yet, I know their thoughts beforehand?"

"Technically, you'll be hearing their thoughts *after* they think them, but yes," Edgar said. "Before those thoughts are turned into actions. The *moment* those thoughts and feelings and emotions are turned into memory, you can access them."

"The Collective is like a library, with the most recent information being the closest. The further back something is, the harder it is to find," Bea said. "But be careful, the sheer volume of information you can access can fry your brain if you try to listen to everything at once. It would be like trying to collect a thimble of water from a fire hose. With you being the thimble. Get it?"

"I— Okay, I still don't understand. If the Collective is like a huge library, then how did I get the warning before? I wasn't looking for information, or listening, or whatever."

Edgar shot Bea a glance. "Sometimes . . . things leak out of the Collective that you can hear without looking for it. Sometimes they're more like predictions than memories."

"How does that work?"

He shrugged. "I don't know. You'd have to ask it."

"It?"

"The Collective."

"I thought you said it was a place."

"It is."

I paused in asking my next question as the long dark passageway opened up ahead. We entered a large circular room that curved downward into a sloping spiral. Looking over the side as we passed, I swallowed. The large cylindrical room spiraled into darkness; I couldn't see the bottom.

The group stopped at collection of secondary passageways chipped into the stone wall. Someone gave a boost to a thin woman in the front, who scrambled into one of the portrait-sized holes six feet or so off the ground. Pulling a metal rod from her backpack, she set it onto the edge of the alcove and stepped back. The rod emitted a series of beeps before it expanded into more metal rods, creating a ladder that extended almost all the way to the floor. She stayed at the top and helped the others over the ledge.

Roger and I waited for our turn near the back as Edgar and Bea had gone forward to take lead of the group.

I glanced at Roger, who didn't seem the happiest of campers. His jaw ground back and forth as he watched Edgar clamber onto the ladder.

"So," I said, "here we are again."

He didn't respond.

"Roger?" I asked.

"You really shouldn't be here," he blurted. "I just— it's great that you want to help, but this isn't the best time to stick your neck out for strangers."

"I didn't realize there was a wrong time for that. But I'll try not to fall into any more Otherworlds, if that's what you're worried about."

"I'm worried about you getting hurt, or worse. I'm worried about you getting into something you never bargained for."

"Like what? Ed said it was just a rescue mission."

He shook his head. "I have a bad feeling about this. Something feels . . . *wrong* here. Are you . . . are you hearing anything?"

"I don't know what I'm listening for," I admitted. "I don't even know if I can access it. Maybe they got it wrong. Maybe I can't hear the Collective. Maybe it was just a bad dream."

We shuffled forward to the ladder. Roger swallowed. "You . . . you didn't hear yourself scream. That wasn't just a bad dream. That was something else. What did you see?"

"I . . . um, I . . ."

The pain in my head flared at the thought of the dream. The black sea, the cold, the hungry waves dragging me under . . . I couldn't think about it. Thinking about it was reliving it. I didn't answer, and Roger didn't ask me to continue.

We followed the group up the ladder. Another dark passageway, shorter this time, led to a blank silver wall. It rippled as we neared, like a liquid mirror.

"What is that stuff?" I asked Roger.

"It's called Spacer Sap. It discourages things from entering this Connector, since Twisting Caverns is home to some pretty nasty species. We put it up as an extra precaution."

The rippling silver liquid warped again as the people in front of us stepped through. I was hesitant to get close to the foreign substance.

"Here." Roger grabbed my hand and pulled me forward. "Just keep your eyes closed. It feels weird, but it doesn't hurt."

I nodded and closed my eyes. As he pulled me through, the liquid clung to me in slippery globs. It reminded me of the oily beads in the barn. That seemed like a lifetime ago.

Roger let go of my hand. "You're through."

I opened my eyes. We were in a large cave system, with stalagmites clustered on the floor and stalactites sprouting from the ceiling. Water dripped steadily from somewhere, echoing off the slick walls and rocky ground. Many openings and tunnels branched off into darkness, but no one had taken them yet. The remaining group had clustered into the center of the cave. Roger and I stood at the back.

Edgar was addressing the crowd. ". . . We'll set up groups here, at the next three Gates, and expand as needed. Anything that suggests recent movement needs to be reported immediately. Any questions?"

No one answered. The constant *drip-drip* of water in the distance echoed.

"Paul and Payton, your teams take the eastern passage," he continued. "Caulder, take your team down the south tunnel. Watch out for Dweller Hounds while you're there. Head back to Giftshop if you get cornered. Same goes for everyone; if things get too tough to handle, don't be a hero. I'd rather have you retreat than dead. Got it?"

The group murmured their agreement. Edgar continued to make team arrangements, answering when asked questions about rendezvous and meeting times. I couldn't understand most of the conversation; the echoes of the cave were too loud. The steady *drip-drip* of water was prominent. I closed my heavy eyes.

Drip-drip.

Maybe my head would quit pounding soon.

Drip-drip.

Probably not. But it was nice to close my eyes for a moment. I was so tired.

Drip . . . tr . . . p . . .

Even the water was beginning to sound like words. Strange.

Dr . . . ip . . . t . . . r . . . i . . . p . . .

My head was full of static.

Tr . . . a . . . p . . . t . . . r . . . a . . . p . . .

"Lily?"

My eyes snapped open.

"You all right?" Roger asked. "You look pale."

I blinked. "I'm . . . fine. Sorry, must have dozed off for a second."

I shook my head to clear the static noise. Edgar had finished giving instructions.

"You all know what to do. Head out."

The group shuffled toward their destinations. A woman in front held up her hand. "I'm getting a heat signature coming from the eastern passage."

"Dwellers?" someone asked.

"No, it looks humanoid."

Immediately the weapons came out in a blaze of light. The group shifted to the outskirts of the cave and waited. Roger pulled me behind a clump of jagged stalagmites.

A shadow danced on the wall of a nearby passageway, and a woman with long curly brown hair emerged from the tunnel, wearing an expression of uncertainty. A large bandage stemmed the flow of blood from a cut on her head. Edgar stepped away from the walls, and the woman's eyes widened.

"Ed!" she breathed. "Boy, am I happy to see you."

"Laura?"

Everyone rose from their defensive positions.

"What the hell happened to you?" Edgar barked, but his face was flush with relief. "We've been trying to reach you for hours! Where is everyone else?"

Laura gave a sheepish grin. "Sorry, Ed, we ran into some trouble on way home. The others are down this way. They're safe. You won't believe what we found."

A general sigh of relief bounced around the room. Even the small sighs sounded like cannons in the echoes of the cave.

The dripping sound got louder again.

"You ran into trouble? Why didn't you answer your Chatterbox?" Edgar asked.

Drip-drip.

147

"I lost it hours ago," Laura said. "We've had one seriously crazy day, Ed. Come see what we found."

Drip...d...r...a...

"What do you mean you lost it? Didn't you send us a message a few minutes ago?"

D...r...a...p...t...r...a...p...

She looked confused. "No, that wasn't me. Must've been a glitch in the system. I'm serious, Ed, you have to come see what we've found. Right now. Everyone's waiting."

T...r...a...p...t...r...a...p...

"All right, all right. We can talk about this later. We're just glad you're safe. We were starting to fear the worst."

The static noise warbled in and out of pitch. My heart thumped against my ribs.

T...R...A...P...

TRAP

"Trap," I whispered.

"What?" Roger asked.

"It's—it's a trap," I repeated. The group had started to follow Laura down the passageway she'd come from, with Edgar in front.

"It's a trap!" I shouted.

The group whirled around. Across the cavern, Laura's head swiveled to me. We made eye contact for a long moment. Her eyes were cold. Dead. Like I was looking into the eyes of a spider, poised for the kill.

Laura stuck her fingers in her mouth and blew a shrill whistle. Stale-tasting wind swept through the cavern. An odd buzzing sound shook the room. Those who lingered by the walls were yanked off their feet by dark tendrils and sucked into the shadows. Those who tried to save their friends were pulled into the darkness with them. Their screams shattered the shocked silence, and the numb group of Jumpers sprang away from the walls, forming defensive positions again.

Black masses crept from the corners, the ceiling, niches, anywhere there was darkness, and seeped into the room like puddles of molasses. The globs undulated and grew, sprouting into people-shaped mounds. It receded, leaving unfamiliar men and women in it's place. They stared down the group of Jumpers with lifeless expressions. The emptiness in their eyes was almost as terrifying as the creeping shadows that made them.

"Oh my God," Roger breathed. "The missing teams."

An older man from the main group stumbled forward to a young boy, barely an adult, who'd sprouted nearby. They had similar features. Someone tried to pull him back, but the man shoved them off.

"Casey!" the man sobbed, running full speed. "*Casey!*"

"Stop!" Edgar yelled. "That's not—"

It was too late. The boy welcomed him with open arms and plunged a knife into his back. The man twitched and struggled until he slumped sideways, unmoving. The boy's expression didn't change. I covered my mouth to keep from screaming. How had that happened so fast?

Laura lunged at Edgar with a long black scythe. He met her with a rust-colored glowing axe, staggering against her blows. He shoved her back.

"Scatter!" Edgar yelled.

The rest of the blob people ran with unnatural speed. They drew the same weapons as I'd seen before, except theirs were jet black instead of colored. The group of Jumpers met the rushing force popping up from the shadows, but they seemed unsure. Most of them pulled out Teleporters and disappeared while their teammates gave them time to escape. Many refused to fight the people they obviously knew, and were cut down.

Roger clamped onto my arm and yanked backward. A dark shape flashed in front of my face, missing me by inches. Someone had come out of the wall, swinging a black blade. A blaze of pink light sent them tumbling back into the shadows. Roger formed a pink shield and threw it into another assailant stretching from the walls.

Something grabbed my arm again, but this time it wasn't Roger. Oozing shadow clamped onto the sleeve of my jacket, pulling me into the darkness. It didn't look like molasses up close but millions of tiny black cubes, falling and crashing into each other. Just like the mass in the Collective.

My arm burned. I pulled away as hard as I could, but it was too strong. It could rip my arm from its socket if it wanted to. My feet slid against the ground as it pulled me into the shadows.

"Roger!"

"Hold still!" Roger shouted. A pink curved shield of light appeared on the back of his arm, and he slammed the edge into the black mass. It shrank back, emitting a horrible sound like screeching metal. My arm was free, but it still burned cold.

Roger pulled me forward as other blobs formed around us. "Go, go, go!"

We sprinted to the other side of the cavern where Terry, Susan, and Bea remained trapped by a wall of shadow people. Bea sliced at the mounds with a small purple dagger to keep them at bay. Terry and Susan did the same with their weapons. Most of the others whose bodies weren't lying on the ground had escaped. Edgar was still fighting Laura.

Roger grabbed the Teleporter from his coat and opened a portal in the ground near Terry, Susan, and Bea. "Get in!" he yelled. "I'll get Ed!"

They nodded and took turns hopping into the portal. As soon as they were in, it closed. Another one opened near us.

"Ed!" Roger shouted. "Let's go!"

Edgar glanced at Roger for a moment and shoved Laura back with a grunt. He ducked a slice at his chest as he turned to run and sprinted toward us. Laura recovered and ran at us, her cold eyes absent of any expression. For a moment, her gaze fell on me, a faint empty smile spreading across her face.

Edgar pushed me into the portal with one hand and Roger in with the other. A screech of metal against stone followed us before the rushing wind silenced it.

Sixteen

Break

Sharp rocks and dirt poked into my body as I rolled to a stop.

I blinked. The strange blue moss below me was familiar, as were the enormous purple trees stretching up to the green-clouded sky. We had landed in the same ravine where I had almost been eaten by the Tigris. The same unnerving sounds of distant animals squawked and cawed like I'd left only minutes ago. I stood gingerly, trying to ignore the stinging pain from the fall through the portal. At least nothing was broken. Probably.

"Ow . . ." Terry groaned. His eye was swollen shut, a large bruise forming on his jaw where he'd been hit.

"I second that," Susan whimpered, rubbing her leg.

Roger rolled to his feet and shrugged off his backpack, tossing Terry a chemical cold pack. Bea stood and brushed herself off, wincing at a cut several inches long seeping through her shirtsleeve.

"I can't believe those were *our* teams," Susan said. "Did you see how they fought? It was like hitting robots. There was no response from *anything*."

"You think they were the real deal?" asked Terry. "Real people?"

"I doubt it," Susan said. "Probably some kind of shape-shifters."

"In those numbers?" Bea shook her head. "Not likely. But I don't want to believe that they, I mean, our friends would . . ." She trailed off. "There has to be some other explanation."

Roger rubbed his shoulder. "They came from everywhere and nowhere. Just . . . out of the walls. I've never seen anything like it." He cracked his neck. "What do you think, Ed?"

Edgar hadn't risen from his knees yet.

"Ed?" called Terry.

Edgar looked up. His hands and upper torso were stained dark red.

"Ed!" cried Susan. The group rushed over as he fell back against the ravine. I stumbled behind them. He seemed confused, his breathing labored. His shirt was soaked with blood.

"Laura." He panted. "She . . . got me good. Thought I had the upper hand too. Dammit."

He closed his eyes. Roger was already ripping his backpack apart, pulling out bandages and clotting them around Edgar's midsection. My stomach lurched; a deep gash ran from one side of his chest to the other, curving into his stomach. Shining white pieces of bone were visible. Nausea rose in my throat. Too many things came out of the wound besides blood. For a moment, I thought I saw black liquid mixed with the blood. I blinked, and it was gone.

"We need to get him to Giftshop," Susan said.

Terry pulled back Edgar's coat, and his face drained of color. "There may not be time for that now," he whispered. "We can't move him like this."

Roger furiously tugged on a pair of gloves and pressed hard on Edgar's wound. He started with one hand, then added the other, but the gash was too big. The bandages were soaked in seconds. He abandoned his strategy and fumbled through a suture kit.

"Don't waste supplies . . . on a dead man, Rog. You know . . . better than that." Edgar gave a shaky laugh. It was cut off by a gasp of pain.

Terry tried to force a smile. "Shut up, you old grouch. You're going to be fine, do you understand me? We'll get you back to Giftshop. It'll be fine."

"Yeah, don't worry, everything will be okay—okay?" Susan stammered. "When we've got you stable, we'll move you."

Edgar shook his head. "I know when I'm got. My time's run out. And that's . . . that's all right." He looked at Terry and Susan, smiling. "I'm glad I got to see you two again. Don't ever change, you hear?"

Terry and Susan swallowed, their faces white.

He shifted to Bea, whose small frame shook uncontrollably. "You . . . do enough, Bea. I know you feel like you don't, but you're the best partner anyone could ask for. Thanks for putting up with me for all these years. Connie would be so proud of you."

Bea's face tightened, her eyes filled with tears.

Edgar gasped another breath and looked at me, his glacier-colored eyes struggling to focus. "You did good back there. See? I . . . told you that you could help." He wheezed. "Listen, there's something coming. The shadows. It's happened before . . . You need . . . to find the others, my old team. They'll explain."

My eyes flooded with tears. "I'm so sorry, I-I shouldn't have—"

He shook his head. "You gave the others a chance to escape. I never should've put you in that position. It'll . . . be different this time. Tell the others . . . we'll do it right this time."

Edgar looked up at Roger, who still gathered up supplies with one hand, keeping pressure on a large clump of once-white bandages stuck to Ed's chest with the other.

"Rog," he said. "It's okay. This was bound to happen eventually. You know that."

Roger shook his head, not looking up.

"Rog."

He sucked in a breath through his nose.

"Roger." Edgar reached up grabbed the side of his face.

Roger finally forced his gaze to meet Edgar's, his face panicked, eyes wide with fear.

"I'm so proud of you. You've come so far. Cliff . . . would be . . . so proud of you. I-I'll . . . tell him . . . you said . . . hi."

Edgar's shaking ceased, the last shallow breath escaping his lips in a wet rattle. His body jerked, his hand falling away from Roger's face. We watched in stunned silence as the light left his eyes, and he was gone.

The world stopped as we stared at Edgar's body. We waited for something to break the spell, waited for time to get moving again, but nothing came to our rescue.

There was nothing.

Just darkness.

Instead, the silence swallowed us whole. I couldn't think. Nothing made sense. Did that really just happen? Why didn't I feel anything? My eyes leaked tears, but there was nothing behind them. Why?

Bea finally exploded in a gasp of violent, racking sobs. It broke the spell, and time ticked forward. Susan stared at Ed's body. Her face looked almost as numb as I felt. Terry's hands covered his mouth, eyes spilling over with silent tears.

Roger's hand was still on Edgar's body, pressing the wound as if it were the only thing keeping him together. His broken expression trembled. He let go of Edgar, pulled off the blood-covered gloves, and sat with his hands in his lap.

Eventually, Bea's sobs subsided. The sounds of the forest returned as thunder rumbled in the distance.

"You," Bea growled. She stood and pointed at me, eyes bloodshot and wild. "This is your fault. If you weren't there, things would've been different. We could've . . . *I* could've . . ." She broke off.

"Bea," whispered Susan, "that's not fair. You know that's not—"

Bea spat a harsh laugh. "Not fair?" Her voice held a dangerous tone. "You want to know what's not fair? That we get stuck with the job of taking care of these *idiots* who are stupid enough to wander into somewhere they don't belong! *This* is what happens!" she shouted, gesturing to Ed's body, "when outsiders get involved. Why should we have to be the ones to die? Our friends? Our families? Why? To protect the scum of the Earth? We should just let them fend for themselves and see how long they last!"

"Everyone knows the risks coming onto this job, Bea," Terry said. "Most of all Ed. It's no one's fault—"

"*Yes it is!*" she screamed. "It's *hers*! And people like her! If she hadn't come poking around where she doesn't belong, none of this would have happened. We would've been watching each other's backs. Everything would've been *fine*!" She looked at Roger. "Tell them, Roger!"

Roger said nothing. He hadn't moved, hands still in his lap. He stared at the bloodstained gloves on the ground.

"I've had enough of people who think they're worth more than us! Think they matter more!" Bea shouted. "I've—I—"

Bea lunged at me, eyes ablaze with hate. Terry grabbed her around the waist, but she elbowed him back. Susan clamped onto her leg, receiving a kick as Bea thrashed. Shoving her off, Bea charged at me, wrapping her hands around my throat. Her grip was inhumanly strong. I tried to pry her hands away, but it was no use.

Roger smashed his shield into Bea's side. She was thrown against the embankment. It didn't faze her, and she scrambled to right herself. Terry and Susan grabbed both her arms and pulled her to the ground. She thrashed and screamed like some wild animal. Her eyes were wide. Foam fizzed at the corners of her mouth.

"Bea, get a hold of yourself!" Susan yelled. "What's wrong with you?"

Roger grabbed her legs as she tried to kick Terry away. She squirmed and yelled, twisting and flopping in the dirt. Shards of rock had stuck into her back and sides, but she didn't seem to care.

A . . . r . . . m . . .

A rustle of static passed my ears. The sound of dry leaves scraping the ground was somehow audible between Bea's wails. I listened closer.

A . . . r . . . m . . .

"Arm," I repeated.

Roger turned. "What?"

"I think— Check her arm," I said.

Terry pushed up Bea's sleeve and recoiled. Black slime penetrated the small cut on her forearm, coating the outside with oozing sludge. A spider-web of black veins surrounded it, snaking just under the skin. They pulsed.

"What the— What is *that*?" Susan quivered.

Bea thrashed in rage, flinging her head from side to side.

"I don't know," said Roger. "Hold her down. *Hold her!*"

Terry and Susan shifted their grip and restrained Bea's flailing body. Roger grabbed an unused bandage and a bottle of rubbing alcohol from his backpack. He swiped the bandage across top of the wound. Even though it looked like hardened black tar, it came away easily onto the bandage. Too easily. Like it was eager to move on to its next host. It squirmed and twitched, reaching out for Roger's hand as he stuffed into a plastic bag and sealed it.

Roger opened the bottle of rubbing alcohol and poured it onto the wound. Bea's screams intensified, her thrashing becoming almost impossible to manage. Roger didn't stop, emptying the entire bottle over the small cut. Slowly, the black veins receded, seeping out of the wound and wiped away. Bea blinked a few times. Her breathing quieted, and her screams ebbed. She lay still, glassy eyes staring at the imposing trees above her.

Terry released his grip. "Bea? You back with us?"

Bea opened and closed her mouth several times. Her fingers twitched, and she jolted up. "What just happened? I don't . . ." Her eyes found mine, and she covered her mouth in horror. "Oh God. I-I'm so sorry, Lily. I don't know what just— I just . . . tried to kill you."

I rubbed my neck, still trying to catch my breath.

"What do you remember?" asked Roger.

Bea shook her head. "It was so strange. I felt normal, until Ed . . ." Her eyes flicked to Edgar's body, and she inhaled. "When Ed died, something . . . broke. All my self-control was gone, and I was left with . . . *hate*. Pure hate."

"Did you black out or something?" Susan asked.

She put her head in her hands. "That's the worst part. I knew exactly what I was doing. The whole time, I knew, and I-I just didn't care. I would have gladly killed you all."

The group fell quiet. Another rumble of thunder boomed from the clouds. A flock of small birds took flight from a nearby tree.

Eventually, Terry rose. "We need to get back to Giftshop, see if anyone else has been infected with this stuff. Should we—" He swallowed. "Should we get on with protocol, then?"

Everyone but me nodded.

Terry wiped his nose on the back of his sleeve. He approached Edgar's body and gently looked through his coat pockets. After a minute, he produced a Teleporter, a Chatterbox, a rabbit's foot dangling from a keychain, and two pens. He turned to Bea and Roger.

"You two should be the ones to bring these back," Terry said.

They accepted them with deep breaths. Bea took the pens, and Roger grabbed the keychain. He clutched the rabbit's foot in his fist so hard his knuckles turned white.

A jolt shot through my stomach. The boxes of pens in the barn suddenly made sense to me.

Terry flipped the Teleporter over in the palm of his hand three times. On the third flip, he held it close to his face and said in a loud, shaky voice, "Fallen: Edgar Montgomery Vasquez. Destination: Necropolis."

The face of the Teleporter changed. Instead of a Metatron's Cube, it displayed a timer counting down from sixty. The numbers engraved on the metal shifted into each other as time ran out. Terry put the Teleporter and Chatterbox on Edgar's chest and folded his hands on top. He carefully closed Edgar's eyes before stepping back. He pulled Susan into a side hug as she cried into her sleeve.

Forty-five seconds remained.

"Okay," Terry said. "I know we usually don't say anything at this part, but I'm ... I'm making a promise." He wiped his eyes again, face becoming blotchy. "If we make it back to our own time, I'm ... I'm letting you beat me in a game of poker, Ed. Like you always wanted. You ... stupid ... kid." His voice broke, and he looked away.

Tears stung my eyes. My bottom lip quivered.

Twenty seconds.

Bea leaned into Terry and Susan. Susan put her arm around her, and they all cried together.

Ten seconds.

Roger stood very still. His entire body was tensed, his jaw locked. No tears spilled from his eyes. I had the sudden impulse to grab his hand, but I stopped myself.

Zero.

The Teleporter buzzed. A bright flash of light blinded me, spotting my vision with black dots. When they faded, Edgar was gone. Only a dark puddle soaked into the ground remained.

The group composed themselves. Bea was the one to finally break the silence.

"We need to get back and tell the others what we know." She cleared her throat, picking up the bag that held the slime-covered bandage. "We can take the—whatever the black liquid is—and get it analyzed. I'll send out a mass message for everyone to return to Giftshop immediately. All right?"

Everyone nodded.

Bea pulled out a Teleporter, and a large oval opened in the air. Beyond it, the dark wooden walls and vaulted ceilings of Giftshop were visible. Terry, Susan, and Bea walked toward it.

Roger didn't move.

He gave a little cough. "I'll meet you guys in a few minutes. I . . . need a minute."

Bea's expression softened. "Rog, you know I can't leave you here by yourself."

"I'll be fine."

"Yes, but . . ." She trailed off, her eyes flicking to me. "Lily, would you stay with him?"

"Me?" I said. "Don't you want someone, I dunno, less useless?"

"Just stay and keep an ear out for anything, would you?"

I glanced at Roger, who was in the middle of rolling his eyes. I looked down. "Sure."

Bea sighed. "If something happens, don't try to fight, just get back to Giftshop. We don't . . . need to bury another body today."

Roger nodded. "Thanks, Bea. We'll see you soon."

"Till again." She waved, stepping through the portal. Terry and Susan followed.

As soon as the portal closed, Roger pivoted and made a beeline to the other side of the creek bed.

I had to jog to catch up to him. It took two of my strides to match one of his. "Hey, wait up!" I called. "Where are you going?"

He didn't slow down. "Ed asked for one thing, and one thing only." He vaulted up the creek embankment and reached down to pull me up by my arm, which he did with ease. "To find his old team and tell them what's going on. I'm *not* putting that on the back burner while everyone else gets caught up."

"So what was all that business about you needing a minute?"

He shrugged. "Bea would've told me to wait for her."

"And I'm here because . . ."

"It's protocol. You're not supposed to leave anyone alone after a traumatic event."

"Why?"

He shot me a look.

"Oh," I said. "Gotcha."

He ducked under a low-hanging branch and stepped onto an animal trail lined with glowing patches of small flowers. "Bea can explain things to the rest while we go through some records."

I ducked under the branch. "What records?"

"If there's one thing Jumpers do well, it's record keeping. If you know where to look, you can find info on *every* team member since 1860."

He paused, looking up at a cluster of huge purple trees. Stepping back, he picked up a rock and chucked it at the trunk of a particularly large tree. There was a metallic clanging sound, and a metal ladder glitched into view. He mounted it and started climbing. I followed, peeking up. A large dark square shape of a building stood high up the tree, the ladder leading straight to it. Eventually, we reached the top, where it connected with a wooden platform.

Opening the hatch, Roger clambered inside and pulled me in. My eyes adjusted to the darkness. The spacious wooden tree house was simple, with wide windows covering all sides like a fire-watch tower. The views overlooking the forest were stunning. Great winding rivers and lakes dotted the landscape. Bright patches of moss and bioluminescent plants created great contrast against the dim sky, giving everything an ethereal backlit tone.

One side of the room was dominated by a table, chairs, wires, cords, and translucent glass tubing. Several bulbous screens sat suspended by rickety shelves and wooden planks. Overall, it reminded me of the design of the Chatterboxes, but on a larger scale.

Roger flipped a few switches, hit a large button, and pulled out a chair. The screens flickered to life, casting harsh blue light over the dim room. A complicated-looking map popped up titled "Sector 14: The Forest of Luminescence." Roger typed in a series of letters and numbers with the old clattering keyboard. Files and photographs filled the screen.

"So what are we looking for?" I asked.

"Anything on Ed's old team members. They're retired now, but their addresses and contact info should still be here."

He scanned through pages and pictures, pulling a few of them to a separate folder. His face had an odd, determined expression. He didn't look well. The shaking of his hands caused him to backspace frequently.

"Hey," I said. "Are you . . . doing okay?"

"I'm fine," he said. The tone in his voice didn't leave room for any questions.

He clicked open a file, and a picture flashed across the screen. A young man beamed at the camera, his eyes youthful and carefree. The name Edgar M. Vasquez labeled the picture. Large red letters stamped the single word *DECEASED* across his face.

Roger froze.

I expected him to keep searching through files, but he didn't move. He didn't even seem to be breathing. After a solid minute, I cleared my throat.

"Roger?" I asked. I put a hand on his shoulder.

Roger buried his face in his arms and sobbed. His entire body shook with every shuddering breath, every whimper. I could tell he wanted to stop but didn't seem able to.

I pulled up a chair and waited, hand still on his shoulder, the word *DECEASED* glaring down at us like a grave marker.

SEVENTEEN

Traps: The Sequel

Eventually, Roger's breathing slowed. He kept his head down, gripped his elbows, and sniffed. Glancing around, I spotted a pile of napkins next to an old bag of trail mix. I grabbed a few and placed them on his arm. After a moment, the napkin pile slid out of sight.

He wiped his face and sat up.

"Hi," I said.

Roger glanced at me, eyes red and puffy. "Hey. Sorry. I just—" He cleared his throat. "Wasn't prepared for, uh, that . . . Brought back a lot of stuff."

He clicked away from the smiling picture of Edgar.

"Don't be sorry," I said. "To be honest, I was starting to think you were a robot. Good to know that's not true."

He gave a small, hoarse laugh. "One can only dream," he mumbled, and sat up. "Okay, here it is."

He clicked on a folder that opened a list of seven people, each accompanied by an older-looking photo. Two of them had the word *DECEASED* stamped on them. One was the photo of Ed, and the other was a woman's face, her already dark skin made more so by the contrast of the old film.

"Hang on, is that . . . Bea?" I asked.

Roger leaned closer to the screen. "I don't think so? Sure does look like her, though. No, it can't be. Look." He pointed at the numbers and letters on the side. "'Deceased. Logged . . . July 20, 1966.'"

"Does it list a name?"

He clicked on the file and scrolled. "Uh . . . yeah, here we go. Durand, Constance M. Durand . . . That's Bea's last name. I didn't know she had a sister. She's never mentioned her before—" He cut off abruptly as he scrolled to a section titled "Details."

He scanned the minuscule text. "Oh," he whispered.

I leaned over his shoulder to read it.

DURAND, CONSTANCE M.
JANUARY 9, 1945 – JUNE 20, 1966
C.O.D: GUNSHOT; SELF-INFLICTED; CONNECTOR,
UNDISCLOSED
L.T.O: COLLECTIVE, AGE 18 AT DISCOVERY
NEXT OF KIN: DURAND, BEATRICE L. (SIBLING)

My eyes focused on the words *Collective* and *Gunshot; self-inflicted*. A strange feeling settled over me. So Bea's sister had been the one to hear the Collective. No wonder she knew so much about it. The database said Constance died in an undisclosed Connector, but why? What happened?

Roger glanced at me but didn't comment. He pulled up a list of five addresses and dragged them to a printer icon. All of them were in Stars Crossing. Sheets of paper slid out of one of the many machines surrounding the curved screens.

He stuffed them in his pocket. "All right, let's get back."

We both got up, and he pulled out his Teleporter.

"How do you use those things?" I asked. "Is there a button you have to push?"

He shook his head. "No, it's more of a mental thing. You imagine a firm scene in your mind where you last established a connection, or Giftshop, and hold it in your hand. Concentrate, and a temporary Gateway will open."

"How do you establish a connection?"

"When you're in a place you want to come back to, just hold the Teleporter and try to capture the moment in your mind. It takes practice. You'll know if you did it right; it gives a little buzz."

I nodded. "So your last connection was here?"

"Yeah, when I came to get you. You know, when you fell out of the sky?"

I rolled my eyes. "Thanks for the reminder."

He flashed a weak smile. "I'm just glad I had one here. When Ed said to scatter, I was worried I'd have to go back to Giftshop."

"Why is that a bad thing?"

"Usually it wouldn't be, but . . . those were our teams. Meaning there was a chance they'd be waiting for us in Giftshop too. Not very likely, but if they can fool us, they might be able to fool Giftshop. People are tricky to read." He nodded to my jacket pocket. "You still have a Teleporter. Do you want to try?"

"What, now?"

"Yeah, why not? We're just going back to Giftshop."

I shrugged. "All right, but don't blame me if I accidentally take us to the edge of the universe or something." I pulled the small metal disc out of my pocket and held it out. "So I just . . . visualize Giftshop, then?"

"Just picture it like you were standing there. You can close your eyes, if that helps."

I nodded and closed my eyes. I thought of the dark wooden walls and endless hallways of Giftshop. I tried to recall the smell of peppermint and old tobacco.

Instead, something very odd happened. A tug in the back of my head. A feeling of vertigo. The sensation of falling backward, then I could see. I could see the room I was standing in. I watched myself stumble back with my eyes closed and felt the vibrations under my feet. I watched the back of Roger's head as he stood with folded arms. I saw the dark room of the tree house, illuminated by the brightly lit computer screens. I gasped. I saw that too.

A small buzz vibrated the Teleporter in my palm. I'd accidentally made a connection here. Whoops.

Roger tilted his head. My vision pivoted so I could see his face. His eyebrows furrowed. "Lily, are you okay?" he asked.

I watched my own mouth move and felt the twang of my vocal cords. "I-I can . . . see, Roger."

"See? See what? The Collective?"

I shook my head. It made me dizzy to watch. "No, the room. I can see us, right now, standing in this room," I said. "Like I'm watching a video of it happening, but it's from a different perspective. I can see everything."

Roger held three fingers behind his back and watched my face—well, my physical face—carefully. "What am I doing right now?" he asked.

"Holding three fingers behind your back. Seriously, this is . . . whoa."

It was also disorienting. And it made me nauseous. I opened my eyes, my real eyes, and blinked. A wave of dizziness hit me. I blinked again. "Whoa," I repeated.

"Yeah . . ." He nodded. "Interesting. Yeah. Nope." He shook his head. "I have literally no idea what just happened. What did you do?"

"I-I don't know, I was just concentrating on visualizing Giftshop, and I could see us instead."

"Like an out-of-body experience?"

"I guess. It's happened before in my dreams of the Collective. Do you think it's connected to it? The Collective?"

Roger raised his shoulders. "Maybe? I guess we'll add that to the list of questions we ask Bea later. She obviously knows more about it than she's let on."

I again held out my Teleporter and thought of Giftshop. A strange electric sensation ruffled the air. A large oval portal opened a few feet away.

We stepped through it, and I looked back into the tree house. I relaxed my concentration, and the portal closed. We were back in the Guest Book room. The large crystal chandelier loomed above. I squinted. It was much brighter here than the Forest.

"Look who finally made it back."

Atop a nearby table sat Catacombs, cleaning bits of dirt from between his paws.

"Where is everybody?" I asked.

"They're meeting in the viewing bay. Bea was about to send someone out looking for you two. I'll tell her you're back."

He jumped from the table and headed for the door but paused. *"I . . . heard about Ed. I'm sorry, Roger. He was a good man."*

Catacombs sauntered out the door.

Roger watched him go, mouth hanging open. "He's never used my real name before," he said. "Come to think of it, I didn't think he knew any of our names. He was always just kind of *there*. What did you call him again? Catacombs?"

"Yeah."

"Why?"

I shrugged. "He was really dusty when I met him, looked like he crawled out of a tomb. It just seemed to fit. Did he not have a name before?"

"No, I usually just called him cat, or fleabag, or spawn of Satan. You get the picture."

I chuckled. "Hi, Giftshop," I called to the room. A light breeze that smelled of lilacs wafted by. I glanced over at the Guest Book.

"Should we sign out now?" I asked. "So we don't have to do it later?"

Roger nodded, pulling a pen from his pocket and handing it to me. "Probably, I'm not sure where we're going after this."

I pulled out my pen. "I have my own this time. But thank you."

We signed out and shuffled down the hallway that led to the viewing bay, avoiding eye contact with the long line of marble statues. Roger opened the door to the next hallway and continued, but I stopped at a framed picture. I wasn't sure if I hadn't noticed it before or if it simply wasn't there until now.

"Lily?" Roger asked, turning back. "What's wrong? Do you hear something?"

I shook my head and pointed to the new picture. Three people sat around a roaring campfire. Two men and one small boy, maybe six or seven. The little boy roasted a hot dog over the flames. One of the men I recognized as Ed.

"Oh my God," Roger said. "I didn't know that picture still existed."

"That's Ed, right?" I asked.

"Yep."

"Who's the other man?"

"My dad."

I blinked. It wasn't hard to see the resemblance. His eyes crinkled the same way as Roger's when he smiled.

"So the little kid, that's you?" I asked.

"Yep."

"Oh. My. God."

"What?"

"Look how adorable you were!"

Roger rolled his eyes. "Ugh, stop."

"Look at those little cheeks!" I gushed.

"Cut it out."

"I just want to pinch those little cheeks!"

He put his hands up and walked away. "I'm leaving. Good. *Bye.*"

I chuckled and jogged to catch up. Roger glanced at me, face tinged red. At least he was smiling a little.

Muffled conversation floated through the ornately carved door as we approached. We pulled it open and pushed aside the heavy purple curtain.

The mass of people became still as we entered. Bea addressed the crowd, who all had their backs turned from the window. They looked somber and resigned. A few of them were crying. I spied Catacombs near the windows lounging under a table. His tail flicked back and forth as he surveyed the room.

Bea spotted us and gave us a nod. "Welcome back," she said. "I was just getting everyone caught up. We're still waiting for Irene's team to get back. There was a situation they had to take care of first."

"Was there . . . anyone else, Bea?" Roger asked. His eyes dimmed as he asked the question.

She lowered her head. "Six of Jacqueline's team, Jonesy, and Mark didn't make it back. We still haven't heard from a dozen others. We can only assume the worst."

Roger stared at the ground. I only recognized one of the names: the man back at Sal's who spoke to us. He vouched for me when I was brought back to Giftshop. Now he was probably dead, or worse, changed into one of those shadow people. Or driven berserk like Bea. Along with how many others? The remaining group in front of me had dwindled in number. Did I even want to know the exact count?

The group continued its quiet pockets of conversation. The low murmur of voices reminded me that I should be listening for the Collective. I strained my ears, but no otherworldly voices reached me. It was a funny thing, trying to hear something that was beyond hearing.

The door opened, and in shuffled Irene and her team. I recognized Leo and Irene but didn't know the four other people's names. They sported bandages and bruises, looking tired and annoyed.

"What happened to you?" Bea asked Irene.

Irene, who had an abundance of small cuts on her face, shook her head. "Ran into some wildlife. No serious injuries, but a waste of time." She scratched the back of her hand. "I *hate* those stupid bat things. They always come out of nowhere. Anyway, what did you find? Any sign of Laura's team?" She looked around. "Where's Ed?"

The group was silent.

Realization dawned on her face. Her shoulders sagged. "Oh . . . no. No."

Bea gave a short nod. A younger girl with blue hair and the three other men in her team gasped.

Clearing her throat roughly, Irene looked up. "What happened?"

"An ambush. Laura's team and . . . others were in the Caverns, and we got caught off guard," Bea said. "Ed didn't make it."

"Laura's team?" asked a man behind Irene. He had red hair and thick glasses. "You found them? I don't understand. Are they alive? Are they okay?"

"Jack, they *were* the ambush."

"What?" the girl with the blue hair squeaked. "There's no way. I refuse to believe that. Laura is one of the most dedicated people I know. She'd never—"

"Something wasn't right with them," interjected Susan, who stood near Bea along with Terry. "They didn't act like themselves. Like robots, or . . ." She trailed off, searching for the right word. "Puppets."

"But if they were just puppets," Irene said, "then who was pulling the strings?"

A silent tension held the room hostage. The gnawing quietness constricted the group.

Until a quiet chuckle drifted from the corner.

Heads swiveled to see the source of the noise.

It was Leo. He stood away from the group, his arms folded, face set in a large smile. He was . . . laughing. The action seemed so out of place, so alien.

"I have to say," he said, still laughing, "I'm *very* impressed with how many of you made it back in one piece. Honestly, I thought that would take care of at *least* half of you. Ah well." He jabbed a finger in my direction. "That's what you get when you leave loose ends, isn't it? Should've taken care of the psychic wonder child when I had the chance. Oh well." He scratched his nose absentmindedly. "What're you going to do?"

The group stared, frozen. No one seemed to know what to do. Leo's fellow teammates were pale, faces full of pained realization.

"Leo?" Bea asked, approaching him. "What are you talking about?"

He shrugged, the unwavering smile plastered to his face. "I'm just saying props to you guys for sticking in there. I mean, it makes it harder for me, of course, but that's all just part of the fun."

Nothing in his mannerism besides his words suggested anything malicious. He simply sounded like he was commenting on the weather. But there was something in his eyes that I recognized, a strange hollowness that made him look inhuman. A darkness.

"Please tell me you're kidding, Leo," Irene said, face torn. "Tell me you didn't do this."

Leo clucked his tongue. "Dear Irene, who do you take me for? I'd *never* lie to you. That's more than I can say for the rest of you."

"What—"

"Didn't I ask you to come along that day?" His smile wavered. "Didn't I *tell* you that we needed help? Didn't I *call* your miserable faces for backup?"

Irene's lip quivered. "Leo, you were out too far. We couldn't get to you in time. Anna was already—"

"Shut up! *Shut up!*" he exploded. "We needed you, and you *weren't there*! That's the bottom line."

For a moment, the rage in his eyes replaced the hollow darkness. His entire body shuddered. He blinked, and the same serene smile returned. "It doesn't matter. I have new friends now, ones who won't abandon us. Never again."

Everyone in the room shifted stances. Hands moved to their weapons; positions pivoted toward Leo. A few people moved to restrain him.

He sighed. "Oh, now that won't do."

He put a hand to his mouth and blew a shrill whistle.

A cold stale breeze swept up from the floor. Leo's long trench coat flapped in the wind, his shadow casting a black shape on the walls. The shadow grew darker, thicker. It metamorphosed into black shifting blobs, stretching outward until the mass coated the space around Leo. It split, globs growing in size and speed, attaching itself to any person it could reach.

The masses moved with horrifying speed. Nobody had time to run or even scream. The instant the darkness touched them, they fell immobile, eyes wide open but unable to move. Like a snake, the black tar engulfed the fallen, encasing them in an undulating cocoon of shadow. Bea, Terry, Susan, Irene's team, anyone standing close was almost instantly taken.

Roger pulled me toward the windows as the darkness neared. "Run, Lily!" he said. "Get out of—"

He froze. A tendril of slime had attached itself to his foot.

"Roger?"

There was no light behind his eyes. He slumped forward into a heap on the floor, covered by black sludge in seconds.

The darkness advanced. I backed up against the windows overlooking the vast cosmos and pressed my hands against the cold glass. The whole floor was pitch black now, and there was no one left standing except me. There was nowhere to run.

"Hold up, guys," called a voice.

The shadows stopped advancing, leaving a small island of untouched floor.

Leo walked through the blackness with no apparent trouble, stepping over the sludge-covered bodies. He flashed a pleasant smile as he approached. It was such a stark contrast between him and the bodies on the floor behind him. It made his relaxed manner even more unsettling.

"Gotta hand it to you," he said. "You've taken to your abilities quicker than we thought. We guessed you would've gone cuckoo by now with all those voices in your head, but look at you! Still going strong. Do you like my new friends?"

I stared at him, scared to move.

"They're not for everyone at first," he admitted. "But you'll learn to get along. You're going to be pals for the rest of eternity!"

My heart pounded. I was shaking.

He considered me, an amused smirk on his face. He turned on his heel and waved a hand. "All right, guys, have fun."

The shadows continued their advance, and I pressed myself against the windows as tight as I could manage. It made no difference.

A low groaning shook the walls. It sounded as if a thousand pipes had burst at once. A strong acidic odor wafted through the air. The many floorboards and wooden panels shuddered. The lights flickered. The air pressurized. A horrible creaking sound cracked the windows behind me.

Giftshop, it seemed, was *not* happy.

There was a moment of peace before books and knickknacks jettisoned off shelves, aimed straight at Leo. Chairs and tables groaned and split apart as they were pulled, flung, and rocked around the room in a hailstorm of furniture. Wind whistled through the bookshelves as the creaking wood panels shuddered violently. Whole pieces of wood were ripped off the walls and splintered into a thousand jagged shards.

The shadowy sludge tore itself up off the floor flew across the room to protect Leo, blocking objects that flew around the room. Leo had pulled out a double-sided poleaxe, slicing at things being thrown at him, just barely keeping up. Even the shadows seemed too slow for the voracity of an angry Giftshop.

I, apparently, was not priority. My little island of clear space grew bigger, bit by bit regaining untainted ground as shadows helped protect their master. I could almost reach Roger as the shadows stripped themselves away. I crawled to the edge and crouched low. A chair narrowly missed me, torn pages of books flapping around my face. I dug the Teleporter from my pocket and waited next to the retreating line of darkness.

A nearby mass of shadow paused, disappearing into the cracks of the floorboards. The groaning in the walls increased. The indoor storm became frenzied. Flickering lamps went out one by one, struggling to stay lit.

With a gurgling meow, Catacombs bounded toward me. Books flew into the air, forming a path above the shadow-covered floor. He jumped from book to book and landed in my clear circle. I held the Teleporter, hoping for something to happen. A hole opened in the wall behind me. The dark surveillance room high in the Forest sat beyond it.

"Get inside!" I shouted over the wind. Catacombs leapt nimbly into the hole.

The shadows had cleared enough that Roger and a few unfamiliar faces were visible. Roger's open eyes were unmoving. I grabbed him by the strap of his backpack and dragged him into the portal. I looked back; the shadows had regrouped as the storm of objects slowed. The lights dimmed, and the walls groaned faintly. I couldn't reach anyone else.

Leo's eyes found me. He wasn't smiling anymore. There was no emotion, no indication that there was a person inside.

Nothing.

Just darkness.

I looked one last time at the room of people I was leaving to die. My view of Giftshop disappeared as the world zipped back together again, and everything was dim.

EIGHTEEN

Hollowed

"Well, that could've gone better."

My eyes adjusted to the darkness. The computer screens had turned off, the only light filtering through the large clouded windows. It cast a muted blue glow across the ceiling.

I stared at the place where the portal had been. How had everything gone so bad so fast? How did we lose everything so quickly? I stepped back. My foot caught on a loose floorboard, and I sat hard on the wooden floor.

Catacombs came and sat next to me. *"Are you all right?"*

"I'm not hurt, if that's what you mean," I said. "Do you think Leo knows where we are?"

Catacombs shook his head. *"I doubt it. And even if he does, he's going to have to deal with Giftshop first."* He stretched, tilting his head in Roger's direction. *"Is tree-boy dead?"*

Roger lay in a crumpled heap on the floor. His eyes were open, and he was still breathing, but that was all.

I shook my head. "He's still breathing. I don't know what that . . . black stuff does, but this is different than what happened to Bea. She went berserk but recovered. This is just . . ." I swallowed. "Spooky. Do you think we could get back to Giftshop it we tried?"

"Hm." He rose and stretched. *"Let me check. Hang on."*

He walked over to the table and disappeared behind one of the legs. He emerged a moment later. *"Nope. Looks like she's closed herself off. Which means your Teleporters are useless, by the way. Hope that wasn't part of your escape plan."*

"That's giving me too much credit," I said. "I didn't have an escape plan. I don't even know how we're going to get out of here."

Saying the words out loud shot a pang of fear through my stomach. How *were* we going to get out of here? The only Gate connecting to Earth was in the middle of the sky. Even if we did manage to get through it, how much time had passed on Earth? Terry had said time works differently between the Otherworlds, and now that Giftshop wasn't around, what would happen? Roger would probably know, but he was unconscious, or . . . worse.

Catacombs sighed. *"This is bad. Really bad. Have you tried waking him up?"*

I knelt next to Roger, untucked his arms from his backpack, and rolled him onto his back. Nothing. I waved a hand in front of his face. Again, nothing.

"He's not asleep."

"*Have you tried using the Collective?*"

"How would that help?"

"*I don't know, I'm just spouting off ideas. Isn't the Collective connected to every human?*"

"I guess."

"*Well, just tap into that connection, get inside his head, and wake him up. Jolt him awake with something. A memory or emotion or whatever.*"

"Look, I don't know if you've noticed, but *I'm new at this*! I can barely hear the Collective! I wouldn't know where to *begin* to access that connection. Ed said that—" I broke off. For just a second, I'd seen a flicker of life in Roger's open eyes.

"Did you see that?" I asked.

Catacombs's ear twitched. "*I did. He must be conscious on some level. What did you say just now?*"

"I just said that I didn't know where to start, and Ed said that one day I'd—" I stopped again. Another flicker. "I think . . . it's because I mentioned Ed." Another flash. A small drop of water leaked from the side of one eye. His arm twitched.

"*He's waking up. Quick, keep talking.*"

"About what?"

"*I don't know, something with Ed, anything he recognizes.*"

"Um . . ." I blanked, suddenly at a loss for words. "I guess I could talk about . . . that picture we passed on our way to the viewing bay?"

There was small movement in his eyes. I kept going even though I wasn't sure it was working. "You were with your dad and Ed. You seemed . . . so happy. And now . . . now you're the only one left in that picture. First your dad, and now Ed."

Another stream of water leaked from his eyes.

"This doesn't seem fair, does it? To lose Ed and then everyone else too. And what if Leo gets back to Earth?" I shook my head. "There'd be nothing to stop him. People would die. Or *whatever* it is that's happened to you. And Bea. And Terry and Susan. And everyone. They're all ... all ..."

My vision blurred. A hot rush of realization hit me, and tears spilled down my face. I was scared. Terrified. I had already lost Terry and Susan once. Did I really just lose them again? Once Leo got back to Earth, how long would it take for the darkness to spread across the world? Probably not more than a few hours. Everyone I knew—my parents, Alice, Oliver, and Dolly—were they destined for this fate too? What if I was the only one to make it out alive? What if it was already too late?

What if I was alone?

I clamped a hand over my mouth and stifled a sob.

Catacombs rubbed his head against my arm in a comforting nudge. "Grmeow."

"I'm so, so sorry about all of this," I said.

On impulse, I grabbed Roger's hand. His fingers twitched, the muscles in his hand tightening. He closed his hand around mine and jolted upward with a gasp.

I fell back onto the floor, startled by the sudden burst. "Roger? Are you back?"

He shook with violent shudders, wheezing. The light had returned to his eyes. He focused on me. "Lily? What did—"

He jolted, an alarmed look passing over his face. He scrambled to the desk and grabbed the small trashcan just in time to vomit. Black sludge poured from his mouth. I looked away. He retched until there didn't seem to be any more slime remaining. He pushed the trashcan away in disgust, falling into a fetal position.

"Ow," he moaned.

I rummaged through his backpack until I found a bottle of water. Approaching him cautiously, I knelt and helped him sit against the wall. He took the water bottle and chugged a large gulp, spitting it out. I was alarmed at the strange chemical smell coming from the trashcan.

"Thanks," he gasped. "That really *sucked*. What happened? Where are the others?"

"Don't you remember anything?"

"Bits and pieces. I remember Leo going all 'shadow puppet master' on us. Not much after that. How long was I gone?"

"Not long, maybe ten minutes?" I said, and recounted what had happened at Giftshop, or rather, that Giftshop had *happened*.

"Wow. She waged all-out war, didn't she?" He chuckled. "I would have *loved* to see that. Did anyone else make it out?"

I shook my head. "I don't think so. I'm sorry, you were the only one I could grab."

He cast his eyes down and took another drink of water.

"It was so odd," I said. "Your eyes were wide open, but it looked like you were dead. What happened to you?"

His posture hunched as he leaned on his knees. "I don't know. I could see and hear what was happening, but I couldn't process any of it. And there was . . . I remembered . . ." Roger's grip on the water bottle crinkled the plastic. "I saw things. Things that I never thought I'd see again."

He swallowed before he continued, his eyes haunted. "Then you mentioned Ed. And everything started to hurt. And then you brought up that stupid picture, and . . . I thought I was dead. But the pain, it gave me something to hold on to. Something to break through the numbness. But it still wasn't enough."

He downed the last gulp of water from the bottle. "And then suddenly, I could move. Simple as that. What did you do?"

I shrugged. "I just grabbed your hand. I wasn't trying to do anything."

"*I told you it might work!*" Catacombs said. "*You tapped into those Collective powers!*"

I rolled my eyes. "I did not."

"Collective powers?" Roger asked.

"Catacombs wanted me to access your brain through your connection to the Collective and wake you up," I explained, shaking my head. "It sounds even crazier when I say it out loud."

"Oh," he said, nodding. "Well, did you?"

"Did I what?"

"Access my brain."

"No!" I stood up. "I don't even know how to do that! I just grabbed your hand!"

"Well, I hate to break it to you." He stood, steadying himself against the wall. "But until the moment you touched me, I was a vegetable. You did something, all right. We just have to figure out what."

"*Great. Psychic Wonder Child gets a prize for being an unintentional weirdo. Can we talk about how we're going to get out of here now that Giftshop's closed, please?*"

"Giftshop's closed?" Roger sighed. "That's not good."

"No kidding," I said.

Roger rolled his neck from side to side. "Well, the nearest accessible Gate is a three-day hike from here. We better start walking."

"Three days? What about the time differential that Terry was talking about? Won't the time on Earth move differently than here?"

"Yes, but not as much as other Gates. This world's time moves similar to Earth's, which is why we use it as a surveillance outpost. We'll lose a week or so, but—"

"A *week*? Earth could be filled with shadow people in a week!"

"We don't have many other options!" he said. "Since the only other Gate that leads to Earth is blocked off, we can't—" He stopped, slapping a hand to his forehead. "Oh my God, I'm such an *idiot.*"

"A fact I have known for years," Catacombs said.

"What do you mean?" I asked.

"Lily, the Gate you came through, the one in Terry and Susan's barn? It's open now. We can get a straight shot back to Earth. Even better, a straight shot to Stars Crossing."

"The Gate is literally in the sky."

"Yeah."

"And you plan on reaching it how?"

Roger grabbed his backpack and headed for the hatch. He pulled it open, a gust of strange-tasting wind swirling into the tree house. "C'mon. We need to find Ed's old team and stop this before things get worse."

"What about the Gate?"

"Don't worry, I've got a plan." His attention turned to Catacombs. He frowned. "How are you getting down the ladder?"

Catacombs flicked his tail and turned his head up. *"That is no concern of yours."*

"Roger's got a point," I agreed. "You can't go down the ladder, and it's too far to jump."

"I'll manage. I, unlike you simpletons, have many ways of getting around."

He sauntered behind the leg of the desk chair and disappeared. He reappeared a moment later, covered in dust, swatting dirt from his eyes. He shook, realized he was in the same spot, and flattened his ears.

"Uh-oh," he said.

Roger unzipped his backpack and held it out for him. "I can take you down. Hop in."

Catacombs thought about this.

"*No,*" he said.

"Come on, it's the only way."

"*No,*" he repeated.

"You can leave your head out if you want," Roger offered. "I won't zip it up all the way."

"*No.*"

My arm itched under my sleeve. I scratched at it, but it only seemed to make it worse. "Catacombs, either get in the backpack, or we leave you here," I said.

He glanced around the tree house and sighed. *"Fine. But let it be known I hate this."*

Roger cracked a smile. "Noted."

Catacombs pounced into the backpack and turned to face the back. His head and front paws peeked out over the zipper. He glowered at us.

Roger put on the backpack, mounting the first step. "If you're extra good, next time I'll bring you a lollipop."

"*Shut up,*" seethed Catacombs.

Roger chuckled and disappeared beyond the hatch. I took a steadying breath and followed him down the cold metal ladder.

Nineteen

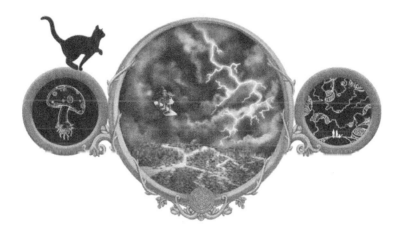

Boxed Memorial

The trip down was uneventful, my foot slipping on the ladder only once. My concentration was constantly diverted by the stunning views of the Forest, stretching into the horizon like an endless ocean. Patches of light radiated from below the canopy, interrupting great swaths of wooded darkness with punches of blue and green.

We landed on the squishy ground and started off on another path.

"Do you want out?" Roger asked Catacombs.

"*Hm . . .*" Catacombs considered. "*I quite like being toted around by you. You're like a chauffeur. Or a pack mule.*"

Roger ducked under some low branches, positioning his backpack so Catacombs got smacked with a face full of purple leaves.

"*Ow!*" Catacombs yelped. "*Okay, okay, I get it! You're not a pack mule.*"

I snickered. Roger turned his head to me and smiled. It was good to see his eyes light up again. Seeing him immobile and lifeless was . . . something I didn't want to see again.

"So what's your plan?" I asked after a few minutes of walking. "The Gate's pretty high. Hope you weren't planning on jumping for it. Maybe that's why you're called Jumpers. Hey!" I said. "I made a joke!"

He rolled his eyes. "Hardy-har-har. You know, if Jumpers relied on our own two feet to explore, we wouldn't get very far."

"So that means . . ."

"That means have patience, grasshopper."

Roger turned onto a faint path, stopping at the base of a large hill. Wooden support beams outlined the shape of a small door set into the side. A cluster of translucent white mushrooms covered the mound, stretching back into the woods. He strode to the door and pulled a key out of his pocket, unlocking a heavy brass padlock with a *click* and heaving open the door. A small dirt-walled cave filled with boxes, barrels, tarps, and equipment peeked from the darkness. Roger plucked one of the mushrooms off the hill and shook it. It glowed, illuminating the cave, which stretched back farther into the dirt than I had originally thought.

"What is this place?" I asked.

"This"—he ducked into the doorway—"is an emergency storage shed. ESS for short. You'll find one in almost every surveillance area. It holds a five-year supply of food, medical supplies, basic equipment, etcetera."

"Why?"

"The whole idea behind these was to give people stuck in an Otherworld during a Gate switch a fighting chance."

"Does that happen a lot?"

"More often than you'd think, unfortunately." He stepped over a pile of boxes in the entrance and rummaged, holding the glowing mushroom aloft.

"Okay," I said slowly. "Why are we here?"

"Because"—he pulled a small ivory box from a barrel, removing a flat chunk of metal the size of his palm—"they also have transport items."

"What is it?" I asked. It wasn't smooth; the small piece of metal was covered in rivets and copper gears. A strange patchwork of grooves adorned the top.

"It's called a Glider. It's how we get around during surveillance runs." He stepped back outside, throwing the mushroom over his shoulder. "Well, at least *I* do. I believe the exact instructions were 'Roger, do not use this under any circumstances because you're going to lose it' or something like that. It's how I got to you so fast when you fell into the Tigris den."

He rotated a copper gear until it clicked into place. Standing back, he tossed it to the ground. The small plate expanded, unfolding lengthwise, widthwise, lengthwise again, curving, stretching, I lost count. I blinked. A large round metal platform a little larger than a surfboard sat on the ground.

Roger tapped a foot on the edge of the board, and it hummed to life. The Glider rose a few inches off the ground and hovered.

"But I mean come on, *look* at it." He flung his arms at the hovering board, clearly enamored by it. "What was I supposed to do, *not* use it?"

I stared at the peculiar device. It emitted a low hum that reminded me of idling jet engines.

"Is this the only one?" I asked.

"Er, no." He shuffled his feet. "There are more of them in other ESSs, but there are three here. I, uh, may have misplaced the one I was using before."

I raised an eyebrow. "So you . . . lost it."

"Hey, I was more concerned about you not getting eaten alive at the moment. I know it's around that ravine somewhere. Anyway, this is our ticket out of here." He stepped on the board, and it hummed. It tilted a little before evening out.

"Come on up. It's not as bad as it looks," he assured me.

"What?"

"Come on up," he repeated. "We need to get going."

"You want me to . . . fly on that?"

"Technically, I'll be the one flying. You just have to not fall off."

"What about the storm?" I asked. "We'll get electrocuted up there."

"That's a chance we'll have to take. I'll try to steer us away from any thunder cells. But this is our only way back."

"But . . . but I—"

"Look, if I have to ride in a backpack, you have to ride on the floating death board," Catacombs called from the backpack. *"Quit your whining."*

I sighed and stepped onto the Glider. It wobbled. I threw my arms out to balance, which did little to stop my legs from shaking. I glanced up at Roger. He hid his smirk quickly.

"I'll go slow," he promised.

I stood with my feet spread apart in a wide stance, hoping to provide more balance. That theory flew out the window as we rose above the ground at an alarming rate. Catacombs crouched deeper into the backpack, only his ears visible.

I tottered as we gained altitude, my arms flailing to stay steady. Roger leaned forward, and the Glider shot forward. I clamped onto his shoulders.

"I thought you said you were going to go slow!" I shouted over the wind. Blue and purple shapes blurred past me. The wind smelled of cinnamon and sage.

I felt his shoulders shake in laughter. "I am!"

He zoomed upward and broke through the canopy with a resounding crack of breaking branches. I put my head down and buried my face into the side of the backpack, clinging to his shoulders for dear life. The ride smoothed out considerably, and the wind became less fierce. I peeked through my hands.

The wide stretch of the Forest arose with shocking immensity. The green of the clouds around us were so deep, they looked almost black. Between the swirling green haze were patches of blue, silhouetting trees, rivers, lakes, and plants strewn about the countryside. Something large rose from the tree line and cawed in the distance.

"Wow," I breathed.

A dull boom followed a flash of light in the clouds. Roger maneuvered the Glider over a large round clearing, the trees surrounding it thick and dark.

"That's the Tigris den," he called. "The Gate should be around here somewhere. Do you remember any landmarks when you fell?"

I shook my head. "Everything happened so fast . . . but it was definitely close to here!"

"Keep a lookout! I'm going to make a few passes over the area."

He flew in large sweeping arcs. A cluster of bright flashes in a nearby cloud bank crackled too close. Roger swerved to avoid it, the Glider pitching upward. My fingers dug into his shoulders as he leveled out. My heart pounded. A dark shape caught my attention.

In the swirling mass of clouds above us was a square door. I recognized the iron bands that held together the heavy wooden trapdoor.

I tapped Roger on the shoulder and pointed. "There!"

We sped up, gradually gaining altitude as we circled up in another wide arc. As we neared the Gate, Roger slowed and hovered. We drifted up to it until I could touch a hand to the rough wooden surface. I pushed upward, but it wouldn't budge. Roger gave it a hard shove. Bright pink light blazed through, disappearing as the door slammed back down. The Glider wobbled as we pushed from opposite sides, disrupting its equilibrium.

I looked at Roger. "Together?"

He nodded, bracing his hands against the door. "One, two, *three*!"

We shoved the hatch. It swung open, bathing us in bright orange light. Squinting, I could make out pink clouds and the floating spherical islands. A wave of relief washed over me at the sight of something familiar.

"All right, you climb up first, then take the backpack," Roger said. "I'll follow you."

The rumble of thunder hung in the air as we hovered close to the Gate. I grabbed the edges, pulled myself up, and rolled to the side. I reached back down for the backpack and set it on the squishy ground.

"*Can I get out of this baby carrier now?*" Catacombs grumbled. I unzipped the backpack, and he hopped out to stretch.

Roger emerged from the trapdoor and swung his legs up onto the ground, leaning into the hatch again to retrieve the Glider, now in palm-sized form. He stood, shielding his eyes from the bright light.

"Wow," he breathed, turning in a circle. "You weren't kidding about the rubber band ball things." He squinted at a nearby orb. "Are those flowers?"

"No idea," I said. "I thought you could tell me."

"I've never been here before."

"Oh. Right."

The wind blew gently, bringing the smell of roses and citrus. The same soft music echoed from . . . somewhere.

"*I have to say, they picked a good first Connector back in the day,*" Catacombs said, skulking over to join us. "*At least the air here is breathable.*"

Roger turned his head. "What?"

"*What?*"

"What do you mean the first Connector?"

Catacombs sat and watched the clouds with us, tail twitching. *"This was the first Gate. You know, the original seven and all that? That was a fun day."* He nodded fondly. *"Lots of jumpy Jumpers."*

"You act like you were there," I said.

"*I was.*"

"How? That was over a hundred years ago!"

"*Yeah,*" he said. "*Only a hundred years ago. Barely a blip.*"

I couldn't tell if he was joking or not. I shut my mouth anyway.

"Where's the Gate?" Roger asked.

I pointed at the far side of the orb. "That way. The pole over there."

We trudged to the base of the pole and stared up at the long ascent. The rope I had left earlier swung in the breeze.

"*Does this mean I have to go in the baby carrier again?*" asked Catacombs.

"How did you get down last time?" I asked.

"*I have my ways, like I said. But for some reason, I can't go through now.*"

"What does that mean?" asked Roger.

"*I think ... something happened to Giftshop.*" He shook his head. "*Before, I thought she just evicted everyone, but now ... now I can't connect at all. This has never happened before.*"

That was worrisome. After the display she showed with Leo, I'd assumed she had everything under control.

Roger held out his unzipped backpack. "Come on, inside."

Catacombs groaned and slinked into the pouch.

I clambered up the pole first, embarrassed at how out of breath I became and how badly my muscles shook. I closed my eyes against the oily brown beads but again forgot to close my mouth. I searched around blindly for the edge of the metal bucket until my hand bumped against it. Grabbing hold, I used it to heave myself out of the Gate and onto the wooden floor. The barn looked almost exactly as it had when I left, silver lighting casting its glow from the clouded sky. Rain continued to fall outside. Was it the same rain?

After a minute, the backpack popped up from the Gate. I grabbed it.

"Those beads taste like death," whined Catacombs. *"I hate them."*

"You and me both," I said, unzipping him from his confines.

Roger appeared from the bucket and hung on the rim.

"This has been"—he panted—"a very long day."

I grabbed his arm and tugged. He shimmied through the Gate, flopping onto the floor with an *"Oof."*

He got up, arched his back, and rubbed his eyes. "I forgot how much I hate Spacer Beads," he murmured, blinking hard. "They stick to your eyes. Like your actual *eyes.*"

We walked toward the door, shoes sticking in spongy puddles of dried paint. Roger spotted the window and skirted around the pyramid of pens. He crouched beside them, out of sight from the dirty panes.

The open box of pens was still there, exactly as I had left it. I pulled down the flap, a heavy feeling settling across my shoulders as I surveyed the hundreds of battered and broken pens. The dark dried spots were not ink, as I had originally thought. They were blood. This pyramid of pens was one large boxed memorial, each pen representing a fallen Jumper.

Roger left his post from the window. "I can't see anyone at the house. We should be clear if we don't stay in the open too long." His eyes shifted to the box. "What's that?"

I opened the flaps wide so he could see. "I didn't know what these were when I first came through here. I . . . I do now."

Roger stared at the boxes. "So this is where they go," he mumbled. "I always wondered . . . Terry and Susan must have collected them for years. I wonder what else they've got here."

"I can answer that mystery: an enormous amount of random junk. I've been packing up the house for the past few weeks, and I feel like I've barely started."

"You're packing up the house? Why?"

"When they . . . died, they left my family the house and everything in it. So we've been—or I guess, I've been—packing up their stuff to put in storage."

"Why? Don't you own the house now?" he asked.

I sighed. "Yeah, but we can't keep it."

He looked confused. "Um, not to sound like a broken record, but why?"

"Look we . . . don't really have a lot of money. And on top of that I . . . there's some medical bills, okay? My parents can't handle the taxes on it, so they're trying to figure out a way to sell it."

"Why don't you just live out here?" he asked. "Have your parents sell their other house and live here?

"First of all, my parents rent. They have nothing to sell. Secondly, there's no job industry out here. It's all retired people and trees. They'd lose all their insurance, pension, everything. I can drop out of school to support them, but even that won't solve anything."

"So . . . what are you guys going to do?"

I huffed a breath through my nose. "That's the question, isn't it?"

"Seriously."

"I really don't know, Roger. Seriously."

"Well, we can't let you guys sell the place," he mumbled. "Not with a literal Gate in your barn. Don't worry about it. I'll talk to someone."

I laughed. "Sure. Whatever you say."

"No really, we'll figure something out. I'll talk to Ed, and—"

He broke off, squeezing his eyes tight for a moment before heading for the stairs. "Well, if we get out of this alive, I'll talk to someone."

We headed into the rain, Roger keeping a wary eye as we trotted to the front door. Catacombs trailed behind us, complaining under his breath about his paws getting wet. The cold wind was oddly comforting; it blew rain into my face and eyes, but at least I knew it was normal Earth rain. Something I knew wasn't going to kill me.

The stairs to the front porch seemed steeper than usual. The house sat in cold gray silence. I pushed the door open, greeted with a puff of warm air as we stepped into the kitchen. I dead-bolted the door behind us. I flicked on the kitchen light above the sink. Nothing happened.

"Power must be out," I said.

Roger pulled down the window shades in the kitchen, the living room, and the dining room before heading to the rest of the house. He returned a few minutes later.

"Okay, all the windows are locked, and the shades drawn. We need to keep any light, candles, flashlights, or whatever, away from the windows. I don't want anyone to know we're here."

"You think someone's watching this place?"

"I don't know, but I don't want to take any chances. It's getting dark. The best thing we can do now is lay low." Roger slung his backpack off his shoulder and collapsed onto the floor, letting his head hit the wall behind him. "I think I'll just . . . sit here a minute."

I joined him. The exhaustion that I'd been ignoring settled over every sore muscle, every lingering bruise. The release of pressure on my feet sent a rush of blood through my legs. My arm burned. I scratched it through my sleeve.

Catacombs spread himself out on the floor with a tremendous sigh. *"Well, here we are. Waiting to be hunted by a crazy person. Whee."*

"Whee," I agreed. I glanced at Roger. His head nodded, jerking up as he slumped forward.

"Hey." I nudged his shoulder. "There's an extra bedroom down the hall. Go use it. You look like you're about to pass out."

He slapped his face with both hands. "I'm fine, I'm fine. We need to figure out a plan. What if Leo shows up?"

"We'll sleep in shifts. I'll take first watch and wake you if anything happens. Okay? You're no use exhausted."

He rubbed his eyes. "Yeah. Yeah, okay."

I stood and stretched. "I'm going to find some candles. I just packed a whole box a few days ago. Well . . . That could also be yesterday. Weird."

In the time I'd taken to stand up, Roger's eyes had already closed again. I prodded him with my foot.

He jolted. "Hm?"

"Go. I'll wake you up in a few hours."

He rose slowly. "You'll come get me if you hear anything? Promise?"

"Promise."

He sighed. "Okay. Just give me an hour, then it's your turn."

"Gotcha."

Roger gave a wave, shuffling down the hallway. "Thanks, Lily."

He disappeared through the bedroom door, shutting it behind him. I looked down. Catacombs had curled into a ball on the mat below the sink, fast asleep. The *tick-tick* of a battery-powered clock read half past four in the afternoon. Was this still the same day I wandered into the barn?

I found my legs shaking, so I sat on the floor. Through the cracks in the curtains, I watched the dark silhouette of trees sway against the clouded sky. I listened for any static but heard none. The whistling of wind and the soft drumming of rain against the cold kitchen window were my only companions.

TWENTY

Nutella Cat

When I next glanced at the clock, it was half past seven.

I blinked at the darkness. Three hours had gone by, and I hadn't even picked myself up from the kitchen floor. Nothing had happened during the past few hours except for the steady beating of rain. There had been no sound that was out of place and nothing from the Collective. Even Catacombs hadn't even stirred from his slumber on the floor mat.

I rubbed my eyes. I was tired, but the thought of going to sleep was worse. The Collective would be waiting for me there. The pod. The drowning. I didn't think I had the strength to go through it again. Roger would probably be getting hungry, though, and it was past time for me to wake him up.

My arm burned through my sleeve again. I scratched it, finally rising from my tucked position. An alarming amount of soreness radiated throughout my body. I ignored it, tripping in the dark over boxes to locate the tub of candles I'd packed earlier. Minutes later, I found it buried under a pile of blankets and tugged it into the living room before I realized I didn't have any matches. Rummaging clumsily in the pantry, I located a box and lit a few in the living room and the kitchen.

I chose a chunky candle that wouldn't tip easily and knocked on Roger's door. A few moments later, Roger opened it looking disheveled, jacket in hand. His eyes seemed more alert than before.

"Morning," I said. "Or evening, I guess."

"What time is it?"

"A little past seven."

He put on his coat. "You were only supposed to give me an hour."

I shrugged. "It was quiet. No reason to wake you up. I figured you might be getting hungry, though."

"Yeah, starving. Don't you want to get some sleep?"

I shook my head. "I'm not tired."

"Really?"

"Yeah."

Roger tilted his head and looked at me funny. "Lily, are you feeling all right?"

My arm burned. I scratched my sleeve. "I'm fine. Do you think the stove will work?"

He nodded slowly, still giving me a speculative stare. "If it's a gas stove, then yeah. We'll just need to light it."

"Oh. Right."

I turned around and headed back to the kitchen, shielding the small flame of the candle with my hand. Catacombs had woken up and perched himself on the counter. His tail flicked as we rummaged through the cabinets.

Roger grabbed the flashlight and opened the pantry, frowning at the contents. "Wow. Haven't gone to the store in a while, huh?"

"It's just me here. I don't go through a lot of food."

"Hm," he mumbled. "Well, you have pasta, and I see tomato sauce in the back. Do you want makeshift spaghetti?"

I scratched my arm. I wasn't hungry, but at least he could eat. "Sure, that's fine. Pots are over there. I'll get the stuff out."

He nodded, watching me gather the ingredients from the pantry and set them on the counter. I measured out a single serving and turned to Roger for the pot. He hadn't moved. Both he and Catacombs were staring at me.

"What?" I asked.

"Uh, shouldn't we make more than that?" Roger asked. "There are two of us."

"*Three of us,*" Catacombs pointed out.

I shrugged again. "I'm not hungry. It's fine. You guys can eat."

Roger folded his arms. "Lily, how long has it been since you ate something?"

I rolled my eyes. Here we go again. "Why is it any of your business?"

"What?"

"Why do you care?"

"Because I don't want you passing out on me."

"I'm not passing out. I'm fine."

"Lily, you look like—"

"I look like what? What's *wrong* with me now?"

Roger's worried expression increased to alarm. "I was going to say you look pale. Really pale."

"*I'm actually with tree-boy on this one,*" Catacombs said. "*You don't look so good.*"

"Ugh!" I threw the spaghetti box on the counter. This was just like before. Why couldn't they just leave me alone? "I'm fine. Just drop it."

"Lily, you're not—"

"I said I'm fine!" I shouted. "Why does no one ever listen to me?"

They were quiet. My arm itched again. I scratched at it.

Roger approached me. "What's wrong with your arm?"

"What? Nothing. It's fine."

He held out a hand. "Can I see?"

I held my arm close. "No, I'm fine. It's *fine.*"

Roger stepped closer. "Lily, let me see your arm."

"No, leave me alone!"

Roger moved fast. His fingers closed around my wrist and yanked up my sleeve. He grabbed my other arm as I tried to hit him. I couldn't break free.

"Let me go!" I yelled.

His face drained of color as he inspected the underside of my arm. He pulled me over to the sink and turned on the water, scraping it with a towel. He tugged something stuck to my forearm, and it pulled my skin. I kicked and screamed, but he wouldn't let go.

"The water's not working!" he called to Catacombs. "Find something!"

"*Like what?*"

He ripped off my jacket. "Something acidic! Alcohol, lemon juice, anything!"

I broke free and lunged for the nearby knife block. Roger tackled me and dragged me to the floor. I screamed, hitting any part of him I could reach. I elbowed him across the face. It didn't faze him as he held me down. I tried to twist and throw him off, but he wouldn't budge.

"Hurry!" Roger yelled.

Catacombs emerged from the pantry, dragging a large glass bottle in his mouth. Roger snatched it and cracked open the cap, dousing my skin. My arm was on fire. The sharp smell of vinegar stung my nose. I screamed again. He was pulling my skin off, I knew he was. He pulled out my blood vessels one at a time. The sickening burning engulfed my entire body until the edges of my vision darkened.

Eventually, the fire dulled. I stopped screaming. It felt like a snake had unwound from my intestines, the crushing force I hadn't noticed before peeled away inch by inch. The strong vinegar smell burned my eyes. The cold kitchen floor beneath me was wet. I sucked in a breath.

Roger loosened his grip on my arms. He sat up, still on top of me. "Lily? Can you hear me?"

I looked at him. His deep brown eyes were so worried, flicking over my face. So full of kindness. I had wanted him dead just moments ago. I was reaching for knives to *kill* him just a few moments ago.

"Lily?"

"I—"

I couldn't speak. The nausea in my throat choked me. Roger untangled himself from me and helped me sit up. I looked at my arm. Even though they had receded, the pulsing black veins underneath my skin stretched past my elbow and disappeared beyond the sleeve of my jacket. The kitchen towel writhed with the weight of the twitching black mass. It inched along the floor, crawling back toward me. Roger grabbed a pair of tongs from the counter and stuffed it into a plastic grocery bag hanging nearby.

"Are you . . ." I cleared my throat. It was sore. "Did I hurt you?"

Roger rubbed the side of his face. His cheek was red and puffy. "You got in some good hits, but I'm fine."

I put my head in my hands.

"Hey." He pulled my hands away, peering at me with a reassuring smile. "It's okay. No harm done."

He grabbed a roll of paper towels and continued wiping off the sludge that oozed from my pores. It hurt, but I didn't scream this time. In a few minutes, the black veins were gone. Only an angry red welt and deep-purple bruises remained. Roger added the paper towels to the bag and tied it closed.

"How long has this stuff been on me?" I asked.

"To take a guess?" He sat down on the floor next to me. "Probably since Twisting Caverns."

My lip quivered at the thought of it being attached to me all that time. "Why did I only react now? Why was Bea so much quicker?"

He shrugged. "Who knows? Maybe Bea had the . . . black stuff introduced through her bloodstream directly. She had a cut, remember? It might take longer if it's only through dermal contact. Or . . ."

"Or what?"

"Maybe . . . it's tied to our triggers. Bea had a reaction when Ed died, maybe that was tied to the loss of her sister. And you seemed okay until I asked if you'd eaten. Do you . . . have problems with that? Not eating, I mean."

I stared at the floor, shame settling over my shoulders. I hated it. I hated how I was still like this. I was a grown adult; why couldn't I take care of myself like one?

"Yes," I whispered.

"Can you stand?"

I nodded, using the edge of the counter to pull myself up. I grabbed another towel from the cupboard and sopped up the excess puddles of vinegar from the floor.

"So . . . if I *were* to make some spaghetti," Roger said, "would you eat some?"

I gave a weak chuckle. "Sure. I'll get some more food out."

"Hey, what else you got in there?" Catacombs said, hopping off the counter. *"I'm not really a fan of spaghetti."*

"Um . . ." I glanced back into the pantry. Roger was right, I did need to go to the store. "We have . . . popcorn, flour, sugar, bread, peanut butter, Nutella—"

His ears perked up. *"Nutella? I love that stuff! Can I have some?"*

"Can cats even eat Nutella?" I asked. "It's chocolate. Won't it make you sick? Maybe you should have something else."

Catacombs's penetrating glare bored into me. He sat.

"I have watched the rise and fall of countless civilizations and seen great men fall to their knees before me to plead for mercy. I have seen the glory of the cosmos and have been worshiped as a god. I am a being of unknowable power that your tiny human minds cannot begin to comprehend." He lifted his paw and stamped on the floor. *"Give. Me. The. Nutella."*

I unscrewed the lid of the container and set it on the floor, backing away. Catacombs licked the sides of the lid before sticking his nose into the jar.

Roger, who was filling a pot with water, glanced at me. He shrugged, a smirk passing across his face.

Soon we had a pot full of cooked spaghetti noodles. Roger drained the pasta while I struggled to work the rusty can opener. Eventually I hacked open the lid enough to pour the chunky tomato sauce into the pot. It looked a little sad, but at least it was food.

Roger grabbed the loaf of bread from the counter and some plates. We sat across from each other at the kitchen table and dug into our makeshift dinner. I hadn't realized how hungry I was, and apparently neither had Roger. We both cleaned our plates twice.

"Okay." Roger sopped up the last bits of tomato sauce with a crust of bread. "I'll keep watch and wake you up in a few hours."

I shifted in my seat. "No, that's okay. We need to make a plan."

"All right." He leaned back. "The plan is I'll keep watch and wake you up in a few hours."

I looked away.

"Look, I know you're exhausted," he said. "Why don't you want to— Oh." Realization dawned in his eyes. "You're afraid to see the Collective, aren't you?"

I nodded sheepishly. "The last few times I've slept . . . things didn't end well."

Roger stood and cleared away our plates from the table. "You can't stay awake forever."

"I know."

"Eventually, you'll have to deal with it."

"I know."

"*Hey, I can watch you if you want,*" Catacombs said, abandoning his Nutella. *"I can wake you up if you start thrashing around like you were in Giftshop."*

"I was thrashing around?"

"Like a mental patient."

After a moment of thinking, I shrugged, scooting the chair from the table. "All right. We can try that. Wake me up if you have any problems?"

Roger nodded. "Don't worry, I'll look after things. Go get some rest."

I gave a wave as I left the kitchen. "Thanks."

Catacombs followed me up the stairs and onto the angled ladder of the loft. I glanced at the bathroom longingly on my way past. I wished the power was on. A shower sounded amazing.

I pulled back the covers and yanked off my shoes. "Okay, if I start screaming, try to wake me up? Or go get Roger."

"You got it."

"Goodnight, Catacombs."

"Goodnight, Psychic Wonder Child."

Twenty One

Jerry the Faucet

As expected, I was trapped.

The stringy insides of the pod pressed against my face. I sat back. I knew where I was, and more importantly, I knew *what* it was. Closing my eyes, I sat still and willed my vision to travel outward. Sure enough, after a moment of concentrating, I could see outside my pod. The dark muddy sky and strange orange clouds pulsed with the contrast of light and dark meeting. Looking down, I saw the rest of my body. It was translucent and pale. Like a ghost.

"Welcome to the Collective, Miss Masters," came a deep voice.

I whirled around. A man with white hair, a mustache, and square glasses was seated at a desk, flipping through the worn pages of an old book. He wore a tweed suit and an impeccable red bow tie. Bookcases filled with knickknacks and dusty books surrounded the desk, acting as a wall. A red armchair sat across from the desk. The man and the objects floated in the air, hovering up and down as I did.

"Um, hello?" I stuttered. "Who are you?"

He didn't bother looking up, flipping the page of his book. "I'm here to make sure you don't lose your mind, Miss Masters."

I waited for him to elaborate. He didn't.

"What's your name?" I asked.

"That's entirely up to you." He closed the book and scrutinized my face. "What do I look like to you?"

"What? How did— What are you doing here? I'm still in the Collective, right?"

"Indeed. You are also sleeping soundly as we speak, watched over by Catacombs. Funny how one can be in two places at the same time without realizing it."

"What—"

"I am part of you, my dear, and part of the Collective. A safeguard that your subconscious and the residents here put in place to protect you from yourself."

"So, you're . . ."

"I am a faucet."

"I— What?"

He gestured forward. "Have a seat."

Not knowing what else to do, I accepted and drifted to the squishy armchair. There was a plain wooden hourglass on the desk, which he grabbed and flipped over. Sand trickled from one level to the other.

"As Beatrice pointed out," he started, "trying to process all the information here would be like trying to collect water from a fire hose with a thimble. I am simply a faucet on that hose. It's still an incredible amount of information to process, but I help soften the blow. Think of me as your own personal psychiatrist delegated to you by the Collective."

"So . . . why is it so quiet here now? What happened to that . . . giant wall of static? All those voices?"

He scooted back his chair and reached for another book. "Ah, you see, that was you trying to listen to everything at once. Impossible to hear anything. Now that you've become more aware of your ability, you can listen for specific information."

"Is that what those . . . voices are?" I asked. "When I'm awake, I mean. I hear things, but I can't control them."

"In a sense. At a basic level, you can now hear the outskirts of the Collective. You are familiar with a ball of yarn?"

"Of course."

"The Collective is in a similar state. It's constantly being wound, getting larger with time. The newest memories and thoughts are nearer the end of the yarn. The further you follow it, the deeper into the past you go."

"So the voices I hear are on the outside of the ball of yarn, where they're the easiest to hear?"

"Precisely."

"But I can't choose when to hear them or even what I'm hearing. It just . . . happens."

"You are young," he said, fixing his glasses. "With time, you'll learn to access us from different states of consciousness and search for specific people, places, memories, or what have you. One day, you may be able to channel thoughts and emotions to others." He glanced at the hourglass on the desk. It was halfway drained. "If you happen to survive that long."

"What do I do now?" I asked.

"You live, you learn, and you listen. Try to use the information to help others rather than for ill. Though, of course, that's the morality side of the Collective talking. There is an infinite number of conflicting moral states here. The choice belongs to you, and you alone."

I sat against the armchair, my head spinning. "Why . . . are you helping me?" I asked. "What do you gain from helping me not go insane, I mean."

He looked at me over his glasses. "Why does anything do anything? Simply because we are in existence. And therefore, since we are in existence, we must continue to exist."

"You lost me."

He smirked. "There are so few points of contact to your world and plane of being that we have learned to treat them with care. We have become immense in our many centuries because humans have become immense. It's a lot for anyone to handle."

"We?"

"Things grow, Miss Masters. Where there is life, there will also be metamorphosis." He flipped through a few pages of his new book. "The good, and the bad, come together to form pure and unbridled humanity. That is 'us.'"

I stared at him, mouth open. None of that made any sense, but he didn't explain further.

The last few grains of sand trickled through the hourglass.

I pointed to the pod suspended by thousands of threads. "What is that? Why am I always stuck inside?"

"That is your connection to your physical body, a manifestation of the separation of your incorporeal form," he said. "Be grateful you have it; otherwise, you'd be adrift in the Planes with no hope of ever returning. But that is a conversation for another time."

"Do I have to . . ." I swallowed. "Do I have to leave the same way? The . . . drowning?"

"That depends," he said. "If you can separate the 'you' in your physical body and the 'you' sitting in this chair. Constance never could get the hang of it. Then again, she never had much time to practice."

I swallowed as liquid entered the pod, and I clenched the arms of the chair. I couldn't feel the fabric or anything else around me. I closed my eyes. The steady beat of my heart, the inflation of my lungs, those sensations stayed with me. I took deep breaths.

Just in.

And out.

I glanced over. The pod was full now, but I couldn't feel it.

"Very good." The man approved. "Maybe there's hope for you after all."

I breathed a sigh of relief, keeping a firm grip on the armchair. The world faded slowly to white. It was a nice change from drowning.

"Wait, you didn't tell me your name," I said.

He leaned forward. "What do I look like to you?"

I frowned, considering the man. Somehow he reminded me of my fourth grade teacher. Maybe it was the mustache. But his name?

"Jerry," I blurted. "You look . . . kind of like a Jerry."

He sat back in the creaky wooden chair and put down his book. "Jerry it is, then."

"Lily?"

A voiced reached me from a distant world. It left paths to follow back to consciousness, and I took them. Someone shook my shoulder.

I opened my eyes a little, and the world blurred into view. The loft was dark, illuminated by a single candle on the nightstand. Roger leaned over me, his hand still on my shoulder.

"Everything all right?" he asked.

I sat up and rubbed my eyes. "I met a guy. I named him Jerry. He's my faucet."

As expected, Roger looked almost as confused as I was. "He's your—What?"

I explained what happened in the Collective between yawns. The aches in my body hadn't diminished, nor did the pain in my head. I felt like I hadn't slept at all.

Roger nodded. "Well . . . okay then. Weird."

"No kidding. Anything happen while I was asleep?" I asked. "Where's Catacombs?"

"Everything was pretty quiet. The cat went downstairs to finish his Nutella. Huh." He paused. "That wasn't a sentence I thought I'd be saying today."

I swung my legs from underneath the covers. Ow. "What's our next move?"

He pulled a crumpled piece of paper from his pocket and smoothed it. I recognized it as the information he got at the surveillance station. Besides the two pictures of Constance and Ed, there were five other people listed: three men and two women. Addresses and names accompanied each picture.

"We find Ed's old team, but we're going to have to wait until morning. It's past midnight now."

"Why wait?" I asked. "Let's go now."

He sucked in a breath through his teeth. "Bad idea."

"Why?"

"These folks, they're—how do I put this—they're notoriously trigger-happy. We'd probably get shot."

"Ah."

"Bad idea to surprise them in the dark."

I blew a breath through my nose. "I knew we should've gone earlier. Who knows how far Leo has gotten by now?"

"I thought the same thing," Roger said. "But while you were asleep, I found an old battery-powered radio in living room, and . . . nothing."

"What do you mean nothing?"

"I mean there's nothing out of the ordinary outside of Stars Crossing. No emergency broadcasts, no evacuations, nothing. Everything in town is dead air, but the surrounding counties don't know anything's wrong."

I frowned. That didn't make sense. With the speed of the shadows, I would've thought Leo and his friends would be all over the world. What was keeping them here?

"So . . . what do we do now?" I asked.

He shrugged. "Sleep, I guess. There's not much we can do until morning."

"Okay, I'll take watch again."

Catacombs hopped up the ladder with a small thump. *"Hey,"* he called. *"You're out of Nutella."*

"You ate the *whole* jar?" I asked incredulously.

"No, but it's getting hard to get to. It's too deep. What are you two simpletons doing?"

"Trying to decide who sleeps first," Roger said.

"I can take watch if you want," Catacombs offered. *"That way you both get some sleep. You look like zombies."*

Roger narrowed his eyes. "Why would you do that? That's almost as if you're being . . . nice."

Catacombs licked a paw and preened himself. *"Hardly. But if you two get yourselves killed, I'll be stuck on this godforsaken planet by myself. It'll be the Stone Age all over again. No. Thank. You."*

I looked at Roger, who shrugged indifferently.

"Thanks, Catacombs, that'd be great," I said.

"Cool." He stretched. *"Could you guys sleep in the same room so I don't have to run back and forth?"*

"Sure," I said. "We can sleep in the living room. That's not filled with boxes yet. You can go get pillows and blankets from your room; there's a couch you can use. I'll grab my stuff."

Roger nodded, heading back downstairs with Catacombs trailing behind him. I pulled off the comforter and pillow, carefully descending the ladder. Roger was already making his bed on the floor, the couch untouched.

"Hey." I dumped my armload of blankets on the floor. "I said you could use the couch."

He looked up from his nest of pillows. "No, you use it. It's your house, technically."

"Yeah, it's my house, and that makes you my guest." I folded my arms. "And guests get couch privileges."

He stood and folded his arms as well, waiting.

"I can see this is going to be a problem," Roger said.

"As can I."

We glared each other down.

"So, what's it going to be?"

Twenty Two

<u>Whispers</u>

We stared at the ceiling in silence.

After arguing for a few minutes, it was clear that neither of us would accept the tabooed couch. We made nests of pillows on the carpet, lay a few feet from each other, and settled under the blankets. For some reason, it was awkward lying this close together.

I leaned over to blow out the lonely candle.

Roger lifted his head. "Hey, actually could you . . . maybe leave that on?"

I nodded and moved it onto the coffee table so neither of us would knock it over. "Yeah, I don't really want to sleep in the dark either. Probably for the rest of my life. However long that's going to be."

"You're both a couple of pansies," Catacombs called from his perch on a nearby bookshelf.

We ignored him.

"Do you know these people at all?" I asked. "Ed's old team, I mean."

"Kind of. They retired about ten years ago. My dad was good friends with some of them. Of course, my dad was good friends with pretty much everyone. They were part of the search party when he went missing. They were the last ones to quit."

"Sounds like people really liked him."

Roger was quiet. He turned onto his side and faced away from me. "We should get some sleep. Wake me up if you hear anything. Or if you . . . need anything."

"You do the same. Goodnight, Roger."

"Goodnight, Lily."

A chilly wind swept across the gray landscape, shuffling the leaves around the gravestones like a deck of cards. Two figures walked hand in hand along the overgrown path between the various stone angels and grave markers. A man, and a child, no more than four. The pair turned off the path and headed for a simple tombstone shaded by a large pine tree.

They stopped at the grave and stood in silence. The little boy sniffled.

The man pulled the small boy into a side hug with a pained expression.

"People are supposed to be remembered in happiness, sport."

The little boy continued to sniffle.

"But it's okay to be sad," the man continued, his voice breaking. "It's what makes everything else worth keeping happy."

The pair stared at the dark gray stone flecked with white. Neat letters had been chipped into it.

'Amelia J. Owens, Beloved Wife and Mother.'

"*Do you begin to understand?*"

I jerked into a sitting position. The voice was harsh, yet soft. Like the scraping of stone against metal, or a wire brush against a chalkboard.

"Who's there?" I asked, looking around.

The candle had gone out. It was dark. Roger was asleep next to me, Catacombs curled into a ball on the shelf. Neither of them stirred.

I stood up and looked around. It was dark. The ticking of a wall clock counted the time. I didn't remember a clock in here. It was blank. No numbers. No hands.

"*Do you see why we come?*" it hissed over my shoulder.

I whirled around. No one was there. "Who-who's there? Who are you?"

"*We have many names in this world.*" It whistled like wind through floorboards. "*We have met before.*"

My blood ran cold. "How did you find us?"

"*We didn't. You found us.*"

"Then . . . then why haven't you killed us yet?"

"*We are restricted by certain rules. We cannot enter unless invited in your world. But this . . . unconscious state of yours allows us inside. Especially if one is connected to the Collective.*"

"You know about the Collective?"

"*Of course. It is near our home. Many have tried to listen in our realm, but none could. It is uniquely linked to Earth. And more specifically, linked to you.*"

"Your realm? Where do you come from?"

"*We exist on a different plane than you,*" the voice rasped. "*One not of physicality but of movement. Of balance. Infallibility.*"

My heart pounded. With every word, the voice cut deeper into my head. "What do you want?"

"*We come as saviors, Lily Masters.*"

"What?"

"*We come to liberate your world from suffering.*" It slithered. "*With you as our link, connecting us to Earth physically, we could help you. Help your friends. Your family.*"

For some reason it was hard to resist the urge to say yes. The word was already forcing itself from my mouth. I swallowed it back. "I-I don't believe you."

The voice paused. "*You lack understanding. You are connected to the Collective, yet you are young. The one before you was just as ignorant.*"

"The one before me?"

"*Such a foolish girl. All she did was delay. But you now have a chance to redeem yourself. You and your kind.*"

The walls around me seemed to distort and move. The voice wrapped around my brain like a spiderweb. I felt dizzy.

"What are you?" I whispered.

A cold stale wind that tasted of mildew and decay swept through the room.

"*We can show you.*"

The room was already almost pitch black, but as the wind became colder, the dark became darker. Shapeless masses surrounded me, just barely visible through the darkness.

No wait, it was the other way around.

They *were* the darkness.

They were the space between things. The shadow between shadows. Pure impenetrable voids that hid in the background. For a moment, I could believe the vaguely humanoid figures were just flat shapes. Paper cutouts, incapable of movement. But then they moved. The space around them buckled, the cold wind sucking the warmth from the room.

My entire body shook.

"Are you afraid?" the voice asked.

I swallowed the scream that had worked its way to my throat.

"Do not fear us. We can work together. We will show this world the true reality of freedom. Do you accept?"

One of the shadows held out an arm to me.

"Accept what?" I asked.

"Us."

"I don't understand."

They were quiet again. A soft sigh swept through the room.

"You have much to learn," it hissed. *"Observe."*

The strange sound of crashing waves against rock came from behind me. A wave of pain slammed into me, so distinct and palpable that I couldn't even scream. Hands tore flesh from my bones. Someone burned me alive. Sickness permeated my body. My lungs were filled with water. I was electrocuted again, and again, and again.

After a few seconds, I found my voice and started screaming. My ears rang and echoed with the sound of my shrieks. I writhed on the ground, reaching at anything to stop the pain.

There was nothing around to help me. No hope of an end.

Nothing.

Just darkness.

"Now do you see? This pain is so . . . unnecessary. Your world suffers for no reason. You could be free. Emotion will burden you no more, and you can help us to free others. All you have to do is accept."

Through blurred vision, I saw the creature hold out a sticklike arm to me. I reached for it. The pain could stop? Of course I'd accept. Whatever it was, it was better than this. Nothing before the pain seemed real. Like a dream I was just now waking up from. Where was I? What . . . what was my name? What was I even doing here?

"We can make you powerful," the voice soothed. *"A general among nations. Imagine it: Commander Lily Masters."*

My eyes snapped open. I was inches away from the creature. A distant memory dragged itself from my mind and into the present.

The playground was bright.

Children laughed and played on the nearby swing set. The occasional cloud of wood chips was kicked into the air by little feet.

On the other side of the playground was a small girl backed up against a wall, two other girls facing her.

"C'mon, give it up. You think we won't take it anyway?" scoffed the larger girl.

The girl shook her head, her eyes wide and terrified.

The other sour-faced girl tapped her foot. "We don't have all day."

The small girl reached into her backpack with trembling hands. She pulled out a purple cat stuffed with clumping bits of cotton. One of its button eyes was missing, and its fur was worn to the thread in some places.

Her eyes filled with tears as she handed it over. The large girl snatched it and knocked her into the wall. They ran away, laughing and throwing the stuffed animal between them. The small girl turned and hurried away, finding an empty spot behind a trash can. She sat, folded her knees to her chest, and cried.

The bell rang, signaling the end of recess, but still she sat and cried. From across the playground bounded another girl, ponytail bouncing behind her. She slid to a stop behind the trashcan.

"There you are," said the ponytail girl. The start of a bruise blossomed behind her eye. She held out her hand. The purple cat stuffed animal flopped forward.

The small girl looked up, face red from crying. She smiled and wrapped her arms around the cat.

"What's your name?" asked the girl with the black eye.

"Lily. Lily Masters. What's yours?"

"I'm Alice, but you can call me Sergeant Alice Minnley: Protector of Recess," said Alice proudly.

The small girl's smile grew wide. "That's a nice name. How did you become a sergeant?"

"Someone has to promote you," Alice explained. "My dad promoted me. Do you want me to do you?"

The little girl nodded.

"All right, then, on your feet, soldier," Alice ordered in her best authoritative voice.

The little girl scrambled to her feet and wiped her eyes with the back of her sleeve.

Alice raised a stiff palm to her forehead. The little girl did the same.

"I now promote you to Commander Lily Masters: Defender of All! Use this title wisely. It is only given to a few."

The little girl nodded with a grave expression. Alice started laughing, and so did the little girl. The next bell rang. They hurried off together back to the classroom.

I stopped screaming. I remembered where I was, and more importantly, who I was. I could feel something inside me that wasn't pain. It was . . . something else. Something warm and soft like a blanket. It gave me something to hold on to other than misery. I clutched at it.

Dark creatures around me shifted and writhed. The walls of the house began to melt and peel away. The ground shook. Sounds of metal against metal screeched through the air. Screaming. The creatures were screaming. The world caved into itself, and everything went black.

"Lily? Lily, please, wake up! *Please!*"

The pounding of my heart slowed with time. A draft blew through the room. It smelled of pine trees and dust, not mold and decay. I opened my eyes and was faced with a bright light. Was I dead?

No, the brightness flickered. It was a candle, and I was lying on my back on the floor of the living room. My skin was damp. My throat hurt. Tears streaked my face.

"Lily? Can you hear me?"

I tilted my head. Roger stared down at me, his face pale, his deep brown eyes bloodshot. I blinked at him.

"Lily, come on, if you can hear me, answer me!" he begged.

"I . . . I don't—"

I couldn't speak. Nothing made sense. The sudden gush of memories from the dream shocked me, and I sobbed. The pain was still fresh. The violation of my dreams—my entire being—made me nauseous. Roger helped me sit up and kept a hand on my shoulder. I buried my face in my knees. I felt a nudge on my side.

"Grmeow."

Eventually, I stopped sobbing and sat up. Catacombs sat against my side, peering up at me with yellow eyes. Roger's shirt was wrinkled and spotted with tearstains. Were those from me?

"What time is it?" I asked.

"About three in the morning," Roger said. "You started talking in your sleep a little while ago, and then—"

He stopped. His eyes closed tight for a moment. "Then you just started screaming. I tried to wake you up but couldn't. All of a sudden, you stopped, and . . . I-I thought you died. Your heart rate dropped. You quit breathing, like what happened back at Giftshop. I tried to bring you back, but you were just . . . gone." He trailed off, clearing his throat. "Then you started breathing again. Just like that. What happened?"

"I-I think I just met Leo's friends," I said, my voice shaking. "They were in my dreams. In my head."

"What did they want?"

"I think . . . to recruit me? They kept asking me to 'accept them.' I think they wanted to somehow . . . use me to get to the Collective or get here to Earth."

"How?"

"I don't know. They kept saying they wanted to liberate Earth or free it or something. They reached out their hand and asked me to join them. I refused, and then . . . then there was . . ."

"What?"

"Pain. So much . . . so much pain."

"Did you accept?" he asked.

I hung my head. "I almost did. But something happened. I think I might have accidentally accessed the Collective."

"What did you see?"

"Something that happened to me in grade school. When I met Alice, when we became friends. And . . . it's kind of hard to explain, but after I saw that, the creatures left. Like they couldn't stand to be there anymore. They screamed, the whole world caved in on itself, and I woke up."

Roger shifted on the floor. "Do you think we're still safe here? Since they found you, they probably know where we are."

I shrugged. "I don't know. I asked them why they hadn't killed us yet, and they said something about having to be invited in."

"Invited?"

"That's what they said. I'm just glad we locked the doors and windows. If they haven't gotten in yet, I don't think they can."

We were quiet.

"So I'm guessing you don't want to go back to sleep?" he asked.

I swallowed dryly at the thought. "If I can help it, I'm never sleeping again."

Roger stood and lit another candle. "Right. Okay." He left the room.

Catacombs stayed by my side and didn't say a word. I stroked his head, and he purred like a motorboat.

After a few minutes, Roger returned with a tray, two mugs, a bowl, and a jar of cinnamon sticks. He set it down on the ground and handed me a mug. It was full of hot chocolate. I looked up in confusion.

He shrugged. "I figured we'd be here for the long haul, and hot chocolate always calms me down."

He slid the tray with a bowl over to Catacombs, who eyed it suspiciously. Roger picked up his mug and added a cinnamon stick.

He held it out to me. "I didn't know if you liked cinnamon in your hot chocolate or not, so I just brought the jar."

I stared at the jar. And the hot chocolate. I knew I was supposed to drink it. I definitely was supposed to drink it. That was a normal thing to do, right? Somehow, I couldn't get myself to do it. It seemed *too* normal compared to what I had just experienced.

Roger cleared his throat. I still couldn't move.

"*Well, I like cinnamon,*" Catacombs said. "*I think you broke Lily. If she never recovers, can I have her hot chocolate?*"

Twenty Three

Moderately Extreme

The next few hours passed in a mixture of conversation and awkward silence, broken up by occasional outbursts of boredom from Catacombs.

While we waited for the sun to come up, Roger studied the list of names of Ed's old team. The list was accompanied by pictures of smiling people and information. All had a Stars Crossing address located on the west and south sides of town.

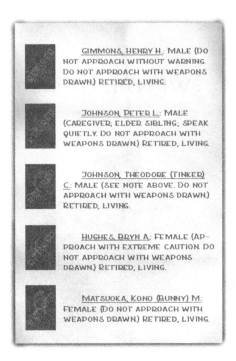

GIMMONS, HENRY H.: MALE (DO NOT APPROACH WITHOUT WARNING. DO NOT APPROACH WITH WEAPONS DRAWN) RETIRED, LIVING.

JOHNSON, PETER L.: MALE (CAREGIVER; ELDER SIBLING; SPEAK QUIETLY. DO NOT APPROACH WITH WEAPONS DRAWN) RETIRED, LIVING.

JOHNSON, THEODORE (TINKER) C.: MALE (SEE NOTE ABOVE. DO NOT APPROACH WITH WEAPONS DRAWN) RETIRED, LIVING.

HUGHES, BRYN A.: FEMALE (APPROACH WITH EXTREME CAUTION. DO NOT APPROACH WITH WEAPONS DRAWN) RETIRED, LIVING.

MATSUOKA, KONO (BUNNY) M.: FEMALE (DO NOT APPROACH WITH WEAPONS DRAWN) RETIRED, LIVING.

"Uh, who writes these?" I asked, looking at the paper again.

Roger leaned against the side of the couch, marking up a series of local paper maps he had acquired while looking around the house.

"Carl," he responded.

"Who's Carl?"

"A friend of mine from back home. He pretty much runs the archives for the northwestern community." Roger folded one of the maps. "New Jumper records, Necropolis entries, team time logs, that sort of thing."

"What's the Necropolis? Is it like a cemetery?"

"It's where you end up if you die out in a Gate somewhere. It's protocol due to contamination concerns."

We lapsed into quietness. He flipped through two maps overlaying each other and compared them, scrawling another annotation.

"*What are you doing?*" Catacombs asked, peering at the papers.

"I"—he made another note—"am marking a route to their houses. And marking some places we might want to avoid."

"Why?"

"The west side of town is pretty rural. That gives a lot of opportunities for walking into an ambush."

"You mean from the shadow things?"

"Um . . . no. From Ed's old team. They've been known to set some . . . traps. I knew one guy who tried to deliver a Christmas plate one year. Didn't even make it to the front door. Lost a few toes, too."

I glanced at the ink-covered paper. "Just how paranoid are these people?"

He held out a hand sideways as a scale. "Moderately extreme?"

"Great."

"Well then. Maybe I should just stay here and guard the house while you guys tackle that particular obstacle," Catacombs said. *"Seeing as I can't really do much anyway."*

Roger looked up and smirked. "You're just scared."

Catacombs bristled but didn't comment.

"But aren't these people—I don't know how to say this—um, old?"

Catacombs and Roger chuckled.

"What?" I asked.

"You know how we were talking about getting compensated for this job?" Roger asked, and I nodded. "Well, we also get . . . perks."

"What does that mean?"

"It means that even though you get older, you don't really get . . . older," Catacombs said.

"On the outside, you age at the same speed, but on the inside you just . . . slow down. A lot," Roger said. "So even though they're into their seventies, I still probably couldn't take them in a fight if I tried."

"How does that work?" I asked.

Catacombs and Roger looked at each other again. "Giftshop," they said in unison.

A few minutes passed, and a dim silvery light peeked though the slats of the blinds in the living room. Roger turned on the battery-powered radio again. He fiddled with the tuner. The dead air was replaced by a forecast of the weather.

"Same thing as yesterday," he mumbled. "Anything outside of Stars Crossing is normal." He shuffled his papers and shrugged on his backpack. "All right, the sun's up. Let's get going."

We took our mugs to the sink. I peered through the kitchen window, expecting to see a legion of shadows awaiting us. Nothing stirred but dripping trees and drifts of fog.

Roger joined me in looking out the window. "We're going to have to take your car unless we want to walk the whole way. Does it even start?"

"Yes," I mumbled. "Most of the time."

He rolled his eyes. "Perfect."

I grabbed my keys hanging from the nail. "Hey, it's our only wheels. Don't knock it."

Roger put a hand on the doorknob, turning back to Catacombs. "You sure you want to stay here by yourself, hairball?"

"*I'll be perfectly fine, thank you,*" he said, ear twitching. "*Have fun getting shot at by old people.*"

"All right, suit yourself." He flipped the deadbolt. He turned to me and lowered his voice. "I don't know what's out there, but no talking once we're outside, all right? Any sign of movement, get back in the house and lock the door."

I nodded.

Roger eased open the door and poked his head out. Nothing happened. We stepped out, and I locked the door behind me. Roger waved me forward, and we hurried to the car. The forest was unbearably quiet. The usual noises of birds and other animals were gone. The occasional dripping of rain seemed to echo in their absence.

I twisted the keys in the ignition and pulled onto the road. Nothing stirred. I checked in the rearview mirrors. Nothing. No one rushed the house. No one followed us.

Roger waited until I was on the main road to start giving directions. After twenty minutes of twists and turns, we ended up on a small one-lane road that led back into a thick forest. I was briefly concerned about meeting another car, but on our drive over, we hadn't passed a single person. The roads through town were deserted.

"Take that road up there," he said, pointing to a tiny mud path.

"Are you sure?" I asked. "I don't think that's even a road."

He nodded. "I'm sure. The Johnson brothers live in the last house. We can start with them, then try the others, if they're not . . ."

"Dead?"

"Yeah."

We passed our first house about a mile in. The windows were boarded up, and the roof was caving in. A few miles later, we passed two others in the same condition.

"These houses have seen better days," Roger mumbled.

We entered a wide clearing where another house had been completely ravaged by fire. Half of the once stately three-story home was gone, the collapsed roof falling onto the charcoal stubs covering its foundation. A faded bunch of fake flowers had been hung on one of the charred posts.

My car gave a strange sputtering sound and rolled to a stop. I tried twisting the key in the ignition, but it wouldn't even turn over.

"Oh, come on," I groaned. "I don't get it. The stupid thing just died completely."

Roger sighed. "Perfect. Just perfect." He opened the door and swung his legs out. "Looks like we're walking the rest of the way. It shouldn't be far. Try to keep quiet. No sudden movements."

We got out and looked around. The large clearing was ringed by towering pines blocking our view of the surrounding valley. The road continued into the trees.

Our footsteps squelched loudly as we followed the wet path. The trees around us seemed older than the ones at Terry and Susan's house. Moss hung from branches like spindly fingers reaching toward the ground for something they'd lost. The twisting branches creaked in the wind, but the overall silence of the woods was disturbing. There was still no sign of animal life.

A sharp cracking noise stopped us. Roger held up a hand and looked around. I glanced at the swaying canopy above. The tree cover was so thick, it blocked out all light.

"Do you hear anything?" Roger whispered. "Anything from the Collective?"

"No," I whispered back. "But what was that sound?"

Something closed around my ankle and yanked me off my feet. The world turned upside down. I tried to reach the cord that had been wrapped around my ankle, but I couldn't pull myself up.

A small group of people emerged from the trees and surrounded us. Two women and three men carried weapons of different colors. They were older, but none of them moved like it.

"You have exactly thirty seconds to explain what you're doing here before we start swinging at you like piñatas," said a man from the group. He was bald, deep crow's-feet around his eyes. "And we won't stop swinging until all your candy comes out. Got it?"

We swung in stunned silence.

"Twenty-six seconds," another man threatened.

"Okay, okay!" Roger said. "We're here to find Ed's old team. My name's Roger. That's Lily. Something happened at Giftshop, and we need your help."

He twisted around to the man who'd first spoken. "Henry! Do you remember me? We were detailed to the same rescue mission? About ten years ago?"

The man, Henry, folded his arms. "Sorry, pal. The only person I remember from that team was the man's kid."

"That's—"

"And I remember that kid saying he'd never go back through another Gate in his life." He gestured to the others, and they advanced. "Have fun with the piñata party."

"No, that's me! Cliff's kid!"

They still advanced.

Roger rolled his eyes and twisted his body up to the cord attached to his foot. There was a flash of pink, and he fell onto his back. He scrambled to his feet. An oncoming woman swung a shaft of light at him. He barely dodged to the side in time. Another man rushed at him. Roger held his two pink shields in front of him, bracing for impact.

"Wait a minute," Henry said, grabbing hold of the rushing man. He pointed at Roger's pink shields. "Now *tho*se I do remember. And now that you're right side up, I'm sure. Roger. Cliff Owens's kid."

The rest of the group stopped advancing and relaxed.

Henry held out his hand to Roger. "It's been a long time. Thought you were gone for good."

Roger hesitantly took his hand. The man leaned in and scrutinized his face, making quick sweeping motions with his eyes.

After a tense minute, he let go and stepped back. "It's all right, everyone. They're not one of them. At least this one's not. And I doubt the girl is either. You said you were in Giftshop?"

Roger nodded.

"I don't know how you got away, but I'm glad you did. We need to get inside. It's not safe out here."

A gust of wind swept through the trees.

"We need to go, now," a stocky man said from the other side of the group.

Henry turned to a small man with white hair. "Tinker, can you get her down, please?"

The little man pulled out a square remote. He fiddled with a few buttons and flicked a switch. The cord went slack, and I fell on the ground with an "*Oof!*" Untangling the cord from my foot, I stood up and rubbed my head. I hadn't been upside down for very long, but the rush of blood was still painful.

"What's going on?" I asked. "Have you heard from anyone—"

"Not here," hissed a woman with a red scarf. "Not outside."

Henry waved the group forward onto the road. "We can talk inside. The longer we stay out here, the more likely it is that one of us will get infected. Okay?"

Roger and I nodded.

"Good. Then let's go. We don't have much time."

Twenty Four

The Bound

We continued on the squishy mud path. No one made a sound as we marched single file like a team of stiff wooden soldiers.

The forest around us continued its usual drum of water dripping to the ground. I still couldn't hear the song of birds or the rustle of other animals. Maybe they were hiding. They were probably smarter than we were.

After what seemed like an eternity of walking in solemn silence, I spotted the outline of a house between the trees. I was expecting it to be another dilapidated building, surprised to see a well-kept white cottage among the pines. It was picturesque, a wooden picket fence lining the perimeter. The worn brick chimney puffed a thin tendril of smoke.

The group shuffled toward the cottage. We paused at the fence and waited for the small man to fidget with the lock on the gate. A soft *beep*, and the gate swung open, as did the front door of the cottage. The old team went in rehearsed single file. Roger and I followed.

Warm air buffeted us as we entered the cozy room. A table and a set of seven chairs dominated the space to our right, and a couch to our left was surrounded by woodsy furniture and fluffy rugs. A fireplace crackled in the corner. The only thing that made me look twice was the presence of many strange mechanical devices attached to the ceiling. Metal cords crisscrossed the exposed beams like spiderwebs, interrupted by gears and pulley systems.

"Sorry about the power," the stout man said. His dark brown eyes were hidden behind a pair of glasses, a black beanie covering his head. "Lousy generator quit on me. I haven't had time to check it over yet."

"Don't worry about it, Pete. We got more to worry about," said one of the women. She had Asian features, her gray hair tied back in a bun. Despite her looks, she carried no accent.

Roger and I hung back by the open door.

"You might want to close that, son," Henry said. "Those things need to be invited in, and an open door is the same as an open invitation."

Roger pushed the door shut, locking all three of the deadbolts that lined the frame.

"Which of you wants coffee?" asked the other woman. She spoke with an English accent and wore a faded red scarf. She looked the youngest out of all of them, features still clinging to her younger beauty. Everyone but Roger and I raised their hands. She disappeared behind a divider in the living room that connected to a small kitchen.

"Have a seat, you two," called the man with the beanie. "You sure took your time when we stopped your car. By the time you got to the checkpoint, we'd been in position forever."

"That was you?" I asked, grabbing a seat at the table.

"What did you think happened? That it just up and died?"

I cleared my throat, ignoring the look that Roger was shooting me. "Uh, actually yeah. It does that sometimes."

A few minutes went by, and the woman with the red scarf brought out five mugs of coffee and set them on the table. The five Jumpers converged and grabbed a steaming cup. They sipped and sat down in the remaining chairs.

"First, introductions," said the man with the beanie. "My name's Peter, but you can call me Pete. This is my brother, Ted, but everyone calls him Tinker. He don't talk much."

The silent man with white hair looked up and smiled. His hands were busy fiddling with a metal contraption. He had the same brown eyes as his brother, alert and intelligent.

The Asian woman with the bun gave a wave. "I'm Kono, but everyone just calls me Bunny."

The woman with the scarf also waved. "My name's Bryn. You can call me . . . Bryn. I was born and raised in Wales. To save you the trouble, no, I don't watch *Doctor Who*, and no, I wouldn't like a crumpet."

The group smirked.

"Well." Henry sipped from his mug. "You sure have some explaining to do."

The statement was directed at Roger, who looked away. "Maybe some other time," he mumbled. "Did you—did you guys hear about Ed?"

Henry nodded, and everyone looked hard at their mugs. "We heard it through the radio last night. Someone in town looked through the archives before everything went down, and—" He broke off and sighed. "What happened?"

I stared at the table as Roger recounted the events at Twisting Caverns. I expected the group to be surprised, but they weren't. They exchanged dark glances.

"It's just like we thought, Henry," Bryn said, shaking her head. "This is worse than before. And we don't have the option of sealing them in this time."

Henry rubbed his forehead. "All right. Why don't you tell us what happened at Giftshop? That at least gives us a starting point."

We both traded off explaining the events that led up until now. Saying everything out loud was surreal; did all of that really just happen? And more incredibly, how were we both still alive?

I took over when we got to the shadow creatures. Everyone listened intently as I described the walking nightmares.

"They just kept asking me to 'accept them.' I didn't know what they meant, but they kept pressuring me. And then they . . . I . . . ." I trailed off. I didn't know why it was so hard to get the words out. Talking about it just brought back the pain.

"Did you?" asked Henry.

"Huh?"

He wouldn't look me in the eye. His hands tightened around the mug of coffee. "Did you accept them?"

I shook my head. "No. I almost did, but then . . ." I trailed off again and looked Roger. I wasn't sure if I should tell them that I could hear the Collective. We'd left that part out during our explanation.

Roger nodded. "It's all right. You can tell them."

I took a deep breath and tried to formulate words. Anything to do with the Collective was hard to describe. When I was finished, I looked up. The old group stared at me like they'd seen a ghost.

Roger seemed to notice too. "What?" he asked.

Bryn glanced up at me. We made eye contact. Something in her expression broke down, and she closed her eyes. "Henry, we can't do this again. Not again. You know we can't."

A heavy silence settled over the table.

"It sounds like I'm not the only one who needs to explain things, Henry," Roger said, studying the group.

Henry sighed and put his head in his hands. "I guess we start from the beginning, then," he muttered.

The wind whistled outside.

"Do you remember the story of the original seven?" Henry asked. Roger nodded, and so did I.

"Well, technically, this all started back then. When the first Jumpers explored their first Otherworld. It was actually a Gate in Stars Crossing, not too far from here. The people who lived there just passed away a few weeks ago . . . real shame. Good people."

"Uh, yeah. We kind of know about that already," Roger cut in awkwardly. "Those were her great-aunt and uncle. That's how she got mixed up with this in the first place."

Henry regarded me for a moment. "Terry and Susan were your great-aunt and uncle? Well, I guess that makes sense, then. Your family is tied into all of this, Lily. They were a part of the original seven all those years ago."

"Really?"

He nodded. "They helped settle the valley after the Shift, keeping watch over the Gate on their land. Your family seems to have a proclivity for abilities . . . out of the ordinary. After observing that particular Gate, they found that it never closed or shifted; it was a constant. They saw it as the most stable and gathered a team to go inside.

"They picked seven people to go in, but only five returned. The Masters family put up a barn to hide the Gate, and that was that. There wasn't much to guard past the first few Connectors, so it mostly went unused for the next hundred years. But . . ."

He clenched his hands together. "But in the late 1960s, some idiot had the stupid idea to map out the connecting Gates in that barn."

Bryn put a reassuring hand on his shoulder.

"We . . . as a team," said Bryn, "decided to map out the Connectors as a kind of bet with ourselves. No one had ever gone far in that Gate, so we decided to map it. We were young, and stupid, and thought we had the upper hand because we had Constance."

She sighed. So did everyone else.

"Constance could hear the Collective as you can," Pete said. "She was amazingly bright and had a natural aptitude for pretty much everything. She was eighteen when she was discovered and only nineteen when she became a Jumper. She joined our team, and we had two wonderful years together, 'saving humanity from the unknown.'" He smiled at the memory. It faded quickly.

"Then one day," Henry said, "we found something. A new Gate, so close to the entrance that we were amazed no one had found it before. Beyond that Gate we found . . . the Tear."

"A tear?" I asked. "Like a Gateway?"

"Gateways are holes in our reality, but they are natural points of opening," Bryn said. "What we found in that new Connector was a gouge. A rip that looked like it had been gnawed open by beasts. And in the Tear, there was a figure."

"Constance tried to make contact," Bunny said. "She said she could hear it in the Collective, so it must be like her. She said it needed her help, and the only way for it to get out of the Tear was for someone to pull it through."

Roger gaped at them. "Are you kidding me? You found unknown intelligent life in an Otherworld, and you guys just *let* her—"

"Try to understand." Bryn closed her eyes. "The rules were different back then. We didn't know what we were dealing with. Constance was our first line of defense, and she didn't raise the alarm."

"What happened?" I asked.

"After a while of her talking to it, she asked, 'Who is your Link?'"

Static encroached on my hearing, and I became dizzy. I jolted forward and opened my eyes.

I could see it. I could see the Tear, and Constance sitting cross-legged in front of it, talking with the figure on the other side, the rest of the team waiting nearby. They were all young, standing with their arms folded, and bright-eyed. The world around them was black and echoing like a soundstage.

"Who's your Link?" Constance asked aloud. She wore a tan suede coat and was seated on the ground, hair pulled back into a long braid framing her dark-skinned face and deep brown eyes. She looked remarkably like a younger Bea.

The Tear rippled like torn fabric in the breeze.

"*We have one who came long ago, but they were unsuitable,*" a voice hissed. "*We need a living Link. We cannot come through on our own. Help us, and we will help you all.*"

I knew that voice. Soft and shrill like metal against stone.

"I can see your intentions. There's no hiding that from me," Constance said. "I know what you would do if you got through."

"We need you," The voice cooed. *"Your connection to the Collective, it is what we need. Most require time to bring us through, but you are in a unique position. We Link with those who have sufficient power to lead us, and the Collective, as you call it, is more than we would need. Allow us in, and we will free your world."*

"You know I cannot do that," she said. "Go back where you came from. Leave now, or I will."

The voice was quiet for some time.

"Did you think you had a choice?" Its voice scratched. *"If you do not accept us, then maybe one of your friends will? They are not as well versed as you are in dealing with matters of the mind. It would be quite easy to break them all."*

Constance glared at the figure. "Leave them alone."

"So which will it be? Help us, or watch your friends die? The choice is yours. You will not be leaving otherwise."

Constance sat quietly for a moment, thinking hard. She closed her eyes. "What would happen if your Link was severed?" she whispered.

"We cannot exist in this realm without a Link and would be sent back. But we will find our way back again. It will take time, but we will return."

The voice paused. *"What you seek to do is foolish. All you would do is delay. Are you willing to leave behind this life for the sake of theirs? What about your younger sister? Yes, we know about her. Will you leave her alone?"*

Constance wiped the stream of tears from her eyes and swallowed. "You're—you're right. I could never do that. I have no other choice but to help you. I will become your Link. I-I accept."

"That is the correct choice." The Tear fluttered again, and a shadowed stick of a hand became just visible on the other side. *"Invite us into your realm, and we will help you be free."*

Constance took a deep breath and wiped her face with the back of her sleeve. She stood and regarded her friends, a hand in her pocket, eyes hard.

"Connie? What's wrong?" asked a younger man. His cold blue eyes swept to the Tear and then back to her. With a jolt, I realized it was Ed. He looked barely a teenager.

She gave a wobbly smile. "I-I'm sorry. I . . . made a mistake. Whatever happens next, just know, I—" She gulped. "I love you all, and I never meant for any of this to happen."

The group made a move toward her but was stopped short by a loud magnetic pulse that rocked the patch of land. They all fell to the ground, unconscious.

Energy still flickered in the air as Constance pulled out a small mechanical device from her pocket and dropped it on the ground. She turned back to the Tear and looked at the hand, still waiting.

"*Accept us,*" said the voice.

Constance took a few shaky breaths and reached for the hand. As she clasped it, the world around her grew dim. A huge shadowy figure emerged from the Tear and regarded her with hollow eyes. The ground beneath her cracked and withered.

"*We have returned,*" it called.

Constance stepped back, put a hand in her back pocket, and pulled out a small pistol. It was almost dainty, but it was enough. She cocked it and held it against her temple. Her eyes retained tears, but her face looked fierce and determined.

"Not really." Her voice cracked.

The shadow figure lunged for the gun, but she had already pulled the trigger. Everything went black with a loud resounding bang.

I jerked again and found myself seated in a chair, clutching the table. My heart pounded, the pain in my head still sharp. The group around the table watched me.

"Sorry." I panted. I hadn't even meant to access the Collective. It just kind of . . . happened. I was shaking. "Sorry, I didn't mean to . . ."

Bryn reached across the table and patted my hand. "It's all right, love. Constance couldn't control the memories at first either. We understand."

I tried to slow my breathing. "How long was I gone?"

"Long enough for us to tell Roger what we know about that day," said Pete. "We figured you were seeing it for yourself."

I looked over at Roger. He seemed pale.

It occurred to me they probably didn't know the whole story since they couldn't hear the voices. They wouldn't understand why Constance had killed herself, because they never knew what she was protecting them from. What would that be like? To be the only thing standing in the way of your friends' deaths? Would I even be able to do what Constance had done if pushed to it? The thought made me nauseous.

"These creatures," I swallowed. "What are they?"

Everyone exchanged glances.

"They have been here since the beginning of time," Henry said. "Otherworldly beings that find weak spots in our reality and claw their way through. We call them The Bound."

The Bound. The words felt cold and dead in the air.

"What are they doing here?" I asked.

"As far as we can figure, they're hungry," said Pete "And they see Earth as a feast. They need a Link, someone on Earth to connect them to this plane of existence, at least indirectly for now. Like how the Teleporters link to Giftshop. It works in a similar way. They can't survive here without a Link to feed on, but once they're able to take physical form without the help of their host. . . I don't even want to think about how powerful they'd be."

"Feed?"

"Think of them . . . as a parasite," Henry said. "They only survive as long as there's a host to sustain them. Humans are full of—well . . . soul, humanity, life energy, I guess you'd call it. They feed on that, slowly whittling away at a person's life until there's nothing left."

"So they eat your . . . soul?" I asked.

"In a sense," Henry said. "They consume the base layer of our being: your very humanity. It's what makes us who we are and gives us such a capacity for good and evil. Take that away from everyone on Earth, what would happen?" He shook his head. "We'd be just like them. Parasites that move on to the next host just to survive."

I shivered, remembering the hollow eyes of the people in Twisting Caverns. And Leo.

"Is that . . . what Leo is?" I asked. "The Link to The Bound?"

Bryn nodded. "It appears so. I don't know how they got him to accept, but he did. And now this might be the end of humanity. The end of existence. For all of us."

"They've already taken the town, save for a few pockets of survivors like us." Pete shook his head. "If not for the boundaries around this valley, I'm sure they'd be all over the world by now."

"Boundaries?" Roger asked.

"Ed set them up a few years ago, with the help of Tinker and a few others." Pete clapped his brother on the back. "Like a moving invisible wall. It stops anything from the Otherworlds with an unrecognized DNA signature from making it out of town. Not many people know about it."

"Of course, no one knows how long it'll hold," Bunny said. "I'm amazed it's stopped The Bound this long."

"I still don't know how they came back so *quickly*." Bryn leaned on her hand. "This seems more like months in the making. Not days."

"I think it has been months in the making," Roger said. "It started out as simple problems around the Gates and escalated when teams started disappearing. I think this was planned from the beginning. It's not an invasion; it's chess. This was strategized."

The wind picked up outside. Despite being early morning, the clouds gathered dark and thick in the sky. It started to rain again.

"How do you know so much about them?" I asked.

"We started doing research," Henry said. "Any scrap of ancient history that mentioned beings like The Bound, we followed up and researched. Traveled the world and gathered intel from countless different cultures."

"After Connie died, we knew we had to act," Pete said. "We took one look at the Tear and knew that even though those creatures were gone, there was a chance that they could come back. So we went to work. We kept the real story under wraps and blocked off all entrances and exits attached to the Tear. Tinker here is the one who found the solution."

Tinker was still fiddling with a little metal contraption with wires sticking out. He didn't glance up.

"He's good with mechanics," Pete said with a proud smile. "Give him time and scrap metal, and he'll figure out a way to make it into a fully functioning car. Anyway, he singled out a specific genetic trait in— What was it, roses?"

Tinker nodded.

"That's right. He merged it with a self-replicating plant found in one of the Otherworlds to block the Gates connecting to the Tear. People started trying to get through at first but found out pretty soon that wasn't working. After a while, it became just another unexplained occurrence, and everyone ignored it."

"Wait, that was you guys?" Roger asked. "Those Gates have been blocked my entire life. How did you maintain that?"

"It's a fairly simple device that stimulates the replication gene. But it's not perfect," Bunny explained, leaning on the table with her elbows. "The power source drains every few years, which wasn't a big deal because we were always around to replace them. A few years before retiring, we realized that we wouldn't be around to switch them out for much longer and started looking for . . . replacements."

"We picked carefully and eventually came up with a replacement who was competent and didn't ask a lot of questions," Bryn said. "But he was smart. He figured it out on his own and confronted us about it. One day, not long after . . . he disappeared without a trace."

"We can only assume he went looking for the Tear." Henry looked at the table and folded his hands. "I'm sorry, Roger, that man was your father."

My eyes widened, and I looked to Roger. Swallowing hard, he stared down at the table and closed his eyes.

"After that, we decided the risk wasn't worth it." Bryn rotated her empty mug. "If keeping the Gates shut meant endangering lives that weren't ours, then it wasn't worth keeping them closed."

"Not worth it?" I said. "You knew the Tear was still out there. Why did you stop?"

"Over fifty years had gone by," Pete explained. "We had no evidence the Tear would cause any problems, so we stopped. We had Tinker design the longest battery possible for one last swap, and we stopped changing them. And for years, everything was fine. The batteries ran out, and no one was any the wiser. We thought all of our worry was for nothing."

"Until a few months ago," I said.

They nodded.

"I guess some adventurous soul found out they were unblocked and poked around," Pete said. "And now everything's gone to hell in a handbasket."

"This is all our fault," Bunny said bitterly. "If we'd have just warned people to stay away from the Gate, then this wouldn't have happened. We kept our big fat mouths shut, and look what's happened."

Everyone was quiet again. What were we supposed to say? They were right. This was kind of their fault. But I could understand their reasoning. They needed to make sure what happened to Constance never happened to anyone else. So her sacrifice wouldn't be in vain.

But to think, the end of the world was put into motion because someone forgot to change the batteries.

"Even if you had warned the community," Roger said, breaking the heavy silence, "you know no one would have listened. Not because they had malicious intent but because they were curious. That's why we're all here. That's why we chose this life. Because we saw something greater than ourselves, and we were curious. That's what my dad always taught me, and that's what I believe. We may be idiots, but we're human idiots. This isn't over yet. We can still fix this. Ideas?"

The group thought for a minute.

Bryn sat up straighter. "We need to think of some way to stop these creatures from getting through the Tear for good. We may not all be rocket scientists, but we're Jumpers. We always think of something. It might be duct tape and paperclips, but it'll be something."

"Even if it doesn't work, what have we got to lose?" Pete said.

Bunny nodded. "We've got more than enough supplies here to work with. And three of the best mechanical minds in the western United States."

Roger nodded enthusiastically. "Good, that's a good start!" He turned to Henry. "Any clue on how to close an inter-dimensional rip in the fabric of reality?"

"I'm going to level with you, son," Henry said. "I've got no goddamn idea."

TWENTY FIVE

Options

Our plan to save the world began with baking cookies.

The timer beeped on the counter, and Bryn donned a pair of oven mitts to pull a tray of warm, delicious-looking chocolate chip cookies off the rack. Because apparently that's how Jumpers did things when the stakes were high; they baked cookies. Or at least Bryn did.

The generator had only needed a small part that Pete had on hand, and there was much deliberation as to whether we should risk going outside to start it back up again. A decision was reached when Bryn declared that baking helped her think when she was under stress. No one had any other ideas, so the generator got fixed, and Bryn baked cookies with the help of Tinker, who silently gathered ingredients and placed them next to the bowl.

"Right, I think I have an idea," she said, dolloping some dough onto the sheet and returning it to the oven.

Pete plopped into a chair. "We're all ears."

Bryn shut the oven door. "So we know that the Tear is just that: a tear. So why can't we try sewing it back up again?" she reasoned, talking with a spoon in her hand. "Undo whatever these monsters did to rip it open in the first place."

"Well." Henry cleared his throat. "That seems logical. But this isn't a piece of fabric; it's reality. How do you sew reality back together?"

"Actually, Bryn might not be far off," Bunny said, putting a hand to her chin. "I don't think we could sew it up . . . but maybe we treat this like a wound, not fabric. Maybe instead of stitches, we could cauterize it. It seems that it originally took a lot of energy to create the Tear made by The Bound, so it stands to reason that another concentrated wave of energy might close it. Of course," she added, "that might make it worse. But at this point, I don't think it could really get any worse."

"The end of humanity is pretty bad," Roger agreed.

Pete closed his eyes and pinched the bridge of his nose. "Now hold on a minute. That's a lot of energy to emit from *anything*. I don't think we could make something to sustain that much raw power."

"It wouldn't have to be sustained," Bunny said. "Just one short blast, like a bomb. The radius wouldn't even have to be big. Just one small, concentrated pocket of energy." She rubbed her chin. "That actually . . . might work. It would be a long shot to even get there, but it might work."

Henry shifted in his seat. "I don't know, that seems risky. Like Pete said, that would take *a lot* of energy to rip open a hole in our reality."

"Maybe not as much as you'd think," Pete said. "I mean, the Teleporters do it all the time, but they're not sustained for long periods of time. That means all the Tear would need is one punch of power to shock it into closing, like the Teleporter does. At least, theoretically."

"Plus, we wouldn't be opening it," Bryn argued. "Just closing our side of the Tear."

"It's risky," Henry repeated.

"What other options do we have?" Bunny asked. "Take the risk or wait until they break through the boundary? There's no stopping them after that."

No one said anything. She had a point. It was either die on the way there or die sitting still.

"Let's ask Tinker, see if he thinks it's possible," Pete said. "Ted, what do you think? Can we build something like that? Like a bomb?"

Tinker stood in the corner of the kitchen, fiddling with one of his mechanical whirligigs. He shook his head and shrugged.

"You don't know where to start?" Pete asked.

Tinker nodded.

Everyone was quiet again. A thought occurred to me.

"Hey," I said. "In the memory I just saw, Constance used some sort of weird electric pulse thing to knock you guys out. Isn't that kind of what you want?"

Everyone stared at me.

Maybe that was stupid. I should probably just have been quiet. "Uh . . . or not? Sorry, it was just an idea."

Tinker looked up at me and smiled, his face coming to life with excitement. He grabbed a notepad and pencil, scribbling furiously.

"Energy Pulsars?" Pete asked. "I'd forgotten about those. They were decommissioned back in the eighties for being too unpredictable. But if we could make the core supercharged for a moment . . ." He trailed off, looking up at his brother. "I think that'll work. I'm not sure about it closing the Tear, but we should be able to make an amplified Energy Pulsar. We'd, uh, have to be careful. If it goes off before we establish a blast radius, then we're all toast."

"Pete," Roger said. "Being toast is better than being an empty toaster, trust me. I would prefer pretty much anything to going back with those things."

The timer beeped again, and Bryn took out the next batch of cookies. Turning off the oven, she put the cookies on a plate and brought them over to the table. The group descended upon them before the plate hit the table. They were hot and burned my fingers, but they were cookies. And to pass up a hot chocolate chip cookie was a sin in my estimation.

"What are you talking about?" Bunny asked, snatching a cookie.

"Back when Leo went all shadow-master on us in Giftshop, I didn't make it out. Lily was actually the one who grabbed me and the stupid cat and pulled us to safety," Roger explained, also grabbing a cookie. "She's the only reason we're alive. I'd still be an empty puppet right now if she hadn't pulled me through."

They all stared at him.

"How did you come back?" Bryn asked in amazement. "How are you even talking to us right now?"

Roger shrugged. "We're not sure what happened, but I only found my way back when Lily made contact with me. It's hard to explain, but it was like I was in a really thick fog that made everything around me . . . distant. But when she grabbed my hand, the fog disappeared and I could remember who I was." He took a bite of his cookie. "I don't know what happened, but I'm glad it did. I don't ever want to do it again."

Henry looked me up and down. "How long have you heard the Collective?"

"Uh, I guess since yesterday morning? I'm not sure how time works through Gates, but technically it was yesterday in Earth time."

Saying that was weird. All of this had begun only yesterday morning. How had things changed so fast? Just yesterday I was complaining to Alice about how much I hated packing. Now I might never see her again.

"Interesting," Henry said. "It seems like you can already transfer emotions and memories to others through contact. Almost the opposite of what The Bound do. It usually takes people years to do that."

That sparked something in my memory. "I think Jerry said something about that. He didn't elaborate, but he said that one day I might be able to transfer memories or emotions to people."

Bunny looked confused. "Who's Jerry?"

"Her 'faucet,'" Roger said, making air quotes with his fingers.

I shot him a look. He smirked.

"Oh, I think that's her Conrad," Bryn said. "Constance mentioned that a few times; I guess he's a person in the Collective that . . . talks to you? We weren't really sure how that worked."

I huffed a breath through my nose. "Yeah, I'm not sure how it works either. I've only met him once."

Tinker made a few more marks on his notepad and set down the pencil. The sharp point had been dulled to a flat stub. He handed the paper to Pete, who studied it.

"Well now," he said, impressed. "That could work. Well done, little brother. This might be your best design yet."

He held out a hand. Beaming, Tinker high-fived it and clapped excitedly.

Pete stood and stretched. "Right, we'd better get to work on this. I would say come check on us if you hear an explosion, but"—he and Tinker strode across the room and opened a door that led to a descending stair-case—"you'd already be dead. So hopefully see you when it's done."

"Be careful you two," called Henry.

Pete waved a hand as he shut the door behind them. "Yeah, yeah. What-ever."

The only sound that filled the space they left was rain and wind. It was nice, the quiet. I never realized how much I liked the quiet before. Or as quiet as it got for me.

"Well." Bunny stood. "I guess now we just wait. I'll try to contact some others through the radio, see if anyone else is holding out."

She shuffled to a desk in the corner covered with old radio equipment. Sitting down, she pulled an old pair of headphones over her gray hair and fiddled with the knobs.

Bryn and Henry remained at the table with Roger and me. We ate cookies in silence.

After a few minutes, Bryn pushed her chair back from the table. "Sitting still is agony. I'm going to map us a route back to the Gate, as we can't use Giftshop or the Teleporters. Where do you think they keep local maps?"

"Beats me," Henry said. "I can never find anything in this place."

"Here." Roger pulled the maps from his backpack. "You can use these. They're pretty old, but they're not too bad for cross-referencing each other."

Bryn opened the maps and looked at the contents. "What were you looking for?"

"Different traps you guys may have set to keep out intruders."

Bryn raised an eyebrow. "You did *what*?"

Roger shrugged. "I've heard some stories. Thought it was better to be prepared."

"All right, we may be cautious, but we aren't *that* bad." She tapped her hand against the ink-covered map. "What do you think this is, the Tower of London?"

Roger held his hands up. "Hey, I was just guessing. Those are just possibilities."

"You marked the entire road! *We are not that bad!*"

I smirked at the table as Roger and Bryn moved their argument over to the couches and spread out the maps on the floor, marking them with new notes.

I felt eyes on the side of my face and glanced up. Henry was watching me, his expression mixed between sadness and something else.

He turned his gaze to Bunny and Bryn. He shook his head. "I've done a lot of things I'm not proud of, but this takes the cake. We never meant any harm by it. We just wanted to make sure that . . ."

"That Constance didn't sacrifice herself in vain," I finished.

He nodded.

I picked at a loose chip of wood from the battered surface of the table. "She was protecting you guys. You know that, right?"

"What?"

"Against The Bound. Her only options were to watch you all die, or free them. The Bound didn't give her a choice. If I were a lot braver, and a better person . . . no, I still wouldn't be able to do it."

Henry clenched his hands together. "I . . . I never knew that. We all thought she got tricked into accepting, and . . ." He put his head in his hands. "What have we done. All we had to do was warn people to stay away from that Connector, and none of this would've happened."

"If it's any consolation, all I had to do was not take a crowbar to that stupid wall in the barn, and I wouldn't even be here right now."

Henry snorted a laugh.

"A lot of things would be different," I continued. "Maybe if I'd gone in the barn earlier, things wouldn't have turned out this way. Maybe I would've had time to learn how to use the Collective. Maybe I would've known we were walking into a trap before it was too late. Ed, Bea, Terry, Susan, and everyone else . . . they might still be alive if I had done things differently. If I had been . . . more prepared. If I had just *heard* what I needed to from the Collective, then I could've . . ." I laughed without feeling it. "I don't know exactly what I could've done."

Henry looked at me sharply. "Lily. You can't think like that."

I shrugged. "I just can't shake the feeling that . . . if things had been better, if *I* had been better, would things have turned out better too?"

Henry watched Bryn and Roger argue for a moment before he spoke. "I've seen a lot of friends die on my watch over the years. For every one of them, I always felt I could've done more. Trained harder, been stronger, quicker, been better at my job. I let that push me for years. I was terrified if I slowed down, it could cost someone their life."

He sat back in his chair. "At some point, I had to say enough. I had to accept that nothing can change the past. Our only recourse is to keep slogging forward. Someday, you're going to have to make hard choices between life and death, and the people you're deciding for won't have any say in it. It's what you do as a Jumper. You try your hardest to save everyone, but sometimes that's just not how it goes."

"But I'm not a Jumper," I said.

"Oh?" he said, smiling. "From what I've heard, you're well on your way to becoming one. You're curious by nature, go looking for answers in unknown places. When faced with a new problem, you choose the answer out of the ordinary. You gave yourself options. It takes a special kind of person to do all that and still ask themselves if they could've done better."

Bunny stood from the desk and set the headphones on a peg, stepping over Bryn and Roger on her way to grab another cookie.

"I found Carmen and her team," she said. Roger and Bryn looked up from their mapping discussion to listen. "They were all together when The Bound attacked. They're taking shelter at her house."

"Did you tell them not to go outside? Not to answer the door for any reason?"

Bunny nodded. "They should be relatively safe for now. I didn't disclose our location, but I know theirs if we need them. At least we know there's a chance some others are safe."

"Good," Henry said, nodding. "We might be able to make a break for Terry and Susan's house. Lily, why don't you go check the progress on the Energy Pulsar?"

I blinked. "Me?"

"Just let them know you're coming down so they don't blow up the house."

I got up from my chair and opened the door the brothers had gone into. The smell of metal and burnt rubber assaulted my nose. Stone steps led down into the basement, and I followed them. A metal hanging lamp illuminated the way, humming with electricity.

"Hello?" I called down the stairwell. At the bottom was another door. I knocked and pushed it open carefully.

The two brothers were sitting back to back on two separate workbenches, assembling pieces of complicated machinery. Tinker held out a hand, and Pete wordlessly handed him a screwdriver over his shoulder.

"Hello?" I called softly, trying not to startle them.

Pete looked up. "Hey. What's wrong?"

"Nothing, they just sent me to check on how you guys are doing." I stepped out from behind the door. "How's it coming?"

"It's . . . coming." He grabbed a pair of tweezers. "These things are simple in design. The only trick is setting the blast radius." He tweaked some wires and reached over his shoulder. Tinker handed him a small metal file. "That, and finding a way to harness enough energy to rip a hole in the fabric of existence. I'm trying to draw comfort from the fact that Teleporters do it all the time."

"Do you have a time estimate?"

"Could be an hour. Maybe less," he said. "We'll try to go fast and be safe at the same time. Can't really pick and choose."

I nodded, walking toward the stairwell. "Call if you need anything. Don't blow up the house."

Tinker smiled, concentrating on his piece of gadget.

"We'll try," Pete mumbled. "Not to, that is."

I smiled and closed the door behind me. The small metal hanging lamp flickered. The sounds of static ruffled past my ears, and I stopped to listen.

O . . . u . . . t . . . s . . . i . . . d . . . e . . .

My stomach dropped, and I ran up the remaining stairs and flung open the door. Bunny, Bryn, Roger, and Henry looked up.

"I think we have company," I said.

Nobody questioned me, springing up to check windows.

Peeking through the curtains, Bryn grimaced. "I've got six people coming through the woods. Anyone else?"

Henry was across the room, Roger looked through the window by the door, and Bunny stared through the blinds in the kitchen.

"Eight over here," Henry called.

"Ten, and more are still coming through," Roger reported.

"Same on this side," Bunny said.

I stepped next to Bryn and watched through the curtains. Emotionless groups of people trudged through the woods and stopped just behind the tree line. None made any movement after they stopped, ringing the clearing like stone-faced guardians. Among the faces were Bea, Terry, and Susan. Blood covered their clothes. I wasn't sure if it was theirs.

My heart sank. "Roger . . ."

"I know," he said. "I see them."

"What do we do?" asked Bryn.

Henry took a deep breath. "Double-check all the windows and doors. How long did Pete say until the Energy Pulsar is finished?"

"Maybe another hour."

Henry let out a slow breath. "There's nothing we can about them now. Let's gear up."

Twenty Six

Over and Under

We shuffled away from the windows. I knew they probably couldn't get in, but I was keenly aware that only a thin layer of wood and glass stood in their way. I gulped as knots twisted my stomach.

"Bunny," Henry said. "Go tell Pete and Tinker."

She hurried to the other side of the room.

"Carefully," he added as she closed the door.

"Do they still keep supplies in the attic?" Bryn asked.

"Despite us telling them to move them for the last thirty years, I'd imagine so."

"What if they finally moved them to the outside shed?"

"Then so help me God . . ." Henry shook a fist at the air.

"One way to find out."

Striding over to the kitchen, Bryn dragged a chair under a small attic hatch and stood on the wobbly seat. It made me nervous, seeing someone elderly teetering on an old chair. I had to remind myself that she was probably more coordinated than I would ever be.

Bryn yanked off a string taped to the ceiling and tugged. A ladder unfolded with a hearty squeak. She transferred herself from the chair to the ladder and peeked her head up.

"Ha, I knew they wouldn't move them for anything!" She leaned down. "Come on up, it's all still here." She hopped up the rest of the ladder. We followed.

It was large for an attic. A single window illuminated the room with gray light. Boxes and crates were stacked in teetering piles around the room, racks of weapon shafts propped against them. Cluttered tables of scrap metal and wires clogged most of the maneuverable space. Everything had a thick layer of dust.

"Wow." Henry waved dust from his face. "They haven't cleaned out a thing, have they?"

"You know Tinker. Waste not, want not." Bryn hefted a long metal shaft engraved with vines. "If there's a hairpin, he'll figure out a way to use it."

"Okay," I said. "I get why his nickname is Tinker, but why is Kono's Bunny?"

Henry and Bryn exchanged looks.

"Well, for one thing, she's fast," Henry said. "Faster than any of us still, probably."

Bryn giggled. "But, uh . . . it's also because she . . ." She broke into a fit of giggles and waved a hand. "You're going to have to tell it. I still can't make it all the way through."

Henry smiled. "On her first day, she was a little . . . nervous. And, uh, there was some rustling in the bushes behind her, and—"

"Are you telling this story again?" A voice drifted up the stairs. The aforementioned Bunny poked her head up the ladder. "For God's sake, it's been fifty years. *Let it go!*"

Henry coughed back a chuckle. "Let's just say she got a little . . . spooked."

Bryn laughed hysterically in the corner. "I've never seen a rabbit look so scared in my entire life!"

Bunny climbed to the top and stepped in. "Hey, I was nervous! All those orientation lectures had me paranoid."

"We hadn't even left Earth yet." Bryn cackled. "Hell, we hadn't left *town*! We were still outside of Sal's!"

Bunny ground her teeth. "Laugh it up. I've got some pretty good stories about you too. Let's not forget the lemonade incident."

Bryn's smile was wiped from her face. "Okay. Point proven."

Bunny smirked. "That's what I thought."

Henry regained his composure. "What did Pete say?"

"He said they'd work as fast as they could and try not to blow us up," said Bunny. "He also wanted me to remind you that patience is a virtue."

"A stupid virtue," Bryn muttered.

Henry sighed. "Let's hope those things are kept outside and don't find a loophole."

"Why do they have to be invited in?" I asked. "Why not just break a window?"

"You know how we have laws on Earth that can't be broken?" Henry said. "Gravity, the rotation of the planet, the force of a moving object, things like that?"

"Yeah."

"Well, as far as we can figure, there are certain laws The Bound can't break directly. If they want to inhabit a place, they need some form of permission. They can't enter by themselves."

"But they were able to visit me in my dreams," I pointed out. "They didn't need permission for that."

"I think it applies to Earth as a physical location. The subconscious, or a dream state, seems to be a gray area."

"Why?"

He shrugged. "Who knows? Maybe it's how things work where they come from."

I watched everyone gather random supplies around the room. Bunny put together a satchel of egg-shaped metal containers, and Bryn rifled through a wooden crate of coats and boots. Roger picked over one of the dusty tables, wiping a small box buried under a clump of cords.

"Hey, check this out." Roger waved me over, holding up the box. "I haven't seen these in years."

"What is it?"

He opened the box and tilted it so I could see. A small triangle-shaped dart the size of my index finger sat inside, the tip dipped in a dry green substance. I reached for it, but he pulled away.

"Careful," he said. "You get any of that on your hands, you won't be using them for a while."

"Thanks for the warning. What's that green stuff?"

"Tigris poison."

I backed away. The scar on my leg twinged. "Who did you have to use as a human shield to collect that?"

Roger snorted. "Tigris shed their quills every season. The Forest is littered with them. These used to be part of standard equipment, but they got discontinued. I never knew why. Do you, Henry?"

Henry glanced up at the box and smiled. "I think the practical jokes got out of hand. I know they did with us." He looked up to the ceiling. "Yes, Ed, I'm talking about you."

The group chuckled.

"What does it do?" I asked.

"It's a paralytic," Roger explained. "A powerful one. They were used for collecting animal tissue samples. One prick, and your target will be completely immobile within seconds."

"For how long?"

He shrugged. "It depends on the size of the animal. Something the size of a"— his eyes flicked to Bunny—"rabbit will probably be down for a few minutes. Anything larger, seconds, maybe."

Roger closed the box and handed it to me. "Here, you can have this."

"Are you sure?" I asked.

"Sure. It'll buy you some time if you're in a bind." He shrugged. "Until I can get to you, that is."

I looked at the floor and shoved the box in my pocket. "You don't . . . you don't always have to be there to protect me."

"Of course I do," Roger said. "That's my job."

"I think your job ended when you dropped me at Terry and Susan's house. The first time."

"Well, technically." He scratched the side of his face. "But . . . I want to."

I raised an eyebrow. "You're not tired of babysitting me?"

Roger laughed, nudging a loose nail on the floor with his foot. His face was tinged pink, his brown eyes glancing up at me. "Not even a little bit."

The way he looked at me made me speechless. A warm feeling settled in my stomach, like a soft blanket wrapping me in a cocoon. He gave a sheepish smile. I returned it.

"Hey, come check this out," Bunny said from the attic window.

We shuffled over, avoiding boxes and scrap metal. From the dust-covered window, we had an uninterrupted view of the small clearing and the soulless, still people who guarded the edge. Except they weren't still. Not completely.

"What's happening to them?" Bryn asked. "Why are they . . . swaying like that?"

The puppet people wobbled on their feet, as if a huge gust of wind were trying to knock them over. Some grabbed their heads, others looked as though they would topple over. Through the windows, the sound of birdsong rang through the air.

And then it was gone. The people resumed their statue-still positions. The birds faltered to silence.

"Well, that was . . . odd," Henry commented.

"Yeah . . . odd," I said.

Thumping sounds bounded up the stairs. Pete and Tinker emerged from the ladder, looking triumphant, their faces streaked with grease.

"We did it," Pete said. "I didn't think we'd be able to, but we got it. If anything's going to close the Tear, this is it."

He held up a small cylindrical object riddled with gears and copper wires. A small red button blinked on the side.

"How did you supercharge it without making it unstable?" Henry asked.

Tinker and Pete shared a sidelong glance.

"Uh, we . . . didn't," Pete admitted. "Technically, this thing could blow at any minute. But it'll work when it needs to. Probably."

We all took a half step back.

"Are you serious?" Bryn asked.

"Okay, it's not as bad as it sounds. Have I ever exploded you guys before?"

"Yes!" Bunny folded her arms. "Multiple times!"

"There was that time in New York—" Henry pointed out.

"And that time in Berlin—" Bryn said.

"And don't forget the time you guys detonated a bomb in Giftshop, and the only reason we didn't *die* was because she sent it out into space before it went off," Bunny complained. "She was *so* unhappy after that. The Pacific Northwest wing was freezing cold for weeks!"

"All right, all right. I get it, not the best track record," Pete mumbled. "But it's not *that* unstable. So don't hurl it off a bridge, and we'll be fine. All right?"

We all regarded the little cylinder warily but nodded.

"Well, we've done our part. What have you guys come up with?" Pete asked. "How are we getting out of here?"

"That," Henry said, "is a good question. Still working on that part. What are our assets?"

The room went quiet as we considered this.

"Um," Roger said. "I have a Glider."

Henry looked taken aback. "What, really? Where did you get that?"

"I've been on surveillance duty in the Forest of Luminescence. We, uh, picked it up at an ESS after the Giftshop incident." He pulled off his backpack and took out the small Post-it Note–sized piece of metal. "I can only take two people on it, though."

"How long does the battery last on that thing?"

Roger heaved a sigh. "With three people on board? Half an hour. Tops."

"I guess that's an option. The only problem would be that they could follow you," Henry said. "The Gate we need to get to inside the Connector isn't far from the entrance point, so you won't have a lot of time to lose The Bound."

"We could send you and two people ahead to the Tear while the rest of us stay behind," Bunny suggested. "Lock the doors behind you?"

"Wouldn't work," Pete said. "Once we open this place up, there's no telling what happens. I don't want to play red-light, green-light with these things."

"So anyone left here would be sitting ducks. And . . ." Bryn trailed off.

Henry shook his head. "Not an option. Besides, they'd catch up with the Glider in a half hour anyway. Neither of us would have a chance. Any other ideas?"

Wind whistled through the chimney as we thought.

"We have the tunnel," said a small voice from the corner. I looked up in surprise. It was Tinker who had spoken. His voice was impossibly small, but clear.

Pete, Henry, Bryn, and Bunny alerted and listened intently to what else he had to say.

"What do you mean, Tinker?" Bryn asked.

"I think he means those old Cold War tunnels the neighbors put in when we were kids," Pete said. "They go back way into the hills, and there's a section that leads to the road."

"How did you find out about them?" Henry asked.

"A girl down the road snitched. We used them to sneak out when our parents were out of town. I can't imagine they're still passable. It's been years since anyone's been down there, and . . ."

Pete trailed off as Tinker shook his head and pointed to himself.

"What do you mean? You *still* go down there?"

Tinker nodded.

"Why?" Pete asked.

Tinker shuffled his feet and shrugged.

"Can we get through to Lily's car? Is the tunnel still open to the old Brenwich place?"

Tinker nodded.

"I guess that's our best shot, Henry," Pete said. "It's not exactly a fun walk, but it should lead us back to a car. The only problem is the entrance is outside."

Henry sighed. So did everyone else.

"I think our only choice is to split up," Roger said. "I can take two people on the Glider and draw attention away from the rest of you. That way, you could make a break for the tunnels, and we could rendezvous at the Gate."

"They can track you," Bunny pointed out. "You'll be making yourself a target."

"I can lose them. If not, then we'll find someplace high and stay up there until you guys close the Tear."

"And if we don't?" Henry asked.

Roger shrugged. "Then we land and pick a place to die."

The attic was quiet. I made eye contact with Roger, shaking my head slowly. I didn't like this plan. It left too much to chance.

Eventually, Henry sighed. "I don't like the idea of splitting up, but I can't think of a way around it. Who wants to go with Roger?" He glanced at me. "Lily, you should stay on the ground, we need you to listen and make sure nobody's following us."

I glanced at Roger. "I guess. I'm not sure how much help I'd be. I still can't tune in when I want to. It just happens."

"You can do it. We can give you tips Constance told us. Who's going with Roger?"

"I can go," Bryn said.

"So can I," volunteered Bunny.

Henry nodded. "You three can take off from the roof. That might be safer. Once they start to follow you, we'll head for the tunnel. Everyone ready?"

There was a collective nod.

273

Without another word, Henry, Pete, Tinker, and I descended the ladder as the others readied themselves by the window. Roger turned and gave me a final wave. I waved back half-heartedly. I didn't like this plan.

The four of us huddled by the back door, out of sight from the windows.

"You ready?" Henry called up.

"Yeah," came a voice from upstairs.

"We meet in exactly one hour at the Gate. You hear me? Don't be late, or we're leaving without you."

I heard a few chuckles from up the ladder, along with the sound of the Glider expanding. A small screeching noise signaled the window was open. A gust of cold stale air rushed into the cottage. It tasted of decay.

Immediately, the formerly still watchmen at the tree line darted from their positions toward the open attic window. I heard thumps against the side of the house as the humming sound of the Glider intensified.

"Go!" commanded Henry.

We burst through the door and sprinted into the woods. I tried my hardest not to trip over anything as my legs pumped as fast as they would go. I was still the slowest of the group.

We rushed through the ferns carpeting the clearing and headed toward the tree line, Henry in the lead. I chanced a look over my shoulder. Three people sprinted toward us. Terry, Susan, and Bea. Their arms and legs moved in an unnatural way, their eyes empty.

"We got company!" yelled Pete. "Now, Ted!"

His brother yanked a wire from a small metal ball and threw it behind him. A great sucking noise followed. Bea, Terry, and Susan were on the ground, struggling to escape the pull of the small metal ball. Sticks, rocks, and nearby fallen branches were pulled into it too. The group grew smaller as we ran forward.

We made it to the tree line, and Pete and Tinker took the lead. I glanced back to see if anyone else followed us. No one remained. The Glider receded over the tops of the trees, with a mob of people pursuing them. I tripped over a branch but kept upright, arms flailing.

Pete and Tinker steered us to a large moss-covered rock formation among the trees. No, it was a crumbling concrete bunker. The rusty metal door hung ajar.

Pete slammed his body into the door. It cracked open an inch. All of us pushed against the metal crank, its corroded hinges letting out a vicious screech. We stumbled into the dark corridor and pushed the door again in the opposite direction. The muted silver rays disappeared as the lock snapped into place, stranding us in the dripping darkness of the flooded tunnel.

Twenty Seven

Phone Calls

We slumped against the cold slimy door, waiting for the pounding noises from the other side to begin.

They never came. Our erratic breathing was the only sound echoing in the pitch darkness. I heard shuffling before being bathed in the glow of a turquoise-colored sword. Henry held it aloft and lit the dark tunnel, squinting against the sudden brightness. Pete and Tinker took out their weapons as well, and our pocket of light expanded. Pete held a large silver mace, Tinker a small white dagger.

The tunnel was filled with debris. Moss and rubble covered the floor, stagnant puddles of muck dotting the narrow corridor. A set of cracked steps led deeper into the darkness.

"Wow," breathed Pete. "I haven't been down here since I was a kid. It's gotten . . . wetter."

"What is this place?" I asked, the sound echoing in the damp air.

"Old man Brenwich made these at the start of the Cold War," Pete said, stepping over a chunk of fallen concrete. "Course, he never got to use them. Died with the rest of his family just a few years later."

"What happened?" I asked.

"Gas explosion." He shook his head. "Real shame. They were nice folks, an old name in the Jumper community, too. You remember them, Henry?"

Henry nodded. "Sure do. They never did find all of the bodies in that mess." He held his sword high, casting light further down the tunnel. "We need to hurry. Tinker, mind leading the way?"

Tinker nodded and scooted past me down the stairs, setting a brisk pace. We walked in silence, concentrating on avoiding puddles of brown water and rusted debris.

"So when we get to the Gate, what do we do?" I asked.

"We find the Tear, set off the Energy Pulsar, and pray it sends those things back where they came from," Pete said.

"What about Leo?"

They exchanged looks.

"Hopefully, closing the Tear will break the Link," Henry said.

"Hopefully?"

Pete stepped over a puddle of murky water. "The Bound haven't been able to take true physical form yet, or they wouldn't need to control other people. So that means coming through is taking longer than they thought."

"That's a good thing, right?"

"It could be," Henry allowed. "It could also mean they're waiting for something."

"What will happen to Leo if the Link isn't broken when the Tear closes?" I asked. "Won't The Bound still be here because he's alive?"

They didn't say anything.

"Guys?"

"We will do what we have to," Henry said over his shoulder.

I swallowed. Pete, Henry, and Tinker looked at the floor. I lost my footing on a slippery patch of moss and stumbled forward.

"How much longer?" Henry asked.

Pete cleared his throat. "About halfway, now."

We came upon a crossroads where a large portion of the cement ceiling had caved in, giving us only one option. Little streams of outside light filtered in from the small cracks between the fractured stone.

"You hear anything, Lily?" Henry asked.

I shook my head. "No. I'm sorry, I can't control when it happens."

Henry turned his head. "Give it time. You've only heard it for a few days. The fact that you can listen at all shows that you have a knack for this kind of thing, like your grandfather did. Not that John ever really tried."

"You knew my grandpa?"

"Sure, back when he was a Jumper. We had a traditional poker night at the Masters house every week. John was lousy at poker, but Terry and Susan usually wiped the floor." He chuckled. "Ed was the worst out of all of us. Except—"

"Except?"

"I just remembered. The one and only time Terry bombed, Ed won the pot. He lorded it over them for weeks." His smile faded. "I miss those days."

"So you knew about my grandpa and the Collective?"

He nodded. "A few years after he Discovered, he told me and Connie. Made us swear not to tell anyone. Even Terry and Susan were in the dark as far as I know. He never did learn how to listen to it, just blocked it out and left the community."

I ducked under a caved-in portion of the ceiling. "You can do that? Block it out, I mean."

"If you try hard enough, you can make your mind believe almost anything. Denial is a powerful tool. He just denied that he could hear it, until one day it became reality. Of course, by then, most of his life had passed him by. But he got his wish, in the end."

We came upon another crossroads. Tinker held up a hand, and the group stopped. He stooped to grab a small pebble and tossed it down the right passage. He listened to the echo before waving us down the hallway to the left.

"When you said my family had a tendency for . . . abilities out of the ordinary, did you mean the Collective?" I asked.

"Partly," Henry said, hacking away some foliage. "There are records of your family having . . . let's just say special abilities. Psychic abnormalities, telepathic tendencies, astral projection, things like that. It seems to come with people who hear the Collective, strangely enough."

Tinker pointed forward. The tunnel curved ahead, becoming considerably narrower.

"We're almost there," Pete said.

"Any info?" Henry asked again.

I strained my ears to hear. Nothing. "I'm sorry, I really am trying."

"Maybe don't try so hard," he suggested. "Just let things flow naturally. Listen to your surroundings. Breathe."

We reached the end of the curved section and stopped at the base of a rusted ladder. At the top was another crank hatch. Closing my eyes, I hung back and listened to the sounds of the dark passageway.

I heard the steady running of water. The occasional draft of wind. Outside, the breeze whistled past the metal hatch. A small puff of air blew down the corridor.

C . . . l . . . e . . . a . . . r . . .

S . . . a . . . f . . . e . . .

I opened my eyes. "I think we're clear."

He smiled. "See? You're getting the hang of it."

Tinker mounted the ladder. He gave the hatch a twist and shoved. It popped open. He peeked over the brim and threw open the hatch. We emerged onto a small grass-covered hill surrounded by pine trees. In the distance, the fire-ravaged house was visible. Well, what was left of it.

"We'll cut through the woods so we stay under cover," Pete said, gesturing forward. "Hurry."

"Keep an ear out," Henry said to me. "You'll be our only warning."

I nodded.

We ran through the woods until we hit the edge of another clearing. I could see my car sitting immobile in the mud, flanked by two people, still as statues.

We crouched behind a close-knit set of trees. Henry huffed a breath. "Son of a *bitch*. I should've known."

Tinker was already rummaging through his pack. Pete pulled out a pair of goggles and a long silver tube. He loaded it with a small gold dart and aimed at one of the sentries. Tinker assembled what looked like a small crossbow. Snapping on a bowstring and placing a small bolt, he lifted and aimed. He flicked a button, and the bolt hummed.

"One, two . . . three," whispered Pete.

They fired their respective weapons, and the two people dropped to the ground; the one shot by the crossbow was twitching.

Henry pushed me forward. "Go!"

We ran to the car as I fumbled with the keys.

"I'm driving," Pete said.

I didn't argue, and tossed him the keys.

Tinker rode shotgun, and Henry and I sat in the back. Pete turned the key, and the car sputtered to life, equally as unhappy as we were.

As he backed up, I looked at the bodies on the ground next to us, two men. I didn't recognize them. An imposing shadowy figure flickered into existence, its hand pressed against the unfamiliar man's shoulder. In an instant, the black figure was gone. My blood ran cold.

I looked at Henry. "Did you see that?"

He nodded, face white. "They're getting close. We don't have much time left. If they regain true physical form . . . it's all over. Nothing can stop them."

Pete reversed and sped down the muddy lane.

The trip back to the main road took less than half the length of time it had taken me. The forest was nothing but a green blur as we rushed toward Terry and Susan's house. We passed over a large bump to turn onto the main road. Pete stepped on the gas. The car sputtered in protest.

"Doesn't this thing go any faster?" complained Pete.

"No," I mumbled.

We sped down the highway. Nothing tried to stop us. No cars, shadow puppets, or roadblocks. Before long, we turned onto the long winding driveway that led back to Terry and Susan's. I clutched my seat as we slid around corners at impossible speeds.

Sliding into the driveway, we pulled up close to the barn. Pete pulled the key from the ignition, and the engine shuddered. I had an uncanny feeling it would never start again.

We raced up the stairs, past the pyramid of pens, and stopped at the tetherball pole in the center of the small hidden room.

"I'll go first," Henry said. "If you hear anything funny, leave me behind and run for it."

Pete and Tinker nodded. He mounted the pole and disappeared through the Gate. Pete waited a minute before sliding through the portal. Tinker gestured for me to go next, which I did. I shut my eyes and mouth against the Spacer Beads, hands squeaking on the freezing-cold metal. I looked down, and my heart sank. Only Pete and Henry waited at the bottom. Roger, Bryn, and Bunny were nowhere to be found. Stepping back from the pole, we waited for Tinker, who slid down, eyes shut, shaking.

Pete patted him on the back as his feet touched the spongy ground. "Good job. That was much faster than last time!"

Tinker gave a small smile.

"They should've beaten us here," I said. "How much longer can we wait?"

Henry checked his wristwatch and grimaced. "They have five minutes."

I looked down.

"I'm sorry," he said. "They knew the risks going out. The best we can do is close the Tear."

We waited in silence for what seemed like an eternity. My stomach knotted and twisted as the seconds ticked by. Were they dead? Infected? If we succeeded in closing the Tear, did that mean everyone who was infected would be released? What if it didn't?

I wrung my hands together. If it didn't, then the entire town of Stars Crossing was already dead. Terry, Susan, and Bea might already be dead.

Roger might already be dead. I kept my eyes fixed on the Gate, watching for any sign of movement. There was none.

After several eons, Henry sighed. "We have to move."

Pete and Henry turned and walked away. Tinker stood with me, staring up at the Gate. He turned to me before joining the others, eyes filled with tears. I swallowed, following behind them.

Henry led us past the ring of trapdoors and onto an adjoining orb. The air here was peaceful, but I found no comfort in it. Would the Connectors be spared from The Bound, or would they spread to the Otherworlds too?

The sound of wind chimes wafted past me. Static mixed with wind chimes.

S . . . t . . . o . . . p . . .

"Stop," I repeated out loud. The others paused.

"Lily, I know you're worried. We all are," Pete said. "But we have to go."

"No." I shook my head. "They—the Collective—"

A shout echoed behind us. We turned to see three figures waving and running down the nearest vine bridge. Bryn, Bunny, and Roger. My sinking heart picked itself up again.

"Wait!" Roger shouted, running across the orb. A moment later, they skidded to a stop in front of us, wheezing.

"You're late," Henry said, exhaling a relieved breath. "What happened?"

"Hold on," panted Bunny, bracing herself on her knees. "Give us . . . a . . . goddamn . . . second."

We gave them a second.

"We led them around for a while," Bryn said, wiping some sweat from her forehead, "trying to give you guys a head start. This one"—she pointed at Roger—"is a *madman*."

Roger flashed a smile between breaths, wincing as he clutched his ribs. "I told you to hang on."

Bunny caught her breath and stretched. "We didn't know 'hang on' meant 'compose your last will and testament.'"

Roger stood, wiping sweaty bangs from his face. "Sorry we're late. Had a run-in with someone guarding the road, and we lost the Glider."

Henry's eyes flicked to all three of them. "Anything broken?"

"No, it didn't last long," Bryn said. "Roger took a few good kicks, though. We had to run all the way from the main road."

"Any troubles on your end?" Roger asked.

Henry shrugged. "Nothing major. Which is what concerns me. It was too easy getting here."

"Speak for yourself." Bryn stretched her back.

Henry scrutinized the area. "I don't like it."

"Well, like it or not, we need to move," Bunny said. "When we dealt with the guard, we saw The Bound. They were . . . controlling him like a puppet. They're almost through."

"We saw it too," I said.

The group exchanged dark looks, and we continued on. Henry led us across three more orbs, over bridges, and under great swaths of vegetation. The white-and-pink material was spongy, compressing as our steps trotted across it. I tried not to look down.

We stepped onto one of the largest orbs in sight, and the group spread out in a triangle formation. Roger hung back next to me.

"You all right?" he asked.

I tried to give him a reassuring smile. "I'm fine. How're your ribs?"

He rubbed a hand over his chest and breathed in. He winced again. "Not broken, at least. Hurts like hell, though."

"I was worried when you guys didn't show up. I thought you might've . . . well, you know."

He looked down. "I was worried too. You guys sure are prompt. One hour on the dot, and you were out."

"You can blame Henry for that," I said.

He gave a short laugh. The brief smile was replaced by a tense expression as he twisted to look behind us. "I hate this, being out in the open. I feel like we're being watched."

"I know," I said. "I feel it too."

"Hear anything?"

"Nothing."

We climbed the steep curve of another sphere. I swallowed and looked around. Every twitch of the vegetation from the wind, every movement in my peripheral vision caused my heart to pound. Any second, I expected a legion of shadow puppets to ambush us.

A buzz vibrated my pocket. I jumped, the others whipping around. I pulled out my phone and blinked.

"I-I actually have service here," I said in amazement.

Henry stopped, chewing on the inside of his cheek. He looked to the others, who nodded, pained expressions on their faces.

"Listen, Lily," Henry said. "I have to be honest: our chances . . . they don't look good. We've all made our peace with that. It comes with the job. But you haven't had that chance."

"I'm not following you."

"If there's . . . anyone you'd like to talk to before you . . ." He shook his head. "If you want to call someone—"

"Oh."

Henry turned. "Make it fast. We don't have much time."

The group stepped away a few paces and left me alone.

I looked down at my phone. The battery was draining at an alarming rate. I had no choice but to be fast.

I found the contact for Oliver first. My finger shook as I dialed.

Putting the phone to my ear, I was greeted by a dial tone. After five rings, someone picked up.

"Hello?" a voice said.

Words stuck in my throat.

"Um, hello?" they asked again.

I cleared my throat. "Hey, Ollie, it's me."

"Lily! I've been meaning to call, but things have been so crazy at work, and . . . anyway. How's the packing going?"

I shifted my weight to my other foot. "Oh, um, packing's good. Just sorting through dust and . . . junk. Hey listen . . ." My throat stuck again. I swallowed. "I just wanted to tell you that . . . that . . ."

"Lily, is everything okay? Did you watch one of those emotional talk shows again?"

I forced a happier tone. "Yeah, everything's fine. I was just going through Terry and Susan's junk, and it reminded me of you, that's all. You've been a really good brother, and I . . ." I trailed off.

A muffled voice from the other side talked over me. "What?" Oliver said, half talking in the receiver. "No, we should wait to tell her with Mom and Dad . . ."

"Tell me what?" I asked.

"Well, we were *going* to wait to get tell you guys together, but I guess it's happening now. So in short terms, you're going to be an aunt!"

I blinked. "I— What?"

"Yeah, Dolly's pregnant! We're adding another member to the Masters family. Can you believe it?"

My mouth floundered for words.

"Lily?"

"That's—that's great, Ollie. Congratulations!"

Oliver laughed. "God, you don't have to sound so down about it. Are you jealous already? I've heard that happens with the first kid."

"That . . . that must be it." I wiped the tears trailing down my face. "Listen, I have to go. Just, uh, I love you, okay? And you're going to be a great dad. I know it. Bye."

Click.

Looking at the depleting battery, I fumbled to dial another number. After seven rings, someone picked up.

"Hello?" a woman's voice answered.

My eyes welled with tears, but I kept my voice steady. "Hey, Mom."

"Hey, sweetie! Oh, did you find a place on the property with service?"

"Uh . . ." I looked around at the enormous pink-and-orange clouds. Technically, I wasn't lying. "Yeah, I did. Just—how are you?"

"We're fine. Your dad's here too. Want me to put you on speaker?"

"Yeah. That'd be perfect."

A crackling sound shuffled through the speaker. "Hey, Lil," he said. I bit back a sob. "You called yesterday, but we didn't have time to chat. We're actually just about to head off to work, sorry."

"That's all right," I said. "I just wanted to say I love you guys, and thank you for everything. I've—I've been thinking, and I realized I haven't said that enough."

"You okay, sweetie?" Mom asked. "Are you watching one of those talk shows again?"

I gave a small laugh as tears rolled down my face. I wiped them away and checked my phone. It was almost dead. "Something like that. I-I have to go now, but have a—have a great day at work for me, okay?"

"Sure thing, honey," my dad said.

"I love you guys," I whispered.

"We love you too, honey. See you before you know it!" Mom said.

Click.

My phone shut down. Shoving it back in my pocket and wiping my eyes, I turned to face the rest of the group. They waited patiently a fair distance away.

"Okay," I said, my voice cracking. I cleared it. "Let's go."

The group continued walking. Roger hung back and walked with me. I wiped my eyes again on the back of my sleeve. He grabbed my hand and squeezed it once before letting go.

We reached a large cluster of the roselike vine formations. The large twining gaps made crooked archways, some big, some small. In the recesses of a deep arch, a staggeringly different scene lay beyond it. Swirling color was all I could see. The hacked-apart remains of pale stringy material hung from the sides of the Gate. The same revolting stench from Giftshop wafted from it.

Henry surveyed the area. "The Tear is just beyond this Gate." He backed up to it, eyes flicking to something behind us. "Something doesn't feel right. Lily, can you hear anything?"

I leaned close to the Gate and listened. "Nothing. I can't hear—"

A thousand whispers swept behind me. Something hard slammed into my side and sent me toppling into the Gate. I scrambled to my feet.

A horde of people and strange-looking beasts stretched into existence from the shadows, surrounding the group from all sides. The many-legged creatures moved in undulating swirls, splotches of black sludge falling from them like rain. They had no faces. Gashes for eyes. Slits for mouths. The puppet people stared blankly at Henry, Pete, Tinker, Bunny, Bryn, and Roger.

For a moment, nobody moved.

I locked eyes with Roger. The raw fear in his gaze was unmistakable. A shadow creature bounded lopsidedly toward the group, followed by another, and another, and another. Henry went down first. Bryn was obscured from sight in seconds. Pete and Tinker hacked and slashed their way to the Gate but were overwhelmed. Bunny flung a spear into the black masses. It missed. She was gone too.

Roger tried to dodge an incoming creature but wasn't fast enough. It unhinged its jaws, revealing sharp teeth made of black smoke, and clamped onto his shoulder. He screamed. More creatures pulled him down to his knees. He clawed at his arm and ripped off one of his bracers, flinging it at me. My frozen hands caught it automatically. I couldn't move. My entire body was numb.

I could do nothing but watch the cavalcade of shadow puppets and monsters devour my frightened friends as creeping shadow obscured the Gate with darkness.

Twenty Eight

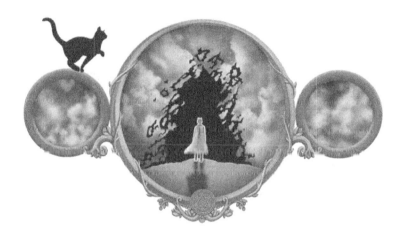

All Colors at Once

Only the cavernous sound of rushing wind penetrated my paralyzed mind.

I stared at the black oozing shadow blocking the Gate, inches from my face. Black blocks shifted and morphed into each other as it grew thicker. Muffled screams and shrieks grew quiet within seconds.

I backed away from the Gate, my heart pounding so hard I couldn't breathe.

"I'll never understand why people fight so hard," said a quiet voice behind me.

I whirled around. The scope of color in my view slammed me with such force that I momentarily forgot to be terrified. Every color in the visible spectrum warped and spun around each other in an ever-shifting dance of clouds. I trembled on a large island of rock surrounded by other floating masses. The frigid air had a metallic tang.

Leo stood at the opposite side of the island, facing the expanse, coat flapping in the wind. Despite being faced away from me, I could hear him perfectly. There was no echo of emotion in his words, just flat syllables strung together into sentences.

"There's no point to it," Leo continued. "One day, everything will be gone, and the only thing that'll remain is them. They are the only constant." He inclined his head in my direction. "I'm impressed you made it this far. I thought for sure the fall into the Forest would've killed you. As per usual, nothing goes as planned."

"You—you were the one who pushed me?" I stuttered. "Why didn't Catacombs see you?"

A nearby floating boulder bounced into our island. The entire rock wobbled. I staggered until it regained its equilibrium.

Leo didn't seem to notice. He chuckled. "My friends are powerful. They like to give me gifts. Abilities. In exchange, I help them. They warned me about you."

"Me?"

"Months ago. They told me you'd undo all our hard work. They said you'd have to be stopped, but I didn't listen. I should've killed you sooner."

"Why . . . why didn't you?"

"You were always with someone," he said matter-of-factly. "If I blew it before they were ready, I could have messed everything up. Almost did, too. Giftshop gave us more trouble than we expected. But we took care of her."

He tugged his coat more securely around him. I finally noticed what he stood in front of.

The Tear. The crude gash in reality warped like ripped fabric in the breeze. Silence leaked from it, sapping the sound from the colorful world.

I looked down. My hands still clutched Roger's bracer. I shoved it on my arm and tried to get it to work. It didn't.

"But you could've killed me in the Connector," I pointed out. "You could've done more than push me, but you didn't."

Leo shoved his hands in his pockets. "I was weak. A push was all I was willing to do. I never was strong enough to do anything by myself." He paused. "Even Anna knew that."

Shadow figures flickered into view. A cluster of them had their sticklike hands on his shoulders and back. They were huge, taller than Leo but not half as wide. Their heads swiveled to stare at me. I stepped back in alarm. Within a blink, they were gone.

"We found this, you know, me and Anna," Leo boasted. "We saw the Gates to this Connector were unblocked for the first time in years. So we went in and found . . ." He trailed off, staring at the Tear. "Anna never did like it, said it'd be safer to leave it be. I even agreed with her. So we let it sit."

Another boulder bumped into the island. The craggy rock tilted again. I dropped to my knees this time, closing my eyes until it steadied. Leo hadn't moved a muscle.

"When she died, I . . ." Leo's voice faltered. He cleared his throat. "I didn't think it was possible to live with the pain. We always had each other's backs no matter what. We were a team. We'd always been a team. Except one day . . . one day I got lazy. She died. And I was stuck here, without her, in my own personal hell."

The levity in his voice dwindled with each word. For a moment, his lifeless tone was laced with tangible sadness. He swayed on his feet, a hissing sound echoing from somewhere. He straightened and shook his head.

"Then *they* came," Leo said. "They visited me in my dreams and told me to find them. Said they could help me, if I helped them in return. So I came back. I talked to them. They listened to me. *Really* listened."

His voice regained its happy tone. "They asked if I could help them with a problem. At first . . . I declined. I just didn't understand . . . I didn't understand what they wanted. They had to . . . to show me what they could do. Everything hurt so much . . ." He swayed again. "When I agreed to help them, they became a part of me. And . . . and . . ." He faced me, arms spread wide, a hollow smile on his face. "And I felt *nothing*. No pain, none at all. Isn't that fantastic?"

I clenched my hands to keep from trembling. His shallow serenity made me squirm. At any moment, he would snap. At any moment, his fragile composure would break, and he'd kill me. I concentrated and tried to get a shield to expand from the bracer, but nothing happened.

"Leo, they're lying to you," I said. "They're going to kill everyone, you know that, right? The Earth will never be the same."

"I know," he gushed. "It'll be better."

The wind shifted directions and blew light puffs of colored vapor across the island. A wall of blue and gold blocked my view. I shielded my eyes. It hurt. The mesmerizing colored clouds stung my skin like acid.

"So I'm going to ask you *one more time*." Leo's voice grew silent, replaced with a harsh hissing. "*Will you join us?*"

"Why? Aren't they already Linked to you? Why would you need me?"

Leo sighed, but it wasn't Leo's sigh. The sound of metal against stone scraped the walls of my skull. "*You still lack understanding. Nothing could send us back to our home if we had the power of the Collective. You will give us an infinite feast.*"

I stepped back and bumped into the sludge-covered Gate. It stuck to my clothes and hair as I ripped away from it. I thought I heard a footstep nearby but could barely see my hand in front of my face.

"Join us, and we will spare you," he hissed. *"Your friends are gone. Soon you will be the last of your pitiful race. There are no options for you here. You understand this, do you not?"*

They were right. There was nothing left to do. The Bound were going to destroy humanity with or without me. What would be gained by saying no? I could at least avoid being tortured to death. The pain . . . I couldn't go through that again. Anything was better than that.

I swallowed. Fifty years ago, on this same slab of floating rock, Constance gave her life to delay The Bound from returning. To protect her friends, her family, and the rest of the world, she killed herself.

How could I let that sacrifice go to waste? If I did, I'd be no better than The Bound.

I stood straighter, trying to calm my shaking hands. "Not. Really."

The clouds rolled past, thicker this time. I squinted against the onslaught of color. It burned my skin.

A glint of light appeared a few steps in front of me.

"Then die."

The clouds shifted. Leo stood in front of me, carrying two halves of a double-ended poleaxe shaft. His old yellow goggles had been pulled over his eyes, the glass glinting in the light. The blades gathered together from the air. They were pitch black.

He swung at me. My shaky legs lunged to the side. I scrambled to my feet and ran until I discovered there was nowhere to run.

Leo moved with no haste, calmly following me around the small island. I backed up to the edge and peeked over the side. I swallowed at the dizzying drop below. No smaller islands. No landmass. Nothing. Just clouds. Only small boulders floated past like an asteroid belt. Straining my eyes, I saw larger islands in the distance. My heart pounded. My visioned darkened around the edges.

"Cease your stalling," he said. *"Your world will soon be ours, and you will be nothing but a fading memory in the Collective."*

I took an involuntary step away and almost fell backward. There was nowhere else for me to go. I glanced at the floating bits of rock.

He neared. *"Goodbye, Lily Masters."*

I turned and leapt onto one of the small boulders, hugging it so tightly it cut through my shirt and pierced my skin in small cuts. It wobbled and tilted but didn't drop from the sky. Scrambling on top of it, I glanced back. Leo followed me, casually stepping from one small rock to another with no indication of fear.

I sprung onto another large boulder, trying not to look down. The wind shifted to reveal a nearby small island. I headed for it, clinging to one small piece of rock after another. The clouds hurt my skin and eyes. Every mouthful of vapor I breathed seemed infused with acid.

After what seemed like an eternity, I rolled onto the small island, shaking violently. I pushed myself up and stood, searching the clouds for Leo. He was nowhere to be seen. A quiet chuckle resonated from the cloud bank.

I looked down at the bracer and shook my arm in frustration. I was concentrating as hard as my panicked body would allow. Why wasn't it working? Roger had probably died to try to give me a fighting chance, and I was wasting it!

A small scrape of the rocky ground behind me turned my blood to ice. I twisted. Leo stared at me through yellow-tinted goggles, inches away. He swung down. My arms came up to block it, but I knew it wouldn't help.

A split second of raw panic erupted inside me.

BANG.

A flash of purple obscured my vision, little dark blotches spotting my eyes. I blinked. Leo was sprawled out on the ground a few feet away, dazed. I looked down at my arm. A translucent purple shield made of light smaller than Roger's flickered out of existence.

Leo rolled to his feet, staggering as he tried to stand. I sprinted for the other side of the island, diving onto a rock as it passed out of a cloud bank. Spotting another larger rock, I readied myself to leap.

Another boulder emerged from my peripheral, knocking me off my feet as I jumped. My fingers dug into the sharp rock. I swung from a single handhold, dangling in the air. I yelled through my teeth and tried to pull myself up. My body was too worn out to manage more than a feeble tug. Swinging my legs, my foot caught a small knob. I swung again, rolling onto my back, heart pounding. At this rate, I was going to fall to my death before The Bound could kill me.

I wanted nothing more than to curl into the fetal position and vomit, but I had to keep moving. I couldn't see Leo, and I couldn't hear him either, but I knew he wasn't far behind. I spotted the island near the Gate and the Tear and headed toward that. A gust of wind blew a bank of clouds into my path. Each jump felt like it would be my last. The island inched closer.

I hopped onto the final rock and lunged for the island. I slipped. My head cracked against the ground. The world went black.

I opened my eyes and pulled myself to my hands and knees. My blurry reflection stared up at me from the polished black floor. My breath came in uneven gasps. Drops of sweat and blood fell onto my reflection.

A pair of leather shoes shuffled toward me. I looked up. Jerry stood above me, hands casually in the pockets of his tweed trousers. His eyes peeked over his square glasses.

I cast my eyes back down. "I . . . can't do it." I panted. "I'm going to die here, and there's . . . nothing I can do."

Tears burned my eyes. I hadn't faced the reality until now. Not truly. Now, it was staring me in the face, and I had no choice but to stare back.

Jerry watched me with an unreadable expression. "Well, my dear, you're quite right. You probably will die here. But saying there's nothing you can do, that's just quitter's talk."

"He's too strong," I gasped. "They're *all* too strong."

"Perhaps. But you are not without strength," Jerry said. "You have abilities that could lend themselves to your cause. Why don't you use them?"

I shook my head. Drops of blood sprinkled the floor. "I don't know what I'm doing! Please, help me! I can't figure it out on my own!"

He turned on his heel. "You're trying to fight like a Jumper, and you don't know how because you're not one. Maybe it's time to stop fighting like others and try fighting like you. Find The Bound's weakness. Use it."

"Jerry—"

"If you want to live, then figure it out."

"Jerry, wait!"

He walked into the darkness, shooting one last glance over his shoulder. "I think it's time for you to choose who you really are, Commander Lily Masters."

Static crackled in my ears as my eyes snapped open.

The world had been turned sideways. A slab of rock pressed against my face. It wobbled, becoming still before too long. I blinked, sucking in a delayed breath. I pushed myself up to my knees and looked around. Leo was nowhere to be found, but I was still alive. I must not have been unconscious for more than a few seconds.

I swiped a hand across my throbbing head. It came away streaked with red. Droplets dripped down the side of my face. I stood on shaky legs. A weakness, Jerry had said. What could The Bound possibly have a weakness to? Beings that fed on people's humanity, their very soul, what stopped them?

I turned in a circle and watched for movement in the swirling clouds. When The Bound visited me in my dreams, what made them go away? A memory. No, it was more than that. It was a feeling. Hope. Love. It reminded me who I was. What made me . . . me. Something that no one could take away, not even The Bound.

Roger described a similar feeling in the surveillance station. He was numb from The Bound's control until he remembered who he was. But only because I touched him. Because I reminded him, through my connection to the Collective, of his humanity, or soul, or whatever it was. It was too strong for The Bound. Maybe the very thing they hungered for was also their weakness?

The Collective . . . That was key. It wasn't enough to tell someone who they were supposed to be. They had to be shown who they were. They had to experience it firsthand.

I could see the Collective. That meant I could show them. I could show Leo.

I stopped turning. If Leo remembered who he was, maybe his Link to The Bound would be broken? I'd have to get close enough to touch him, which didn't seem likely. Throughout our little chase, I knew he could've killed me at any time. This fight was on his terms. He was playing with his prey, just like the Tigris in the Forest of Luminescence.

Wait, the Tigris. The poison. The paralytic.

I reached into my pocket. My fingers closed around the little box. The small dart rattled inside.

I couldn't sneak up on Leo, not with The Bound watching. But maybe he could sneak up on me. It was a gamble. Playing chicken with inter-dimensional shadow beings was the last thing I wanted to do. But it was my only option. What choice did I have?

I slowed my breathing, stepped to the edge of the island, and closed my eyes.

Concentrating, my vision moved outward. I watched myself click open the small box in my pocket. I was careful not to touch the end of the dart, and clenched it in my fist. Overwhelming fear clutched at my shaking body.

I swallowed it and waited.

A few minutes passed before Leo slunk into view on a nearby rock. He pushed back his yellow goggles onto his forehead and melted from sight into the shadows. He reappeared on the island, just steps away from me, stretching out of the minuscule patches of darkness between the cracks in the rock. He moved without sound. I tried to stop from shaking as he stepped behind me.

He pulled back the jet-black axe and swung down.

I opened my eyes and whirled around. My arm flew up to block the strike, a purple translucent shield coming between Leo and me.

BANG.

The dark blade shattered into shards of black. He stumbled back. I pulled the dart from my pocket and stabbed it into his shoulder. He yelled and yanked it out, but it was too late. Within seconds, his entire body shuddered, muscles seizing. His pupils flicked back and forth as I approached him.

I planted my hand on his chest and closed my eyes.

I dug deep, reaching out to the prickly noise of static and the cacophony of the Collective. The orange clouds and muddy red sky flew past me. Strings hung from everywhere, all leading to the same place. I listened. Too many voices. Too many people. My head split open with the weight of them. My nerves caught fire. My brain had been ripped from my skull.

Too many voices. Too many. Too many, too many, too many, too many—

"*Lily.*"

Too many, too many, too many, too many, too many, too many, too many, too many, too many, too many—

"*Focus, Lily,*" Jerry's voice whispered.

I grasped onto a single thread. Leo's thread. A tsunami of memories slammed into me. Years went by in an instant. An entire life. Leo's life.

I lived every second of it.

Every good day, bad day, birthday, first day of school, every vulnerable conversation, every embarrassing moment piled onto me in an unrelenting stream. Love, pain, desperation, hope, fear, ecstasy, agony, disappointment, grief—

Leo's entire life was funneled through my brain, merging his existence into my own.

The pain in my head increased. I watched Anna—my little baby sister—get caught under a falling boulder. Her legs crushed, the rest of her body broken. How had I let that happen? She was just a kid still. Just a baby. Why hadn't I been faster? I held her bleeding hand tightly as she rattled her last breath. I screamed and cried until there was nothing left to do but die. I stumbled to The Bound. They tortured me when I didn't do as they asked. The pain was unbearable. I looked through fuzzy eyes at the things The Bound made me do. The friends they made me kill.

No, I didn't do those things. Leo did. Not me.

My name was Lily. My name was Lily Masters.

I tightened my grip on Leo's string in the Collective. Somewhere, far away, my hand was still on his chest. I pushed the tidal wave of his life back to him. His heartbeat struggled. He gasped.

I opened my eyes.

Leo's entire body shook. Tears streamed from his wide eyes as he realized where he was standing. What he had done. What he had almost done. He stumbled backward, watching me with a horrified expression. Relief washed over me. He had light in his eyes again. He was the same little kid who'd snuck brown sugar into his oatmeal when his mom left the yellow-tiled kitchen. The same boy who'd shielded his sister from the bullies at school. The same man who had led countless rescue missions, putting himself in danger for the sake of others. He was Leo again.

His mouth moved, as if he were trying to say something. His body shuddered, and his legs gave out. I watched in shock as he fell over the edge.

I lunged over the side. "No!"

My hand found the sleeve of his jacket. I clamped down on it. My left hand grabbed hold of a rock so I didn't slide off with him. My shoulder jerked, and I screamed as it was pulled from the socket. The edges of my vision pulsed red.

He dangled freely for a moment before looking up. He looked dazed. "Lily? What did you do—"

"Leo, you need to climb," I said through gritted teeth. "I can't pull you up on my own. Please, hurry!"

He blinked, the color draining from his face as he looked down. "No. I can't. This is your only chance. You—" He took a shuddering breath. "You have to drop me."

"What?"

"Drop me!"

"No! You'll die!"

He gulped. "I-I know. This is the only chance you have to break the Link. You can still end this. You . . . you don't have much time left."

I looked down at his face. I knew that face. I'd seen him grow up from a child. His life had merged with mine. How could I be expected to kill him?

It would be like killing a piece of myself.

Tears burned my eyes. "I-I already broke the Link, right? Isn't that why you're back?"

He shook his head. "I'm awake, but . . . still connected. There's nothing that could break it now. They're too strong. The only way to break it is . . ." His voice cracked. "Is for me to die."

I shook my head. My shoulder felt like it was being torn in two, but I held on as tight as I could. "No. No, I won't. Come back up. We can . . . we can figure something else out."

Leo looked me dead in the eye. "If I come back up there, I *will* kill you, Lily. I'm barely in control now, and I can—" He shook his head as if clearing away cobwebs. "I can feel them trying to get back in. I can't hold them."

I tightened my grip on his arm. He loosened his grip on mine.

"Don't make me take you with me," he whispered. "Please. I've already got enough blood on my hands."

The light of the clouds around us changed. The colors swapped places, giving the light another hue completely, like an inversion of film. The saturated pinks and blues turned to pastel purples and greens. The world darkened as the light of the clouds shifted to night.

My hand was going numb. I couldn't hold him anymore. Tears streamed down my face. "I'm sorry," I sobbed. "I'm so, so sorry."

He looked down as he dangled with one hand. "This is my fault, all of it. Please . . . tell everyone I'm sorry. I never meant for any of this to happen. Can you do that for me?"

I nodded.

He tilted his face back, watching the change of color. "You were right after all, Anna," he said to the sky, closing his eyes, "I guess there is a night."

Leo let go of my wrist. My hand shook as he slipped from my grasp and fell into the clouds below.

I was frozen. My arm was still slung over the edge, hand still wedged in the rock behind me. I sat up and unstuck my fingers from their position. Deep cuts lined my palms, blood dripping from the tips of my fingers. I barely felt it.

A screeching shriek rocked the air. The Tear rippled and warped violently, distorting and writhing until it was still—a gouge in the universe contained. For now.

Time passed. Muffled shouts called from beyond the Gate. Someone yelled my name. I couldn't seem to turn around.

"Lily?"

The voice became clearer. Hacking and chipping noises followed. More people called my name.

"Lily!"

"Lily, can you hear us?"

"Wait, Rog, stop—"

"You don't know what's in there! *Roger!*"

Someone fell to the ground. Fast footsteps grew closer.

"Lily!" they called. The voice was Roger's. A wave of relief passed over me. He was alive. "Thank God you're okay. Are you—"

The footsteps slowed. "Um, Lily?"

A hand pressed gently on my shoulder.

The shock of the last few days crashed into me. I sobbed. Loud, uncontrolled, racking sobs. My hands were covered in blood, so I cried into the edge of my sleeve.

Roger knelt next to me and put an arm around my heaving shoulders as I cried to the colored clouds for the man I'd killed.

Twenty Nine

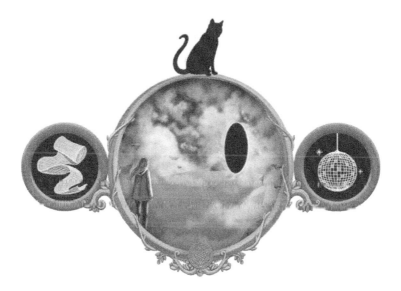

Counterweight

Eventually, my tears ran out. Roger had stayed quietly by my side until my sobs subsided.

My shoulder hurt, as did a lot of other things. The pain sharpened as the adrenaline in my system faded. I swiped my forehead with the back of my hand. It stung. Blood covered both the back and palms of my hands now. Roger pulled my hands in front of him and took off his backpack. He doused the aching cuts with a bottle of water before dabbing at them with alcohol wipes. That stung worst of all. Pink water soaked into the ground beneath us.

Roger wrapped gauze around my hands and inspected the wound on my head. He glanced behind me. "Henry, can you get her shoulder back in while I get this ready? I think it's dislocated. Again."

I turned. Henry limped toward us. His face was marked in gray splotchy bruising, but he was in one piece.

He knelt next to me and prodded my shoulder. It flopped horribly as he moved it around. "This is going to hurt," he warned. "Probably more than it did coming out. I'll do it on the count of three, all right?"

I nodded, bracing myself for a new wave of pain.

"Okay, one—"

He shoved my shoulder forward, and it went back into socket with loud and painful pop. I blinked the spots of red from my eyes.

"*Ow!*" I yelped. "What happened to two and three?"

He shrugged. "Whoops."

I rubbed my shoulder and looked back at the Gate. The black sludge had hardened to an odd grayish material. A sizable hole had been excavated in the top. Pops of light flashed beyond it as it was slowly chipped away.

"I thought you guys were dead," I whispered. My voice was hoarse. "I didn't have time to get back through the Gate before The Bound closed it. I . . . I thought you were all dead."

Henry stood gingerly. "We thought we were dead too. The Bound started to appear physically, and I thought that was the end. But . . . then they was gone. Just like that."

Roger shuffled forward with a bottle of cleaning solution and another roll of gauze. I glanced up at him. He had the beginnings of a black eye forming and a series of claw marks on his face.

He gestured for me to lean forward. "This might sting."

"Great."

Smirking, he cleaned around the cut on my forehead. It hurt worse than my hands.

I jerked back. "Ow."

"Quit squirming," he chided. He pulled out a few small butterfly bandages and taped them down.

"Lily . . . what happened to The Bound?" asked Henry. "How'd you send them back?"

I looked down.

Roger cleared his throat. "Henry, maybe now's not the best time—"

"It's okay," I said. "It's okay. I can . . . try to explain. Everything happened so fast . . ."

I tried to condense the events of the last hour into coherent sentences, stumbling when I tried to explain the encounter with the Collective. Henry and Roger exchanged looks.

"So you accessed the Collective to break the Link?" Roger asked.

"I almost didn't make it out of the Collective," I mumbled.

"Huh?"

"I guess the best way to explain it is . . . it's what happened to you back at the surveillance station, Roger," I said. "After the attack at Giftshop when you were . . . empty? And you came back? I tried the same thing with Leo, to try to break the Link. It didn't break it, but it did release their control for a moment, except . . ."

"What?" Roger asked.

My eyes welled with tears. "I saw everything. His whole life. I saw it all, felt it all, just like it was my own. I knew him like I *was* him. Do you—do you understand?"

Roger looked confused, but Henry nodded. Pity settled on his bruised face.

"And he fell over the edge, and I grabbed him, but I had to . . . I had to—"
I broke off and cradled my head.

"Oh," Roger said, looking over the island.

Henry put a reassuring hand on my shoulder. "There was nothing else
you could've done. The Bound were too powerful. It was too late for him."

I sniffed. "He wanted to tell you all how sorry he was. He . . . he never
meant for any of this to happen. Do you think . . . do you think you could
tell everyone, Henry? I don't think they'll believe it coming from me."

Henry nodded, turning his head to watch the Gate being excavated. "I'd
better help them get through."

Henry limped away, leaving Roger and me sitting on the ground.

I looked down at the bracer still wrapped around my arm.

"Thank you, by the way, for giving me this," I said. "I would've died
without it."

He smiled. "I was hoping you'd find a way to work it. I'm glad you did.
Can I see?"

Nodding, I took it off and handed it to him.

"No." He pushed it back to me. "Can I see you use it?"

"Why?"

He shrugged. "I like to guess what people's colors are, see if I'm right.
I've got a good guess for yours. Go ahead."

I put it back on. After a minute of concentration, a purple translucent
shield flickered weakly into existence.

He put his hands in the air in triumph. "Called it. Called it *way* back in
Giftshop. My winning streak continues!"

I smiled a little and handed the bracer back to him.

"Hey!" called a voice from the Gate.

We turned. Bea was suspended between Terry and Susan, who waddled
toward us with big smiles across their faces.

My heart leapt. Roger helped me stand, and we met them halfway, where Terry and Susan pulled us all into a big group hug.

"I don't know what you guys did," Terry said, muffled against everyone else, "but good job."

We pulled back. They were all covered in dirt, cuts, and bruises, but the only one who looked like they had any serious injuries was Bea.

"What happened to your leg?" I asked her.

"Tinker's implosion bomb," she said. "It fractured it. Running around for the rest of the day finally broke it."

"I'm glad to see you're okay, at least." I wiped a stray tear with the back of my gauze-covered hands. "I wasn't sure I'd ever see you guys again."

Susan pulled me gently by my sleeve. "We're glad to see you too, Lily. Come and see what happened!"

Roger stepped under Bea's arm and helped Terry carry her back to the Gate. People had stopped hacking at it and had left a sizable hole to walk through. I shielded my eyes from the bright light of the rose world Connector.

I blinked. People. Jumpers. They were everywhere. Some I recognized from Giftshop; most I didn't. There must have been at least a hundred of them. Most seemed injured and confused, others rejoicing and crying into the shoulders of their teammates. Teams had set up medical stations and patched each other up. A nearby woman ran past me and jumped into the waiting arms of a man as the people around them cheered. Another woman clutched the remains of a bloodstained jacket, consoled by the blue-haired girl from Irene's team.

Among the group, I spotted Laura and the ambush party from Twisting Caverns. She sat cross-legged on the ground, head buried in her hands.

"Where did they all come from?" I asked Roger.

"These are the missing teams. All of them," he said, smiling. "We all thought they were dead, but I guess they were in reserve for . . . you know."

I looked around at the smiling and laughing people. This was a much different scene than I thought would await me on the other side of the darkness.

"*Thanks a lot for coming to get me, traitors.*"

I looked down. Catacombs sat in front of me, tail flicking.

"Sorry," I said. "We kind of had to stop the end of all humanity."

He tossed his head. "*Whatever. It's not like I care. You peasants can do what you want.*"

Roger laughed. "Oh, come on, stop pretending. You *like* being out with us. Admit it."

"*I admit to nothing. These last few days have been torture. You're lucky I didn't annihilate you in your sleep.*"

I raised an eyebrow. It hurt. "You didn't seem to mind the Nutella."

"*Well, I . . . I—*" He sighed. "*Shut up.*"

Roger chuckled.

"How did you even get down here?" I asked.

"*Giftshop opened up again.*"

"Oh, so you don't need—"

"*I can get around without the stupid baby carrier, thank you very much,*" he grumbled.

Henry approached us, accompanied by Bunny, Bryn, Pete, and Tinker. They all wore different wounds and the same splotchy gray bruises. Pete held the Energy Pulsar in his hands. The little red light blinked.

"We have some unfinished business," Henry said.

Roger and I nodded and squeezed back through the Gate. The Tear remained at the edge of the island, quiet and unassuming. We walked toward it.

"You controlled the blast radius for that thing?" asked Bryn. "You're positive?"

Pete rolled his eyes. "You worry too much. It's not like it's going to explode for no good—"

Pete's foot caught on a small rock, and he tripped. The bomb fell out of his hands with a loud *clank*.

Everyone stopped in their tracks, and we prepared for death.

"Peter. Lyman. Johnson," Bunny hissed. "I swear to God, you blow us up, and I'll bring you back to life so I can kill you a second time!"

Tinker stooped and inspected the device. He gave a thumbs-up. Everyone let out a breath.

"Well." Pete wiped his forehead. "I guess it was less sensitive than I thought. Boy is that a relief."

We all turned to glare at him. Bryn punched him in the arm.

"Ow!" He rubbed his shoulder. "What? We didn't die. Quit your whining!"

Henry strode to the Tear. "Let's just get this over with."

We followed as Tinker set the bomb (carefully) below the Tear. He flipped a switch, and it hummed to life. Tinker pulled out a small remote and waved for us to back up. We shuffled back toward the Gate.

"Do you think this will close it forever?" I asked Henry.

He shrugged. "I think so. I'm just concerned . . ."

"Concerned with what?" Roger asked.

"Never mind." He inhaled a nervous breath. "I guess there's one way to find out. Whenever you're ready, Tinker."

Tinker fiddled with another switch on his remote. A high-pitched whine arose from the other side of the island. An electrical crackle erupted. The energy coursing through the air made my skin tingle. A flash of light blinded me, the whining noise rising to a screech of metal against stone.

I blinked the spots from my vision. The Tear's flaps closed one at a time, as if someone on the other side had pasted it closed with wallpaper glue.

Henry clapped both Tinker and Pete on the shoulder. "Well done, you two. I really wish we'd thought of it sooner."

"Amen to that," Bunny said.

They shuffled through the Gate.

I turned to go, stopping at the sound of the wind. It carried a flicker of static. I listened.

O . . . p . . . e . . . n . . . e . . . d . . .

F . . . r . . . e . . . e . . . d . . .

I turned around. The clouds swirled with the wind, blowing a patch of vapor across the island. There was something. A feeling. Something felt different.

Roger poked his head back through the Gate. "Lily? What's wrong?"

I shook my head. "I don't know. I heard something, but I don't see—"

I froze. The air warped where the Tear used to be.

"Did you see that?" I asked.

He nodded, face pale.

The air rippled and distorted.

"Not again," I mumbled.

I expected reality to tear itself open. I expected the claws of horrific shadow beasts to break through the air. Instead, a large oval freed itself with a flash, identical to those made by a Teleporter. We squinted into the darkness beyond.

"What is that?" I asked.

Roger shook his head. "I don't know. It looks like—"

He broke off. People emerged from the portal. They wandered out of the hole, dazed, shielding their eyes from the light. There weren't many, less than twenty in all. A few people were dressed in old-fashioned clothes, others in modern-day garb.

A man in his forties was the last to stumble from the hole, a Teleporter still clutched in his hand. He tilted his head to the sky and squinted at the colored clouds. The portal closed after him, the air still once more.

Roger stiffened, gaping at the man. I did a double take between the two. They . . . looked similar. Extremely similar.

Roger staggered forward. "D-Dad?" he called.

The man looked up, his eyes without recognition. He blinked, a smile spreading across his face. "Hey, sport."

There was a long moment of silence.

Roger bolted through the small crowd and threw his arms around his father. His shoulders heaved with shocked tears as he buried his face into his shoulder.

The man almost tipped over as Roger slammed into him. He wrapped his arms around his son, tousling his hair. He blinked and looked up at the sky. "Look at you, all grown up. When did that happen?"

I stood, mouth open, staring at the dazed people. Henry returned through the Gate and looked around in confusion. "What's going on? Who are all these people?"

My mouth wouldn't work. I pointed forward.

Henry's eyes widened. "Ah. Well. All right then. I guess my theory was right."

"Theory?"

"The universe has a way of keeping things balanced," Henry explained. "One door closes, another gets left open. Like a counterweight. When the Tear closed . . ."

"Another door got unblocked," I finished.

"Exactly," he said. "Though I didn't expect *this*. Well." He cleared his throat. "Let's go see if Cliff holds a grudge."

We approached as Roger and Cliff broke apart. I stared at him. He looked older than he was in the picture in Giftshop. His eyes flicked to Henry, who clapped him on the back.

"Good to see you again, Cliff," Henry said.

Cliff smiled. "Christ, Roger isn't the only one who's gotten older, is he? You're a walking museum!"

Henry laughed. "Don't knock it till you try it. It's better than the alternative. I could still kick your ass, though."

Cliff chuckled, glancing at me. "Who's this?"

Roger cleared his throat and wiped his eyes. "Dad, this is Lily Masters. Terry and Susan are her great-aunt and uncle."

Cliff stepped back, eyes wide. "No kidding? You finally get a girlfriend, Rog?"

Roger's face turned red. "God, you haven't changed, have you?"

Henry and Cliff laughed while I tried to ignore my face heating up. I glanced at Roger. His black eye had swelled in the last few minutes, but he smiled at me anyway.

Cliff extended a hand to me. "It's nice to meet you, Lily."

I shook it. "Nice to meet you too."

"Do you remember anything, Cliff?" Henry asked. "About when you disappeared?"

Cliff shook his head. "Just bits and pieces. I remember switching out the replicating mechanism on the first few Gates, until I got to this one." He pointed behind Henry. "Then I thought . . . I thought I heard someone calling me. I went over to investigate, and then . . ."

Cliff trailed off. His eyes glazed over as a haunted expression passed over his face.

"Dad?" Roger prompted.

Cliff jolted out of his haze. He smiled. "Then nothing. I can't remember a thing after that."

I glanced at Cliff, maintaining eye contact for a moment. He looked away, the same haunted look hiding deep in his eyes.

"Well, we're just glad you're back," Henry said. "We need to get moving. Damage control for the last few days is going to be hell, not to mention the state of town."

"What about the other people who came through?" I gestured to the small group looking around the island in confusion. "What happens to them?"

"Don't worry about them," Henry said. "We have resources set aside for victims caught in between the Otherworlds and their . . . complications," Henry assured me. "I should get those wheels turning before people head back to Giftshop. 'Scuse me."

Henry disappeared beyond the Gate. Cliff spotted an older man in the group and waved to him.

"I'll be right back," he said to Roger.

"You've said that before," Roger called as he walked away.

Cliff grinned and tapped the older man in the shoulder. The man's eyes widened, and the two conversed low and fast.

A man and woman approached us hesitantly. The man wore a crumpled suit. His small black mustache matched his neatly combed black hair. The woman was strikingly beautiful, light brown hair pinned in a curly updo. She was dressed in a conservative long-sleeved dress and sturdy laced boots. Both looked like they had walked right out of a silent film.

"Pardon us," said the man. "Do you know where the others are? We were part of an exploration team sent to investigate an anomaly and, well, I suppose we find ourselves here now. Wherever 'here' happens to be."

"Exploration team?" Roger asked.

"Yes," said the woman. "There were seven of us all together, but I think we may have been the only ones who ran into trouble."

"Seven of you?" I repeated.

"Indeed."

I looked at Roger, whose mouth hung open. "You don't think—"

He shook his head to stop me. "I'm officially taking myself off duty."

"But—"

"One crisis at a time, Lily."

Henry entered the Gate, accompanied by three people I didn't recognize.

"Excuse me, everyone," a woman called to the confused group. The group turned. "I know you're probably very confused, but you're safe, and if you'll listen to me, we'll try to get things straightened out."

Cliff said goodbye to the older man and followed Henry, Roger, and me out of the Gate. The man and woman dressed in old-fashioned clothes watched us leave with baffled expressions.

Henry and Cliff walked ahead and drew surprised looks and claps on the back. Henry opened a portal with a Teleporter and led the group into Giftshop. The large group trailed after him, clearing their supplies and teammates from the world. Roger and I were the last in line, shuffling forward with everyone else.

I looked around and tried to take some comfort in all of the smiling faces and reunited Jumpers. I tried to feel some kind of relief that the ordeal of the last few days was finally over. I couldn't. The pain was still too fresh, too deep. I had just killed someone. Did that even matter to anyone? Did anyone care that he was dead? It didn't feel like it. Maybe they were relieved they hadn't had to do it themselves. I looked down at my gauze-covered hands. Splotches of blood had seeped through the layers of fabric.

Roger nudged my arm. "You okay?"

I looked down.

"Lily?"

"I'm fine," I said. I chewed the inside of my cheek and laughed without feeling it. "Actually, no. No I'm not. Not really."

We were next in line. I stepped through the portal, inhaling the scent of dust and pine trees. We were in the viewing bay, and not a book, couch, or table was out of place. The wood that had splintered from the walls was restored, the lights unbroken, and the cracks in the glass mended.

The group was dead quiet. A large banner had been strung across the windows.

A small yellow smiley face marked the dot on the exclamation point. Underneath the banner was a large table filled with bowls of chips and other snacks, plus a smaller table dedicated completely to juice boxes, all of which looked to contain grape juice. Little party hats and streamers decorated the tables. A sparkling disco ball hung from a long cord in the center.

The group of stunned Jumpers stood immobile. Even Henry was looking around in confusion. The room was silent as we considered the scene of an inexplicable party.

Somebody burst out laughing from the corner.

It was Tinker. He leaned on his brother for support, who looked equally surprised as everyone else.

The sudden absurdity of the situation struck me also. *This* was what made these people hesitate. Not the fact that most of them had just been possessed by Otherworldly shadow creatures, nor was it the fact that they had almost witnessed the end of humanity. It was because there was a party with a disco ball waiting for them at the end of it all.

I couldn't help it. I started laughing too. Everyone looked at me like I had finally snapped.

"I'm sorry, I'm sorry, it's just—" I giggled. *"'Congratulations.'"*

Roger cracked next, then Terry, then Susan and Bea. It started a chain reaction around the room. The large hall was soon filled to the brim with uncontrollable howls of laughter.

Thirty

Till Again

The box of grape juice sloshed as I swished it around.

I set the crust of my sandwich down on its plate and waited. I glanced down. It had reformed itself. I smiled. It was my third sandwich, and my stomach had stopped growling long ago, but there was something . . . satisfying about an infinite peanut butter and jelly.

The remainder of the Jumper party had passed out on the various couches and squishy pillows situated around the viewing bay. Bryn, Bunny, Pete, Tinker, and most other teams had returned to Stars Crossing to start on damage control, but a few people were sticking around until their wounds could be healed by Giftshop. I was one of them.

Roger had spent most of the last few hours talking with Cliff, Bea was currently asleep on a nearby couch, and Terry and Susan were caught up in a lengthy discussion with Henry. Shortly after arriving in Giftshop, Terry and Susan discovered their Teleporters had swapped the Metatron's Cube for a set of numbers counting down. Their time remaining in this time-stream.

I sat against the couch and listened to the muffled conversations around the room. Nothing prodded at me from the Collective, which was perfectly fine. Even though I felt more connected to it after my last excursion, I wasn't eager to return anytime soon.

Roger and Cliff stood from their seats by the window and wandered over to me.

"Hey," Roger said, plopping in a nearby chair.

"Hey," I said. "Everything okay?"

Cliff pulled up a footstool and sat across from me. "Fine, fine. Just catching up on ten years of lost time. No biggie."

"I'm sorry."

He waved a hand. "Don't be. No use wasting more time feeling sorry for myself. Not going to have time for it, anyway. The higher-ups called, and some idiot"—his eyes flicked to Henry—"just recommended me as temporary region leader here."

"Oh. Congratulations! Wait, congratulations, right?" I looked to Roger. "Is that a good thing or a bad thing?"

Roger laughed, rubbing the dwindling remains of a yellow bruise around his eye. "Yes, it's a good thing."

"Just temporary, though," Cliff said. "Just until they find a replacement for . . ." He trailed off, closing his eyes. "For Ed."

I looked at the floor.

Cliff swiped a hand across his face. "So Roger tells me your family is the new owner of Terry and Susan's place?"

"That's right."

"And that you're looking into selling it?"

"Well, *I'm* not, but my parents are. They need the money and can't handle the taxes on it. Don't even get me started on that."

"I'm guessing Terry and Susan set up conditions on the property in their wills?"

I rolled my eyes. "No kidding. You aren't going to believe this, but if we try to sell the house, it defaults back to some historic preservation society, and we lose it. The lawyers said they're an old firm, established in the early 1900s or something, and they've got properties all over the world, and—"

Cliff and Roger exchanged smirks. My mouth dropped open.

"Are you kidding me?"

"Lily, we—"

"Are you *kidding* me?" I gestured to the entire room. "That's you guys? The 'historical preservation society' is a damn *Jumper* organization?"

Roger chuckled. "I told you not to worry."

I sat against the couch. "Unbelievable. You guys are *unbelievable*."

Cliff laughed. "Don't worry. We'll work something out."

I ground my teeth together. "I seem to have heard that sentiment before."

"For real, this time," Roger said. "Promise."

I sighed and took another bite from my replicating sandwich. It reformed before it touched the plate.

"So . . ." Cliff's eyes wandered around the room. "You going to school?"

"Yeah."

"What are you studying?"

"Uh . . . I'm still figuring that out."

"Do you like college?"

"Yeah, I guess. I just . . ." The lie caught in my throat. I hated college. It was more soul-sucking than high school, but now I was going into debt for my own personal torture. "No, actually. I hate it. But it's the only way to get a decent career, so I'll just have to deal with it."

He nodded, gaze finding its way to the ceiling. "You want a job?"

"I— What?"

"Do you want a job?" he repeated. "It pays well, and you'll never be bored. From what I've heard, you've certainly proved yourself in the last few days. What do you say, Lily; you want to be a Jumper?"

I was speechless. Was he delusional? Was someone lying to him about the past few days? I couldn't keep up with these people! How many times had I almost been killed? I'd lost count. Even my connection to the Collective made me a liability. How could I handle myself in the Otherworlds when I could barely handle what was in my own head?

But the thought of returning to life before stumbling into the barn made my stomach churn. How could I return to a normal life after everything I'd seen? Not just with the knowledge of the Otherworlds but the people I'd met. The people I'd seen die. The man I'd killed. I would see them every waking moment from now on, of that I was sure. Could I function in a normal life with that knowledge? I really didn't know.

"I-I don't know," I stammered.

Cliff nodded. "Think about it. Give it some time. It's a big decision. Just thought I'd offer." He stood. "I'm going to iron out some details with Henry about assignments. See you around."

Cliff waved and crossed the room to Henry, Terry, and Susan.

Roger sat on the ground with me and scratched at the healing claw marks on his face. "Sorry about that."

"Why?"

"I didn't think he'd try to recruit you," he said. "I was just letting him know about your situation and catching him up on . . . stuff."

I shrugged. "It's all right."

He was quiet again for a minute. "So what do you think?"

"Honestly?" I shook my head. "I'm not sure. There's so much to think about. So many things could go wrong."

"True," Roger agreed. "But things could go right, too."

I twisted to look at him. There was a peace on his face that hadn't been there when we met. A resolve. The constant exhaustion in his kind brown eyes had lessened.

"You think you could stand babysitting me *all* the time?" I asked.

He tilted his head back to the ceiling and leaned against the couch. "I dunno   you've been a horrible burden . . ."

I slapped his shoulder.

He laughed. ". . . but I'll find a way to suffer through it."

I smiled. Terry and Susan caught my eye from across the room and waved as Henry and Cliff took their discussion to another table. I sighed. In a few minutes, I would lose them again. I tried to take comfort that they were going back to a full life ahead of them, filled with adventure and mystery. It didn't last long. I knew a grave waited for them in the Stars Crossing cemetery back on Earth.

"I should talk to them," I said. "Before I don't get another chance."

Roger nodded. "Probably a good idea."

I stood, surprised at the lack of pain in my body. Unwrapping the gauze taped to my hands, I flexed my fingers. Thick white lines had replaced the deep cuts.

Terry and Susan smiled as I approached.

I forced a small smile back. "Hey."

"Hey," Susan said. "How're you doing?"

"I'm okay," I assured her. "How much time you guys got left?"

Terry raised his Teleporter. "'Bout ten minutes."

My heart sank. "Oh."

Susan reached across the table and took my hands in hers. "We're so proud of you, Lily. You were pushed into all this—literally—and you've done better than we could've hoped. We always wanted to find a relative to keep the Jumper tradition going, but when John left, we'd lost hope. Maybe it's not too late."

I looked down.

"Hey." Terry nudged my arm. "You just saved the world, you know. Take some credit where it's due."

I squirmed in my seat. "The ones who should be taking credit is you guys. I couldn't have figured all this out without you. I . . ." I swallowed the lump in my throat. "I'm really going to miss you guys."

They glanced at each other.

"We wanted to give you something," Terry said, rummaging in his coat pockets. His eyes widened with panic. "Susie, I think I lost the—"

Susan rolled her eyes and pulled a strange-looking key from her jacket and handed it to me. The shaft was carved from blue stone. Shards of finely cut crystal made the prongs.

"What's this to?" I asked.

"Let's just call it the family safe," Susan said, eyes twinkling. "The entrance is in the study. You'll find it."

Terry's and Susan's Teleporters buzzed. Terry flipped his over. Only a few minutes remained.

"Well, would you look at the time," commented Terry. He stood. "You ready to get back home, Susie?"

She sighed and pushed herself from the chair. "I suppose." Looking at me, she smiled. "Well, at least we'll get to see you again, even though you won't know who we really are. Anything you want us to teach teenage Lily?"

I laughed. "I'm sure you guys will think of something. Just smack Grandpa for not telling you about the Collective."

"I call dibs on that," Terry announced.

We laughed, Susan pulling us both into a long hug. We broke apart as Cliff, Henry, and Roger approached.

"It was good to see you two again," Henry said, shaking hands with Terry. "I'm not sure how much of this little trip you'll remember, but try not to mess anything up for the rest of us, all right? We got enough problems to clean up." He pointed at Susan. "That means *no* trying to prevent these events, got it?"

Susan rolled her eyes. "You're such a killjoy, Henry. Quit with the protocol."

I glanced at the Teleporter in Terry's hand. Two minutes remained.

Terry heaved a deep breath. "I guess this is it."

I swallowed. "You guys are the best great-aunt and uncle anyone could ask for."

"The bestest?" Susan asked.

I laughed. "The bestest ever. Oh!"

My hand went to my back pocket. My fingers closed around the wrinkled card I had stuck in my pocket days ago. It had traveled with me through different worlds, though I had forgotten it was there. I pulled it out and flattened it against the table. The words *Bestest Great-Aunt and Uncle* were smudged, the crude portraits crinkled and distorted.

I pressed it into Terry's hands. "You're going to get another one someday. Keep this in the meantime."

The Teleporter buzzed at the thirty-second mark. Susan pulled her Teleporter from her pocket, and they stepped away from the group.

"Till again, everyone," Susan said with a wave. "It's been fun, despite being the almost end of the world."

I took a deep breath through my nose. "I love you guys. Thank you for . . . everything."

Terry dramatically pointed his arm in the air. "To back home, and wherever else fate takes us!" He smiled. "Till again, Lily. We love you too."

The Teleporters buzzed. A large ripple of electricity danced through the air. There was a bright flash of light, and when we looked back up, Terry and Susan were gone.

EPILOGUE

Light

"You want to know something?" Roger asked.

"What?"

"This lock is over-the-top, even by Jumper standards. Your 'family safe' is locked up tighter than most maximum-security prisons."

"That's the Masters family paranoia for you."

Roger laughed and ducked under a spiderweb. He pulled another crate from his path, and I scooted it out into the study. It hadn't taken us long to discover the small crawlspace in the study. A cluttered table of old books and insect specimens had blocked the entrance to a hidden passageway between the walls. The crawlspace was littered with old crates, obscuring a sturdy metal door at the end painted with a Metatron's Cube.

It had been four days since Terry and Susan left. With a firm promise from Cliff, Henry, and the others that the house would be secure in my family's ownership, we began the arduous task of sifting through the packed boxes and (much to my despair) unpacking everything that wasn't going to the donation pile. It took five teams of Jumpers a matter of hours to undo my three weeks' worth of solo work. A thought I tried hard not to dwell on.

I clutched the blue key to my chest as Roger moved the last of the boxes aside. He bent to examine the overly complicated bronze lock lining the doorframe and clucked his tongue.

"I mean, there's paranoia . . ." He flicked the edge of a copper gear protruding from the lock with his fingers. It hummed. ". . . and then there's *this.*"

"I guess it's hiding something important," I said. "Let's find out what."

Roger shuffled out of the way as I approached with the key. I slid the crystal prongs into the bizarre lock and turned it. There was a loud clanking sound from just behind the door face, and the patchwork of metal plates twisted, revealing an underwork of tumblers, gears, pulleys, and springs. The plates flipped, locking into place with a definitive *click.*

Roger pulled out a flashlight as I grasped the handle and pushed. The door swung forward with a loud squeak.

The metal-lined walls glinted in the flashlight beam. It was a small room, empty except for a large metal chest in the middle. A trapdoor sat in the back, covered with a thick layer of dust and cobwebs. A yellowed envelope sat on top of the chest, the word *Lily* scrawled on it.

I broke the heavy wax seal stamped with the letter *M* and carefully unfolded the thin, brittle paper.

> *Salutations, dear grand-niece!*
>   *Terry spilled coffee on the last note, so this is a rewrite.*
>   *We hope this letter finds you well. You should be opening it just after we gave you the key in Giftshop, so there should be no time for things to go horribly wrong. Emphasis on the word should.*
>   *Terry and I have retained our memories from the events in your time, as far as we know. We can only use this knowledge to try to help you out in the future. Well, your present. Time travel is confusing.*
>   *We made the decision to leave you the house, which you already knew, but we also decided to include a little extra help. Please use the supplies in the basement for whatever you need. We pooled our savings over a few years. It's yours to do with as you please.*
>   *Whatever you choose to do with your life, be safe and find happiness. Whichever path you decide to trudge down, know that we'll be behind you every step of the way.*
>   *We love you. Live and love your life as best you can.*
>   *Love,*
>   *Terry and Susan*
> *P.S. We found the wrapped item while we were cleaning out the basement. We thought you might like it. Use it if you need it. (Or for fun!)*

I handed the letter to Roger when I finished. He folded it while I clicked the latches on the chest. The lid swung open with a poof of dust. My breath caught as I saw the crinkled card, words *Bestest Great-Aunt and Uncle* still visible but faded. A small drawing of a Metatron's Cube and a smiley face stared up at me. I smiled back.

The chest was filled with books and photo albums, bound together with brown twine. Dates, names, and places labeled the sides. Another note lay on top titled *Masters Family Records*. A brown paper package lay next to it.

Picking apart the wrappings, I took out the box inside and opened it. Resting on a piece of cloth was a strange-looking bracelet . . . or bracer, I wasn't sure which it qualified as. Two long pieces of metal snaked their way into a spiral, making a loose form that looked like you could wear it on your arm. A leather strap and buckle folded across where your wrist would sit.

"What is this?" I asked.

Roger shook his head. "I dunno . . . maybe a weapon? It looks like it's been modified. Why don't you try it on?"

"Really? Isn't this kind of your thing? I might explode it somehow."

He snorted. "I think you'll be okay."

I picked it up. It was lighter than it looked. Pulling it onto my arm, I adjusted the metal pieces to fit against my skin. A leather ring fit on my middle finger, securing it to my hand with a flap of leather. Without warning, a small purple disc appeared on the back of my hand, floating in stasis an inch above the device.

"Whoa," I said. "I wasn't trying to do that."

The little purple disc didn't disappear. I shook my hand to try to get rid of it.

"Careful," Roger warned. "Don't—"

The disc shot from the back of my hand and sank deep into the wall. It would have been less terrifying if the wall hadn't been made of metal. It dissipated into particles of light a few seconds later.

I held the device away from my body as I tugged it off. "Whoa."

"No kidding," Roger said. "I wonder where they got a long-range weapon. You hardly see those anymore."

"Is that because they're portable death traps?"

"Actually, yes."

I stood. "Let's go see what other horrors lurk in the basement."

We stepped around the metal chest, and Roger tugged open the trap-door. Rungs of a ladder were just visible in the darkness.

"Can I see the flashlight?" I asked.

Roger handed it to me and crouched near the opening.

Leaning forward, I shined the flashlight down the hatch. Something glinted. A lot of somethings.

I blinked, handed the flashlight to Roger, and pointed down the ladder. He peeked inside.

"Oh my God." He laughed. "Pooled their savings? More like robbed a bank. Wait . . ." He squinted into the hole. "Are those what I think they are? They *are*!"

He stuck the flashlight between his teeth and descended the ladder.

"Hey, Roger!"

I climbed down after him. A *clunk* preceded the flicking glow of hanging lamps attached to the ceiling as Roger located a light switch. I landed on the concrete floor and looked around in amazement.

Crates upon crates of stacked cash bills lined an impressive number of shelves. Bars of gold sat on lower shelves, sagging under the weight. The floor was occupied by cases full of ancient-looking artifacts, filled to the brim with cloth maps, old pottery, and thick leather-bound books. Roger stood at the back, rummaging through a box full of Gliders in folded form. These ones looked older and clunkier than the one from the ESS. Roger looked giddy.

"Look at all of these!" He waved a handful of Gliders in front of my face. "And they're older models too, without speed reducers. I . . . yep." He sniffed. "I think I might cry."

I laughed. "Just try not to kill yourself on those things."

He put the box down. "These will be *so* handy when we're out in the field. I may be able to convince my dad to make them standard equipment again."

My stomach flopped at the thought. "I might be the one to cry now."

He waved a hand. "Oh, come on. I could teach you how to use one, easy."

"No way."

A smile crossed his face. He grabbed two Gliders from the box. "Yes way. In fact, I'll teach you now."

"Wait, what?"

He grabbed my wrist and pulled me to the ladder. "Come on, we're having a lesson."

"Right now?"

"Right now."

The grassy field behind the house was slick with leftover drops of rain. Despite the blue sky peeking through the lazily drifting clouds, the sun's warmth bathed the entire clearing in bright light before being obscured by a passing cloud. It poked out again. I shielded my eyes against the rays. It was first time I'd seen the sun since arriving at the house.

Roger tossed me a folded Glider. "Okay, first things first. You flick this gear—" He tilted his Glider toward me. "And let go as you throw it, so its spring engages."

"Look, Roger, I don't think this is such a good idea—"

"Oh, come on, humor me."

Shrugging, I flicked the small brass gear and tossed it onto the ground. It expanded and emitted a low hum as it hovered above the grass.

"Okay, good. Now just step on."

I crossed my arms. "No way. I am *not* getting on that thing by myself."

He sighed and stepped up on the expanded Glider, holding out a hand. "Come on, you'll have to learn to do this sooner or later. It might as well be now."

"It could also be never," I pointed out. "Never is good."

He rolled his eyes. "Listen, if you're going to be a Jumper, you're going to have to—"

"Whoa." I put my hands up. "I never said I was joining up."

"Oh, really?"

"I'm still . . . mulling it over."

"Mulling it over and stalling are two different things, Lily."

I looked down at the wet grass.

"Tell me honestly," he said. "Can you imagine going back to the life you had before? After everything you've seen, is that even a possibility right now?"

I swallowed. "I don't know. At this point, I don't even know if *normal* life is a possibility. What if I join up and realize that I can't handle it?"

"You can handle it."

"You don't know that."

"I can guess."

"What if it's a huge mistake? What if get killed on my first day? What if I join and end up quitting because I wasn't good enough? I'm going to have to live with myself either way. Normal life or otherwise. Maybe . . . maybe the best way I can do that is to try to forget all of this. Put it all behind me and move on. Try to, at least."

Roger huffed a breath, staring at the floor of the Glider. He closed his eyes and stepped back onto the grass. The Glider's hum decreased.

"Look," he said. "After my dad disappeared, I ran away from the community. I thought if I could just move on with my life, forget everything I'd seen, forget all the pain, then I'd finally be happy. I drifted for five years, looking for *anything* to help me forget what I'd left behind. I . . ." He tugged on the edge of his jacket, pulling his sleeves past his wrists. "I did a lot of things I'm not proud of. I hurt . . . a lot of people."

He swallowed, a dark expression flashing across his face. "But forgetting what's happened to you isn't an option. Neither is running away. Accepting it and moving on is the only way to survive. You can't live your life because of a whole lot of what-ifs. You just have to pick a direction and take what comes."

"My choice of direction hasn't always been the best."

"So change it."

"It's not that easy."

"Why? Give me one good reason."

I sighed, chewing on the side of my cheek. "You remember when I told you one of the reasons my parents needed to sell the house was because of some medical bills?"

Roger nodded.

"They're because of me." I looked down, a wave of shame squeezing my insides. "They're in that mess because of me. My senior year of high school, I . . . well, the doctors had a fancy name for it, but it's a form of anorexia. It got bad. I almost died. I spent months in the hospital, and in therapy, just to be able to walk again."

Roger looked horrified. "I'm sorry," he said. "That must've been . . . God. I'm so sorry."

"The worst part was my parents' insurance didn't cover it. They lost their entire life savings because of me. Because I couldn't take care of myself.

Now they're stuck working crap jobs for the rest of their lives just to survive. Just to be able to eat. And it's my fault."

"Lily . . ."

I cleared my throat, blinking away the burning in my eyes. "So forgive me if I don't trust myself to make life-changing decisions. If I drop out of college to chase after the Otherworlds—which, I may remind you, will most likely end in my death—they're going to think I wasted their sacrifice on a whim. And who's going to take care of them if I get killed? They won't be able to work forever, and I'm not going to turn my back on them because *I* wanted to do something different." I shook my head. "I can't do that to them. I just can't."

Roger blew a breath from his nose. "I can understand that."

"And if you think that's a stupid reason—"

"I don't," he said. "You're worried about your family. I get it. It's an admirable thing you're doing, giving up an opportunity to explore the universe for them."

I closed my mouth. I had expected him to challenge me. I had a whole argument ready to go. It was almost disappointing not to use it. "Oh," I said.

He folded his arms. "Here's a question, though: Do you think your parents want to you to run your life to please them? Or do you think they'd want you to be happy?"

I looked down.

"Plus, I think you're overlooking an important point," he said.

"What's that?"

"This job pays. Well. Like, super well. You'd probably be able to pay off those medical bills in a year or two. Or you could just, I don't know, use the *gold bars* in the basement if things get tight."

I chewed my lip. He had a point. Today's discovery had changed a few things.

"And if you still need help"—he shrugged—"you'll get it. Jumpers take care of each other, no questions asked. We're family. It's what we do."

"Oh my God," I breathed. "Alice was right. Terry and Susan *did* belong to the mob."

Roger chuckled. He stepped back on the Glider, holding out his hand. "Come on. You ready to learn how to fly this thing?"

I sighed, grabbed his hand, and stepped onto the floating death board.

An hour later, I could make a loop around the field without falling off. It was easy enough to balance, similar to riding the subway. Lean one way to go fast, lean the other to break. I came back around from another pass in the small field and slowed next to Roger, who was waiting on his Glider, looking proud.

"See?" he said, beaming. "I told you; it's not as bad as it looks."

I wobbled to a stop, trying to look more confident than I felt. "Thanks for being a patient teacher. Even after the sixth time falling off in the same spot, you didn't give up on me. As a commander, I salute you, sir."

Roger chuckled. "How and when did you become a commander?"

I smiled. "Someone has to promote you. My best friend did me. Do you want me to promote you?"

He shrugged, still laughing. "Sure, why not?"

I shifted my stance. "All right then, soldier, attention!"

He stood straight, the Glider drifting up and down. I put a flat palm to my head. Roger did the same.

"I now promote you to . . . uh . . . Captain Roger Owens, Keeper of Gates. Use this title wisely, as it is only given to few."

He nodded with a serious expression. We held it for as long as we could before bursting into laughter.

"You want to make a run to Sal's?" Roger asked. "All this promoting is making me hungry."

"What, on *these*?" I pointed at the Glider. "Are you serious? I'll break something! Can't we just drive?"

"In whose car?"

I chewed the side of my cheek. My car hadn't moved since the incident with The Bound. Or rather, it had been *unable* to move, due to bits of the engine falling off at random intervals.

He hovered near the tree line. "We'll go slow. Promise."

"You said that before," I grumbled.

He held up three fingers. "Scouts honor, or something."

I sighed, leaning forward to join him over the treetops. He waited for me at the edge of the clearing, wind whipping his hair around.

"You ready?" he asked.

I crouched forward. "As ready as I'll ever be."

Smiling back at me, he took off over the treetops. I took a deep breath, accelerating over the cloud-shadowed foothills. Valleys of emerald-green trees and rushing rivers expanded before me. I inhaled the cold aroma of rain. The wind swirled low-hanging mists over the peaks below. I spotted Roger ahead and sped up to join him among the blue patches of sky.

END OF BOOK ONE

Acknowledgments

This book was made possible by all those who participated in The Otherworlds: Book One Kickstarter campaign. For your support, faith, and patience, you will forever have my everlasting gratitude. I will strive to be worthy of your trust as my journey continues.

I'd like to thank the wonderful editors at Enchanted Ink Publishing for providing an incredible level of professional service. Arin Hanson, Dan Avidan, my favorite grumpy grumps, thank you for keeping me company through the thousands of hours of work that went into this book. To my friends and family, throughout the years of me asking you to read through my terrible first drafts, thank you. You gave me the push I needed to continue forward. Stewart, my love, thank you for your support and patience through the good and bad days, as there were many.

And finally, thank you to Grandma and Grandpa B, to whom this book is dedicated. I wish you were both here to receive this book in person, for which you were instrumental in making. Hopefully they have libraries in heaven.

About the Author

RJ Kinner is an author and illustrator who resides on the ruggedly beautiful Oregon Coast with her husband, and overly-enthusiastic Siberian Husky. Her hobbies include hiking, rock-hounding, occasionally panicking over crippling self doubt, and baking. In addition to her published works, she has illustrated a tarot and corresponding oracle deck (The Kinner Tarot, and The Echoes Oracle) from two successful Kickstarter campaigns. With questions or inquiries, contact rjkinner@rjkinnerart.com.

Also By

Coming Soon:
The Otherworlds Series
Catchers Series

Made in the USA
Monee, IL
28 September 2023

43576955R00193